T0165618

Earth-Watching: A Seductive Pleasure in a Perfect World

Linda Novak

iUniverse, Inc.
New York Bloomington

Earth-Watching: A Seductive Pleasure in a Perfect World

iUniverse books may be ordered through booksellers or by contacting:

iUniverse
1663 Liberty Drive
Bloomington, IN 47403
www.iuniverse.com
1-800-Authors (1-800-288-4677)

ISBN: 978-1-4502-6058-9 (sc)
ISBN: 978-1-4502-6059-6 (ebk)

Printed in the United States of America

iUniverse rev. date: 10/14/2010

Chapter 1

Palala

As he watched the blood drain out of the body, Kebeck shuddered. *Earth beings do such strange things to their dead.* He would have to send a recording of this to the other committee members. He had watched funerals and autopsies on Earth TV shows but witnessing this method of preparing a body for burial performed on a real body disgusted him, especially because he knew this particular Earth being. He had known Carol since she was just a child. He had been curious about how they would dispose of her body.

Fortunately, he had accessed a computer monitor in the back room of the funeral home that allowed him to view the procedure. The female Earth being who was working on Carol's body moved in front of the monitor, blocking his view for an instant. No matter; he had seen enough. Kebeck pushed the record button on his computer. *I do not want to see any more of this ritual.*

Chapter 2

Earth—2 days later

As Adeline reached the high point of the bridge, a thought crossed her mind. *If I was to turn the steering wheel right or left at this moment, I would plunge off this bridge and fall to a sure death. I would cease to exist. Like Carol, I would be dead, gone.* The thought alone scared her and made Adeline hold on to the wheel a little tighter. She glanced over to the right at Lake Ontario, where the wind was whipping up little whitecaps more than a hundred feet below her. The tall chimneys of the Hamilton steel mills flamed to her left. Adeline certainly didn't want to die, but the funeral had reminded her of her own mortality. *All that talk about Carol being in heaven…she's not in heaven—she's not anywhere. She's just gone. I wish there was a heaven; it would make it easier to face death, and life.*

Driving home from her best friend's funeral, Adeline felt a tear run down her cheek and tasted the salt as it touched her lips. She had known Carol since the fourth grade. Part of her didn't really believe that Carol was gone. She found it difficult to accept the fact that there would be no chatty phone call tomorrow, or ever. There would be no more popcorn grabbed out of her bowl as they watched a corny old movie together.

Carol and Adeline had been so close for so long. Adeline's mother used to call them "the twins." It wasn't that they looked alike; they were just always together. Carol was tall and lean with straight brown hair. Adeline had curly blonde hair. Carol was captain of the girls' basketball team in high school and was a high scorer in the university league, while Adeline had no interest in sports at all. Some people thought they looked funny together because Adeline was more than a foot shorter than her friend, plus she had the boobs and hips that Carol was missing. Though Carol wasn't beautiful, she certainly wasn't ugly; she just had average looks. Still, back in high school, some idiot boy once had yelled, "Here come beauty and the beast." Adeline was thinking of that silly, awful incident when the sound of a car horn startled her and she realized that she had just gone through a red light. Adeline straightened up in the seat and tried to concentrate on her driving.

As she pulled into her driveway, Adeline managed to smile as she looked at her pretty little saltbox two-story. The leaves on the maple tree beside the porch were turning red; it was a nice contrast with the new yellow paint on the house. A black squirrel scurried across the power line that ran to just below the roofline. Her fiancé had painted the house before going to England. It was his way of apologizing for accepting the three-month assignment that sent him so far away. But only one more month now and he would come home; they would do the wedding thing and supposedly never be apart again. She missed him. Their daily emails and weekly phone calls were the only things that made their separation bearable.

She had almost decided that men were just accessories that she could live without when she had met Jim at a conference two years earlier. Though doing a newspaper story on an education symposium seemed to her like a big waste of time, her editor insisted that she head over to the university to write an article on some guy named Jim Shannon, whom she had never heard of. A real nobody. As usual, she got busy with some other matter and arrived at the university fifteen minutes late. When she entered the lecture hall where Shannon was speaking, he paused for a moment and then said to the audience, "Let's talk about how we might handle students who come in late." She eased into her seat, red-faced, and smiled up at him, thinking, *he's going to pay for that!*

But her attitude changed as she listened to him talk. He was smart and funny. He knew how to hold the audience's attention and he had some great ideas about working with students. As she approached him after the talk, she couldn't help but notice that he was quite good looking, just a little taller than she was, with wavy brown hair and green eyes. And he was really well built; not too skinny or too thick but just right, with muscles in all the right places. She ran her hand through her hair and introduced herself. A year later they were living together.

Adeline heard the phone ringing as she approached the front door of her house. She refused to let the ringing phone make her rush. As she turned the key in the lock, she thought *life's too short to hurry.* She paused. *Or maybe life is so short and I want to do so much that I need to hurry to get it all in.* The phone kept on ringing. It had to be Dalton Clark, her editor. The old bastard had ink in his veins. He probably picked up the phone the minute he got back from the funeral: "Got to get the paper out." The ringing stopped just as she closed the door and she heard his voice on the message machine: "O.K., I know you were close to Carol and we will all miss her. And you probably need some time off right now, but ... there's something weird going on here, and we need to deal with it now. I want to know why all of Carol's files are missing."

Adeline picked up the phone, "Dalton, what do you mean her files are missing?"

"Ha! You *are* there ... screening your calls ... just as I suspected. But I guess you've had it rough today."

"Yeah, and you're calling me about missing files?"

"This is the thing. When I came back to the office just now, I went over to Carol's desk to see where she was at on some stories. I need to reassign some pieces. And all her files are gone! Someone came in here while we were at the funeral and took every piece of paper out of the story folders on her desk."

Adeline was mystified. "Why would anybody do that?"

"I have no idea," Dalton fumed. "It wasn't anyone from here; I already checked with everybody. It had to be someone from outside the office. I always said we've got too many people coming and going around here. We've no security in this damn place. I'm going to call the police; it could be related to her murder."

"But the police said she was killed in a robbery gone wrong." She paused and took a breath. "You think Carol was murdered because of something she knew ... maybe because of some story she was working on? Is her laptop there? Look in her desk. Sometimes she sticks it in a drawer."

"Let me look." She could hear Dalton walking across the room. She heard him open the drawers and then bang them closed. "It's missing too. The whole desk is empty."

"Shit! It should be there. A lot of stuff should be there."

"There is nothing in this desk. Do you know anything about this? Remind me ... what was she working on? Did she mention anything special?"

"No, the last time we talked was the day before her murder ... we mostly talked about my wedding. I think she said you had her doing a story on that donut guy who's running for Mayor ... and she mentioned researching the demographics of subway riders ... but I don't see why anyone would want to kill her over something like that. I don't know."

"Well, think about it. I'm going to call the cops right now. I'll call you back if I find out anything." Dalton hung up the phone.

Adeline slowly put the phone on its cradle and walked over and flopped down on her couch. She grabbed the remote and mindlessly flipped through the channels as she struggled to recall her most recent conversations with Carol. *The wedding ... the subway story ... the donut guy ... a silly blind date. Was there something going on that she didn't tell me about?*

Chapter 3

Palala

Kebeck was working with all four of his hands, trying to pry open a large juice container without spilling it, when he heard a buzz come from his computer. He placed the container on a shelf with one hand and with two others he simultaneously reached for a towel and clicked a key on his computer. As he wiped all of his big green hands with the towel he thought, *good, she's home.* His computer screen came on just in time to see her enter the living room. He felt a surge of joy to see his Adeline, the Earth girl he had watched since she was a baby. He had been worried about her. She had taken it hard when she heard about the death of her friend Carol. He would also miss Carol. She had been good for Adeline and she had been an entertaining being to watch. He had been saddened by her sudden death. He wasn't used to unexpected deaths. In his world most deaths usually were planned. There were, of course, occasional fatal accidents. But murders, they were extremely rare; he could not remember the last murder that occurred on Palala. Kebeck listened as she talked with Dalton about the missing files. *These Earth beings have such complicated lives,* he thought. *But, that's what makes them so interesting to watch.*

Many people in Kebeck's world watched Earth beings for amusement, but his own interest was more serious than most. Kebeck and five of his colleagues had been assigned the job of studying the planet and the effects that Earth-Watching was having on the sociology and psychology of his fellow Palalans. His specialty was Earth ecology.

It had all started around Earth year 1950, when a Palalan scientist developed a way of watching Earth beings through Earth television sets. It had been easy enough to tap into their radio and phone systems (some Palalans had been doing that long before Earth year 1950). Though people had been watching the Earth television shows since they were first broadcasted, the new invention enabled anyone on Palala to watch the Earth beings through any Earth television set or computer monitor, whether these were turned on or not. As long as the set was connected to a power source, they could watch and hear anything that happened in front of the screen. Soon, almost everyone was tuned in to Earth. Many Palalans learned to speak English, while some studied other Earth languages. The Japanese were a popular group to watch; some claimed that they were the most civilized of all Earth cultures. But most seemed to prefer watching the Earth beings located in the United States. They had more televisions, phones, and computers than most locations, and they seemed to be curiously uncivilized and spontaneous compared to the other developed areas on the planet.

A light flashed on the corner of Kebeck's screen. Someone was sending him a message. He clicked a button and the screen displayed a video message from a fellow he had met a couple of times at the Earth Museum. He couldn't remember the person's name; he talked to a lot of people at the Museum.

"I thought you might like to view a live Earth execution. I have tapped into the video system at a prison in Texas and we should be able to view the government killing of an Earth being deemed too vile to live. It is to take place at 22:20 our time today. Please do not think that I in any way take pleasure in seeing any creature killed. But I am curious. It amazes me that a government kills beings to punish them for killing other beings. I find the concept of punishment odd. I guess we have been taught to think more in terms of logical consequences. But I must admit that the violence of the Earth beings intrigues me. Maybe it is because we have so little violence. Before I started watching Earth, I have never really thought of it as an option for handling conflict. It is unfortunate that Earth children are not taught conflict resolution methods. But then if they were like us, Earth television shows and the Earth beings' ways of living would not be so very interesting.

Recently, I have started to watch the interactions taking place at a bar in the city named Chicago. I am sure you know that a bar is the gathering place where Earth beings consume the liquid chemicals that free their inhibitions, but I had no idea of the purpose of such establishments when I first started watching it. I am growing quite fond of the bartender named Harold. From watching how he handles difficult customers, you would think he had taken some of our conflict resolution courses. I think also that ...."

Kebeck stopped the video. He was in no mood to listen to an amateur talking about Earth-Watching theories. He had already spent enough time listening to his friend Sheme yesterday. She watched a financially disadvantaged family of dark-skinned beings who lived in an area called New Jersey and she was very upset because the fourteen-year-old male was injured by a metal projectile while sitting in his home. Many people got caught up in the lives of the Earth beings they watched. Though Kebeck himself tried to maintain an appropriate level of objectivity necessary for his research, he still had developed strong feelings of affection for his Adeline, a strange creature, so far away, that he had never touched or spoken to.

Kebeck had watched Adeline's birth. She was born in her parents' bedroom, with a midwife assisting. Adeline's parents had televisions in the bedroom, living room, and kitchen, so it was easy to follow Adeline's life. The most difficult part was watching her mope and moan through her teen years. She got a TV in her own room when she was fourteen. He wished he could have talked to her when she was suffering through her teens. Unfortunately, communicating with Earth beings was not allowed.

Adeline survived her adolescence and became a lovely, intelligent woman. Now, at age twenty-eight, she was going to marry. Kebeck had watched her date some young males that he found to be lacking the intelligence and consideration that she deserved. He very much approved of the male she had now selected to marry. He enjoyed watching them together. This male was thoughtful and loving towards her. He pleased her sexually. They laughed a lot together. Kebeck saw no reason why he would not be a good husband for her, and maybe the marriage would last until they died.

People found it strange that some Earth beings promised to live together until death. The custom for Palalan couples who wanted to procreate and raise a young one together was to sign a twenty-year contractual agreement. Each female is allowed to bear two children during her 300-year life span, so most people spent the majority of their lives unmarried. Few people stayed together most of their lives, though occasionally a 200-year anniversary was in the news. Most people simply found it difficult to partner with one person for such a length of time. With their centuries-long life expectancies, Palalans normally had different partners at different stages of their lives.

Though Kebeck thought fondly of his two contractual partners and one unofficial partner whom he had lived with during his 156 years on Palala, for the time being he did not desire another partner. There had been unpleasantness when it became evident that he no longer enjoyed the company of his last partner. Still, he had two friends that he enjoyed occasional sexual stimulation with, and his male friend Yerf had shared his house for the last few years and Kebeck found him to be good company. So marriage for life seemed like a silly idea to most Palalans.

Nevertheless, from watching the Earth beings it was apparent that long marriages seemed to be desirable to them. It also appeared that their ability to deceive was a positive factor in maintaining a long marriage. Kebeck had watched Adeline's parents as they interacted. He could see by their actions that although their affection for each other ebbed as they got older, they both seemed to lie about their true feelings.

When Palalans first started watching Earth TV, they marveled at how the Earth beings' skin color did not change when they stated untruths. Palalan biologists attributed this to the Earth beings' evolutionary progression from their earliest forms as sea creatures to apes to their present state. Palalans, on the other hand, evolved directly from their sea-dwelling ancestors. The anxiety felt by any Palalans telling an untruth resulted in an increased heart rate that turned their necks a red color. From watching Earth television, some of Kebeck's colleagues determined that people on Palala were almost like Earth beings permanently outfitted with lie detectors. After discovering that Earth beings could so easily lie, Palalan historians, sociologists, and political-science specialists devoted countless hours to exploring how their own built-in lie detectors might have affected the development of Palalan society in contrast to the development of civilizations on Earth.

Kebeck looked at Adeline sitting on her couch, a sad look on her face. Her dull eyes seemed unaware of the television in front of her. He was concerned about his Adeline. He knew she would eventually get over the death of her friend Carol. He had already watched her mourn the death of her parents. He knew Adeline could handle this, but the news of the missing files and computer made him wonder if Carol's murder might be more than a random robbery gone wrong. Kebeck had watched many Earth murder mysteries on television and this sounded like one of them. He drummed the fingers of his four hands on the slantboard, thinking about the murder. Carol had worked at a desk beside Adeline. They often discussed stories they were working on. Could his Adeline be in any danger?

Chapter 4

Earth

I'm not stupid, Adeline thought to herself. *I want to go to Carol's apartment and see if her computer and papers are still there, but what if ....* Adeline looked out the window and then at the clock on the wall. *I'm not going to go over to her apartment alone, just as it's getting dark. That's what they do in the movies, and I always sit in the theatre thinking, "this is stupid. Nobody would do that. That's just bad writing."* She looked out the window again. *I'll call the policeman who interviewed me the morning after Carol's death and get him to go to the apartment with me. They also do that in the movies, but at least it's safer and not stupid.*

Adeline rolled off the couch and rooted through the apartment for her yellow purse. She remembered she had been wearing yellow the day Carol died, so she thought the card from the cop who interviewed her must be in that purse. She opened up her closet and surveyed her two shelves of purses. There it was, tucked between her dark green leather bag and her new pink silk clutch. And there was the card, plain, with just a name and number. Nick Hawes. When she looked at the card she remembered the guy. He was sixty-something, average height, with a little belly over his belt. He was bald on top with hair around the sides, like a monk. In fact, now that she thought about it, if he put on a brown robe and sandals, he would make the perfect 12th-century monk.

Adeline sat down in the chair by her desk, picked up the phone, and punched in the number listed on the card. She patiently worked her way through four levels of the automated answering system before she had Detective Hawes on the line.

"Yeah, this is Nick Hawes."

Instantly, she envisioned the monk in a brown robe. "Hi, I'm calling concerning the death of Carol Stafford." It hit her. The moment she got it out of her mouth, the grief that she had been holding back made her weak and nauseous. Adeline leaned back in the chair and took a breath. Tears welled up in her eyes.

"Yes?" Hawes asked.

Adeline couldn't make her mouth work. She took another deep breath.

"Are you still there? Who is this?"

"My name is Adeline. I am … was Carol's friend. You interviewed me at the office, the newspaper office."

"Yeah, yeah … I remember you. Good friend, worked with her. What can I do for you?"

Adeline's notion of a monk was quickly being replaced with more of a Joe Friday image. She wiped her tears and replied, "I'm calling because all of Carol's papers and her laptop were stolen from the office and…"

"Yeah, your boss called with that info. I sent a guy over to look for prints on the desk."

"So, it's not just a mugging anymore, right?"

Carol had been murdered late at night, beside her car in the parking lot of her apartment building, and her purse had been taken. The police had assumed that she was killed during a mugging. But normally muggers don't steal all your files out of your office three days after they kill you.

"Yeah, it's a full-fledged murder investigation now." Detective Hawes paused. "Did you just call to tell me about the office papers or is there something else?"

"Well … yes. I was wondering if you had checked to see if her papers and other laptop were still in her apartment."

"Hey lady, we do know what we're doing, okay? As soon as she was identified, we checked out the apartment. Everything was fine there."

"Were there papers and a computer on her desk?"

Detective Hawes hesitated. "Uh… I don't remember. We thought it was a mugging. The place looked normal. Look, you've got a point. I'll go over to the apartment in the morning. Give it a look-see."

"But that might be too late," Adeline said. "Whoever took her stuff from the office could be over at the apartment clearing it out right now!"

"Maybe … but probably not," he grunted. "Listen, that building has a good security system. When I was in there I noticed that it had an alarm system that was connected to the nearest police station. Taking stuff from that newspaper office was easy, but her apartment is pretty tight. Plus, I've got supper waiting for me at home."

"But I have a key to her place. I could get someone to go with me to check it out right now!"

"Not a good idea." Hawes let out a big sigh. "Well … I gotta go over there anyway. Okay, let's do this … you knew her really well, didn't you? And you know what should be in her apartment. So I'll meet you in the parking lot of her building tomorrow morning at nine and we can look it over together, alright?"

"I would rather go now."

"No."

"I have a key. I can …."

"NO!" he barked at her. "You may have a key but I have the law. As of this minute I am declaring that Carol Stafford's apartment is now a crime scene, and that makes it off-limits to you and to any other civilians. Step one foot in there and I will charge you. Am I clear?" he asked.

"All right, tomorrow at nine," Adeline surrendered.

Adeline wandered over to the couch and plopped down. Then she got up and started toward her computer with the intention of sending her fiancé an email. *No, I'm not going to tell him about Carol's missing papers; he'll just worry. I'll just write my usual lovey-dovey, miss-you stuff.* Adeline sat down to write

She had only had typed a few words when the sound of the fall wind whipping leaves around caught her attention and she turned to look out the front window. Her eyes moved to the big comfy couch that dominated the room. An image came into her mind. She saw Carol lying on the couch, in one of her usual convoluted positions, with one long leg hanging over the couch arm. In her mind's eye, Adeline saw Carol wearing a scoop neck lavender blouse with a dark green pair of big-leg pants. Adeline wouldn't have left the house in those colors but Carol could pull it off. That was the outfit Carol wore when they went out to dinner two weeks ago. She remembered their conversation from that night. A bottle of wine had inspired a bout of soul searching. Carol had read some article that said a person who lived to eighty-five would have only have lived 744,600 hours. Carol had added up what she had left: "I have about 500,000 hours left and I must not waste them." She had lifted her wine glass in a salute and continued: "The pity is ... I write my life in the sand knowing the tide will erase all traces of me." That line had bothered Adeline at the time, but she had dismissed it and told Carol to lighten up. Now, as she envisioned Carol draped on the couch, the line haunted her. Carol was an only child. She had had friends, but no real close friends, except Adeline. *After Carol's parents die, she'll be gone forever except for the memories in my head*, Adeline thought. *Maybe a few other people will remember her, for a while. But soon it will be as if she never existed.* A tear slowly ran down one cheek. *Shit, I don't want to cry again.* Adeline sniffled and wiped her face with the back of her hand.

When Carol had said the line about writing in the sand, she had been concerned that she would never do anything of significance. More than once she had said, "I just want to be really good at something, anything." Twice she had started writing a book. The second time she had over a hundred pages when she decided that it was drivel and burned all of it in a bonfire on the beach. *And now she's dead. Alive one day and dead the next. Shit! I've got to make my life count for something. It would really piss Carol off to know that she died before she had a chance to leave her mark on the planet. Maybe that's the good thing about death being the end of consciousness ... no regrets. What we do, we do and when we're done, we're really done.*

Adeline realized that her shoulders had tightened and her hands were tensed over the computer keys, but she had written almost nothing. She got up and stretched as she wandered over to the couch. Her eyes gazed at the blank TV screen in front of her. She didn't want to think about the unfairness of life. She didn't want to think at all. Adeline picked up the remote. She didn't know if she would sleep much that night; she hoped her TV would keep her company and help get that line about "writing your life in the sand" out of her head.

Chapter 5

Palala

Kebeck had listened and watched as Adeline set up the appointment with the Earth policeman. He then set the time device on his computer to connect to the cameras, television sets, and phones in and around Carol's apartment building and parking lot for the next day. Now he could relax. At nine a.m. Earth time his computer would notify him so he could watch and hear everything.

Kebeck flipped to his video messages and noticed a name he didn't recognize. He clicked it on. It was the same fellow from the Earth Museum again. *Now I remember his name.* It was Nodge Copa Ule, a regular visitor at the museum.

"Greetings Kebeck. I hope my messages are not an intrusion, but you are the only Earth expert that I know. I have come across something that bothers me greatly. Now that my English has improved to the point where I can read the language, I decided to read a book that is much discussed on Earth television. Fortunately, I was able to find the entire text on the planet's Internet system. In this book there was a story in which a god kills every living being on Earth except one family and the creatures they had aboard their ship. I understand that this book, the Bible, is the basis for their Christian religion and that many Earth beings think everything in it to be true and real. How can it be that this god was thought of as a good and loving entity when he had murdered almost all the beings on the planet? I do not see logic in the story. And, was there once such a being ... one that was powerful enough to do that? I would be most grateful if you would explain the logic in this. I thank you for your time. I look forward to seeing you at the Museum."

Kebeck's shoulders drooped. *He wants me to explain the logic of a legend out of one of their religion books.* Then Kebeck smiled. *I'll refer him to Leto, he's the religion expert, not me.* Nodge was good at coming up with difficult questions. Last week he had asked why female Earth beings wear shoes that are raised in the back. Kebeck had explained to Nodge that because the females are generally shorter than the males, they wear the tall heels in an attempt to be as tall as the males. Evidence showed that on Earth, beings of short stature were not as well respected as the taller ones.

As he backed away from his computer he heard Yerf enter the house behind him. The dripping sound that accompanied his footsteps meant that once more Yerf hadn't bothered to towel off before coming in. As he pushed the off button on the computer with one hand, he pushed his slantboard back with a second hand and threw a towel at Yerf with a third hand. He waved his fourth hand at Yerf in a sign of exasperation.

"You agreed to not drip water inside when you come in from a swim," he said.

Yerf grabbed the towel out of the air and started to dry the big shiny scales on his body. "Sorry, I was thinking about my votes and forgot." Yerf ran the towel over his sleek oval head. His eye, ear, and nose membranes closed as he dried the small scales on his face.

"Yerf, all your adult life you have voted on eight-day. How does it still sneak up on you?"

Yerf sighed. "I guess I just take longer to make decisions. You know some societies have rulers or committees who decide what is best for their people. They don't have to personally vote on every issue. All the thinking makes my brain tired."

"Well, if you are too lazy to think about it, then just vote as I tell you. Vote no on the issue of whether to allow limited hunting of the maets on the Gnilles nature preserve island. I think we should not interfere with the balance of predators and grass-eating animals on a nature preserve. Also, you should vote to keep four hours as the maximum paid work time allowed per day. And vote against allowing government buildings to be used for religion meetings. If some of our people want to adopt some of the Earth religions, I guess they can. They are free to think what they want. But we should not allow them to use government buildings. I would think by watching the Earth beings and studying their history, any logical person can see that religion has not been a good thing for any of those concerned. We should not encourage it. We outgrew that type of misplaced causality centuries ago. I can't see how anyone could take any of the Earth beings' religions seriously. But, they seem to amuse some people."

"I have not decided how I feel about the religions, Yerf replied. "I cannot take them seriously either, but the kneeling and praying seems to make some people very happy. It seems to be something akin to meditation. The religions fit into our philosophy of letting people do whatever they want as long as it hurts no one. From studying Earth history, religions have, on the whole, been harmful for the Earth beings, but we are different. We are more logical and less violent. If you can reserve a government building for a hands-ball game, then I do not see why we should not allow people to reserve rooms for their religious activities."

"You know, you are wrong on this one," Kebeck growled. "These Earth religions can be harmful to our people. Believing in a religion changes the way you think. As we study how Earth-Watching is affecting our people, the two big things that concern us are religions and violence."

"I can see not wanting to adopt their violence, but how are their religions going to harm us?"

"Most of their religions are full of violence. The Christian ones have as their main symbol a person being tortured to death, and their main ceremony is symbolic cannibalism. They kneel and eat something that symbolizes the dead body of their god's offspring. Is that not disgusting and rather primitive?"

"All right," Yerf conceded. "You are the expert. No public buildings for religious meetings. If you are through with the computer for now, I will register my votes and be done with running the world for seven more days."

Kebeck moved away from the computer and over to the food area. As he reached into the refrigerator and grabbed a handful of raw vegetables, he thought about Earth's eating rituals. He wondered how Earth beings had developed the custom of having specific, formal times for eating. Some time in their development they had quit eating whenever they were hungry and ritualized eating into a virtual ceremony performed three times a day. Kebeck wondered why that had happened. Somehow it seemed to have been accepted all over planet Earth. One of his colleagues, Samot, put forth the theory that such ceremonial eating habits were one of the main reasons many Earth beings in the more economically developed parts of the planet weighed too much. It was a logical assumption; one may tend to overeat if one were prohibited from eating again for five or six hours.

"I was thinking, Yerf, maybe we should go to the restaurant that has been opened in town."

Yerf growled at Kebeck: "Just a minute, I am almost through registering my votes."

Kebeck took a piece of smoked fish out of the refrigerator and put it in his mouth.

Yerf turned to face Kebeck. "Now, let me get this straight. Somebody has opened a place where people go just to eat food, like the restaurants we see on television on Earth? Why would I want to go to a special location to eat food? There is food at home, food at work, food almost anywhere you go. Do they do something special to the food?"

"I understand they cook the vegetables and that they put spices on the vegetables and the fish," Kebeck replied. "Vegetables should be eaten raw. I have tried heated vegetables; not good, and they are mushy, as though they were spoiled. I agree with cooking or smoking fish; it kills parasites and germs and preserves it. But spices, they cover up the flavors of the food. Why should we go to this place?" Yerf twisted his head to one side and gestured the hand signal for "What?" Because Palalans spent so much time in and under the water, a language of hand signals had evolved. It was common for people to talk with their hands and their voices when they were agitated or excited. One knew Yerf was not happy when his hands were in motion.

"It makes an occasion out of eating," Kebeck said.

"Why should it be an occasion?" Yerf asked. "Do the Earth beings also make a ritualized occasion out of disposing of body waste or drinking water?"

"So you do not want to go to the restaurant."

"Of course not," he sighed. "I don't understand why people would want to adopt the Earth beings' food customs. Unlike Earth, food is not a problem on our planet. Our age-old system of using the government to supply food, water, and body waste facilities to every building is a plan the Earth should adopt from us."

"So I will go to the restaurant by myself," Kebeck said.

Yerf got up and walked over to Kebeck. He was much taller than Kebeck and a lighter tone of gray. Yerf looked down at his friend: "I do not want to be seen as grumpy or unsocial, so if you want my company when you visit this restaurant place, I will go with you. But just this once, because it is a silly idea to sit and eat at a special location."

"Good. Then get dressed and we will go visit it now."

Yerf shook his head in disbelief. "We have to put on clothes? Why? It is not cold outside."

"It is the custom to wear nice clothing when you go to a restaurant on Earth."

"And what is considered nice clothing? I have three pieces of clothing designed to keep me warmer and two pieces of clothing that are designed to protect my body when I work with hot metal or glass blowing."

"Just wear something."

"All right," Yerf said. "But if it gets hot, the clothing comes off. And I guess we will have to bicycle there, because we cannot swim to town if we are going to wear clothes."

Kebeck stopped and smiled to himself.

"What is the big smile about? Share the joke."

"Well," Kebeck said, "there is an axiom that came about when a group of female Earth beings were expressing their right to be equal with their male counterparts: 'A woman needs a man like a fish needs a bicycle'."

"And that is funny because ...?"

"Because to an Earth being, we would look somewhat like fish and often we ride bicycles."

"You have been doing too much Earth-Watching. I think I understand why some people want it outlawed."

Chapter 6

Earth

The building that had been Carol's home for the last nine months was a square brick five-story with an asphalt parking lot on two sides. A road ran along the third side. The fourth side was a gaudy attempt at a grand entrance, with trees and grass on both sides of a cracked walkway that led up to a six-column portico. Bits of rusted metal were visible where the cement had fallen away at the bottom of the columns. Adeline arrived exactly at nine, pulled into the parking lot, and sat waiting in her car. She looked around to see if the policeman had arrived. *He's late.* She didn't want to look at the parking lot, so she looked around inside her car. Candy bar wrappers and parking lot receipts littered the passenger-side floor. *I should clean this car.* She loved her zippy little Mazda and usually she kept it in perfect condition. She glanced at the time. As she looked up from her watch, Nick Hawes pulled up beside her. She didn't like being in this parking lot because this was where Carol had been killed. She didn't want to look at the asphalt because she was afraid that she would see the dark spot where Carol's blood had seeped onto the pavement. She got out of the car looking straight at Detective Hawes. He was wearing a brown suit.

"Hi, how are you?" he asked.

"Could be better," was all she got out.

"Shall we go in?"

She nodded and followed Hawes across the parking lot. She was surprised at how tense she felt at being here. Over the years, as a reporter, she had been to crime scenes many times. This was just another gray asphalt parking lot, divided into numbered spaces by faded yellow lines, but it spooked her. As she fumbled with the keys to unlock the outside door to the apartment building, she reminded herself to *just breathe normally.*

"Are you all right?" Hawes asked as they crossed the foyer to the elevator.

"Yes and no. I found being in the parking lot where Carol was murdered a bit upsetting, but I feel better now that we're inside."

"Just warn me if you feel like you might pass out" he said. Somehow he managed to sound both concerned and sarcastic at the same time.

Adeline wasn't sure what she thought of him. *Is he a good cop, sincerely wanting to find out the who and the why of Carol's death or is he just going through the motions to get by until retirement?*

As soon as they opened the door to Carol's apartment, Adeline knew someone had been there. Directly across the room from the door sat Carol's desk. Adeline had never seen the top surface; now she saw that it was a nice oak with bits of inlaid marble. There should have been a computer and three to five inches of papers covering that desk.

She turned to Nick. "Everything is gone."

"What's gone?"

"Everything. Her computer and all her papers."

"This is the way it was on the night she was killed. We had the super let us in here an hour or two after we found the body. I thought she was just a neat person who kept a clear desk."

"No!" Adeline threw her hands up in exasperation. "She was … a pig, sort of. I mean she was a wonderful person and my best friend, but she was not neat. Look at the kitchen. Look in her bedroom, clothes everywhere. We used to say that Carol had evolved from being a hunter-gatherer to being a gatherer-hunter. She gathered everything and then had to hunt through it to find things. Her papers and computer are gone."

Hawes pulled a pair of thin rubber gloves out of his jacket pocket and put them on. He then opened every drawer in the desk and found nothing except a few paper clips and dust balls.

As Adeline dropped down on the couch where she had watched countless movies with her friend, Hawes shouted, "No! Don't touch anything! Don't even put your hands on the couch to push yourself up. The crime scene guys have got to go over this place."

Adeline froze. Then she clasped her hands in her lap as her eyes traveled around the room.

Hawes put out his rubber-clad hand to help her up.

"Sorry," Adeline said as she let him pull her up off the low couch.

"Okay, stand right there and don't move."

He pulled off the rubber glove and stuffed it in a pocket, then reached under his coat. When he pulled out a gun, she stepped back.

"Just stay here. I've got to check out the rest of the place. I don't think there's anyone here. The gun's just a precaution. But who knows … we found a guy hiding in a closet last month. That was freaky. That guy had spent two days in a closet. No toilet, no food. Unbelievable."

Adeline stared at the gun. She couldn't remember ever seeing anyone, in real life, pull out a gun. She of course had seen probably thousands of guns in movies and on TV, but this was different. *This is serious*, she thought. *Carol is dead and I'm in her apartment with a cop with his gun out.*

"Better idea," he said. "You wait in the hall."

Using the edge of his coat, he opened the door and waved Adeline out.

The door closed. *I'm scared*, Adeline thought. She looked up and down the hall. It was empty. *Here I am standing in a place as familiar to me as my kitchen and I'm scared shitless.*

After five or ten minutes, Hawes came out the door and tucked his gun back under his coat. Adeline was relieved and almost wanted to hug him, but he didn't seem like the type who would feel comfortable with that. So instead she just moved a few inches closer to him. He whipped out his cell phone and called the crime investigation unit. "I need a unit over here at..." He paused and looked over at Adeline. "Where are we again?"

"1362 Willowdale, unit 17."

"Right, thanks." He repeated the address to the person on the phone.

Adeline stood there and listened, thinking, *what next?* As he put his cell phone away, he turned to her and said, "Are your fingerprints on file with the police?"

"What?" she asked. "Why would they be on file? Do I look like a criminal?"

"Uh...yeah, now that you mention it, you do look like a criminal because criminals just look like regular people. But that's not why I want your fingerprints. You've spent a lot of time in that apartment, right?"

Adeline nodded.

"The crime lab will need your fingerprints to differentiate between your prints and others found on the crime scene. So, I want you to drive down to the nearest police station and get fingerprinted. That would probably be ... uh ... the one at Fifth and Welland."

Adeline stood staring at him.

"Now, please."

"Now?" she asked.

"Yes, now. I have to stay until the CSI guys get here." He held out his hand. "Give me the keys to the apartment and go. Get fingerprinted. Then, get on with your life. I'll call you in a couple of days, after I get their report."

"That's it? Just get on with my life like nothing's happened?"

"Besides losing a close friend, nothing has happened to you. I understand that all this scares you." He cocked his head to one side and studied her carefully. "Do you have any reason to think that you're in any danger?"

She hesitated and thought for a minute. "No."

"Then go do whatever you normally do and call me if anything unusual happens. Still got my card?"

"Yeah."

"Then go." He gently nudged her toward the elevator. "I'll call when I know something. I've been doing this for almost thirty years. I'm a good detective. I should be able to find your friend's killer."

Adeline did as she was told and walked over to the elevator. And then she did something she had never done before. When the doors opened she paused and carefully looked inside the elevator before getting on.

Chapter 7

Earth

The thing Erwin had liked best about being a professional killer had been the hours. The money had been pretty good too. Now he worked ridiculous hours just to keep his business afloat. Sometimes he thought that maybe he had selected the wrong business in which to invest his hard-earned money; the coffee shops turned out to be more complicated than he had thought. Fifteen years ago, Erwin had taken every penny he had earned as a hit man and invested it all in two dozen coffee shops, and now he was fighting hard to keep the big franchise chains from putting him out of business. If he was just up against one-owner stores he literally could just kill off the competition, but he knew that wouldn't work with corporations. *Friggin' multiheaded dragons just grow two new heads when you cut off one.* Fortunately, he had stowed away enough of his early profits in other investments so that he would always be able to live somewhere between comfortable and very comfortable. But he hated fighting the big guys in order to keep afloat.

"Charles, where are my notes from the last Metro meeting?" he called out. The sound echoed off the walls of his big oak-paneled office. Erwin rifled through the stacks of papers that covered his desk.

His assistant came into the room with an electronic notepad in his hand. Charles had the appearance of a classic nerd: tall, pale, and skinny and already losing his hair at twenty-seven. "I downloaded all those notes into your laptop this morning."

Erwin turned toward Charles and shook a finger at him, saying, "I want it on paper. I can't go into a meeting at City Hall and wave a laptop at the other councilors. Print it out. Put it on my desk. I'll come back for it after my meeting with the Parks Committee."

He hadn't planned to get into politics. He had planned to keep a low profile, just be a successful, quiet businessman. But five years ago, he decided to build a new shop on Bloor Street. So he had to go to City Hall to get a building permit. Then, he had to go to a City Council meeting to get a minor adjustment to the permit approved. Erwin had to sit through almost three hours of the meeting before they got to his request. When they finally got to his spot on the agenda, they quickly agreed to the minor adjustment. But after sitting in the lofty, circular council room and listening to the councilors make decisions that determined the future of the city, Erwin realized that he wanted to be part of it all. In fact, he wanted to run the show. *I want to be Mayor of this city*, he thought. *I'm bored. Battling the chains is getting pretty tedious. I want this type of power. It'll be fun!*

Getting elected to Council was relatively easy. It was fortunate for him that the incumbent in his district just happened to die in an accident a mere two months before the election.

When Erwin had worked as a hit man, he always liked to make his killings look like accidents. And he didn't like to touch his subjects. Only once did he have to use his hands to personally finish off a victim. The target in question was allergic to pine nuts; they supposedly made his throat swell so he couldn't breathe. So, Erwin laced a hamburger with pine nuts. The doomed man was fighting and struggling to breathe but he just wouldn't die.

Of course, Erwin had to make sure the subject was dead before leaving the scene so he had put a plastic bag over the fellow's head and held it tight. After that one Erwin decided to never again depend on food allergies for his dispatching activities.

With the soon-to-be-deceased incumbent councilor, Erwin came out of retirement and staged a drowning accident. As usual he studied his subject's habits, hobbies, and work activities. He discovered that the councilor liked to swim and snorkel and had booked a trip to the Mayan Riviera. It had been easy to check in to the same hotel and watch his subject's swimming habits. Erwin noticed that the hotel beach staff insisted that all snorkelers wear a little safety vest that could be inflated in cases of emergency. On the fourth day of this "vacation," Erwin put on scuba gear and was waiting underwater when the councilor went for his daily snorkel tour of the reef adjacent to the hotel. Erwin had already discovered some enormous concrete blocks in the shallow waters of the reef that were used by the local fishermen to anchor their boats. After threading a rope through a metal ring in one of the blocks, Erwin had simply looped the rope through the belt on the hapless snorkeler's safety vest and pulled him down to the bottom. The councilor struggled for two or three minutes, then went limp. Erwin looked at his watch and waited ten more minutes before he released the body and gathered up the rope.

The election, of course, was a breeze.

Chapter 8

Earth

It itched, all of this lace and tuttle or tootle or whatever they called the net-like stiff fabric that seemed to be part of every wedding dress.

"Stand still," said Nina.

"I'm still. Now take the picture and let me get out of this thing. And I'm not trying on any more."

"I only have one more."

"No thanks!" Adeline carefully undid the first of the twenty little silk-covered buttons on the bodice of the dress as she turned to go back to the dressing room.

Nina called after her, "This one could be the perfect one."

Adeline was not in the mood to fiddle with lace and fluff. But then she had never been into the whole wedding scene. She was doing it in a church with bridesmaids just to make Jim's mother happy. She would much rather run off, just the two of them, and get married at some resort in Mexico or the Bahamas.

As she pushed past a pink satin stool and exited the changing area, Nina snapped another picture.

Adeline glared at her friend. "Enough. Let's just sit down and look through the photos and pick a dress."

"But you should be excited. This is big! You're picking out your wedding dress!"

Adeline pointed toward the pink and blue brocade couch by the door: "Sit."

Nina made a childish face at Adeline, tossed back her curly red hair, then flopped her round little body down on the seat. "You're no fun," Nina huffed. "I know things are bothering you, but you need to let it go and get into the moment."

"I'll try." Adeline sat down beside her. As Nina flipped through the photos on the digital camera, Adeline realized that she just didn't care. "All right, the third one will do. You really liked that one." Adeline waved to the clerk who had been watching them from the counter. She came over and Nina showed her the picture of the chosen dress. The clerk gushed on about how beautiful Adeline was going to be and went to the back to wrap it up.

"All right, what's wrong?"

"I'm scared. And I don't like it. You know, when I first heard of Carol's death, it was a mugging. And I'm a reporter, right? There are muggings and robberies in the news all the time. It happens. So, I figure if I'm careful I won't become one of those statistics. It's basically a nice world and if you're not in the wrong place at the wrong time, you should be okay. But now... Carol's death seems to be a murder that could be related to her work. Well ... I feel at risk. I've always tried to live as if strangers are just people I don't know yet. I didn't always lock my door in the daytime. I expect most people to be nice most of the time. But now maybe there's some person out there, maybe some person I walk past every day, who for some reason killed Carol and took all her papers and computers. I don't know why he killed Carol. I'm guessing it's a man; most murderers are men, but it could be a woman.

But what could Carol have known that would make someone want to kill her? She had no big secrets. Carol and I talked about everything, really. Everything. I knew all her secrets. And they were just normal stuff ... nothing to kill over. Her biggest secret was that she had been groped by a neighbor when she was seven. The old man died five years ago, had a heart attack. I was the only person she ever told.

Carol wasn't into drugs. She didn't gamble, said it was just giving money away to big corporations. Her biggest vice was an appreciation for Margaritas. I'll never be able to drink a Margarita again without thinking of her." Nina reached out and took Adeline's hand as she went on: "I have no idea why someone would want to kill *her*, of all people. But now I'm not only sad, I'm scared. If it's related to the newspaper, maybe I'm next, or maybe it'll be Dalton. I don't know. But I'm frightened, and I hate it."

Nina took a big breath, looked down at the floor, then back at Adeline. "So ... as my shrink says, what're you going to do about it?"

Adeline thought for a second. "I guess ... not much. What am I supposed to do, leave the country? Maybe her death has nothing to do with the newspaper or me. Who knows? Of course, I hope the police find the killer as soon as possible. I am being extra cautious, locking doors and avoiding underground garages. I've got lots of work to keep me busy. I'm going to try to live a normal life." Adeline stood up. The clerk was coming toward them with two large white and silver bags. Adeline turned to face Nina. "But, my world has changed ... and it really pisses me off!"

Chapter 9

Palala

Kebeck and Yerf parked their bicycles under a huge tree next to a round dome-shaped building. Kebeck liked Tew trees because their big leaves would keep the back supports and seats of their bicycles dry from any rainfall.

"Look, they put up a sign in English," said Kebeck.

"Does that mean that we will get English-type food?" asked Yerf.

"I hope not," replied Kebeck. "On television shows, negative things are said about food from the island of England."

"I have come to the conclusion that they use the word "English" too many different ways. It seems to refer to things from the island of England or as it is also called, Great Britain, and to a language spoken in several different countries. Confusing."

"Let us go in and see what style of food is being offered. If it is food of a kind they like to eat in England, then it might be Indian food," said Kebeck.

Yerf had his hand on the door as he turned to Kebeck and said, "What? Did not the English kill the majority of the Indians to take over the country they made into the United States of

America? Did they then take the food of the Indians back to their country?"

Kebeck paused, closed his eyes for a moment, and then explained: "There is a rather large country located somewhat between the lands known as the Arab peninsula and Thailand that is called India. However, when European Earth beings started exploring the oceans, they sailed to North America and assumed they were in India. Thus, they misnamed the local people and called them Indians. For centuries both groups were called Indians. But now, the Indian people in North America are usually called Native Americans."

Yerf still stood holding the door handle, looking confused. "So which Indian food will we probably be eating?"

"The people of England like to eat food from the country of India."

"Why? What is wrong with the native foods of England?"

"Native English foods are not spiced; they are said to be plain or dull," Kebeck explained.

"I might like English foods," said Yerf.

"Enough speculation. Let us just go in and see what they have."

The round room had ten tall tables, each table equipped with four 70-degree slantboards. Attached to the wall at the far end of the room were shelves, a preparation counter, and a cooking unit. The room was dim. There were candles on each table. Only the cooking and food preparation area offered brighter lighting. Kebeck was surprised to see pieces of fabric patterned in red and white squares covering the tables. Dyes were rarely used on Palala, but now, after seeing the bright colors of fabrics common on Earth, people were starting to use more colors. As Yerf and Kebeck entered the room, they were approached by a female wearing pink fabric adorned with sparkles. Bits of light were reflected in Kebeck's eyes.

She stretched out her hands in the customary greeting. "I am the one with the role of welcoming you. I assume you have come to eat food with us. There is a charge of four credits each."

Yerf looked at Kebeck. "I have to pay credits for food? It is wrong to pay for food. Do you also want me to pay for water and air?"

"We are paying for the experience," said Kebeck. "If you will cease all negative comments so that we might enjoy this, I will also pay for your eating experience."

"As you wish; I will only see sunrises and not sunsets," said Yerf.

Kebeck turned to the pink-cladded female. "Do you want me to authorize the transfer of credits now or at the end of the eating experience?"

"It is the custom to pay at the end of the meal. There is a computer by the door that you may use as you leave. Now, as they say on Earth, please be seated." She motioned toward a table surrounded by its four slantboards.

Yerf and Kebeck climbed on the slantboards, tucking their feet into the foot troughs. A recording of horn and drum music played in the background; they sat quietly, just listening. Kebeck watched as Yerf ran his hands over the fabric on the table. Yerf picked up a plate and flipped it over to examine the bottom, then sniffed the water container.

"A problem?" Kebeck asked.

"Yes and no. Time, effort, and materials were wasted to make these unnecessary objects. This is counter to what our society values. I understand that this place allows us a unique experience and is somewhat of an experiment, but I am not comfortable here."

"Change is never comfortable."

"Are we supposed to just sit here and wait for food? I do not Earth-Watch that often. Is there not more to this?"

"Yes, I apologize." Kebeck shrugged his shoulders as he raised his upper hands toward the ceiling. "I was thinking ... and not being in the moment. During Earth-like dinner occasions we are supposed to discuss pleasant subjects. Like ... like ... sports. I see in the news that the bigball team from Kaffa is coming to play against our village team. Does our team have a chance against them?"

Yerf's posture changed and his face brightened. Anyone could see that he loved sports. "The Kaffa team has some injuries, so it should be an even match."

"I would never play that game. I do not want to be run over by a ball, half filled with water, bigger than me. If you remember, my son Prigo played it in school and not only was he run over by the ball but two of the fellows pushing the ball stomped him. He was in an injury recovery unit for three weeks. But, I must admit, it is fun to watch. Did you ever play bigball? I do not remember seeing you play."

"No one my size should get on a bigball field; those guys are huge. I would be crushed to a pulp." Even though Yerf at times acted big and tough, he was actually a little thinner and shorter than most male Palalans.

"Good point. You know what would be fun to see? I would like to see a bigball game between two of those Earth football teams we see on Earth TV."

Yerf huffed. "Can we not have a conversation without you talking about Earth?

"Of course we can. But Earth-Watching shows you new ways of doing things.... They pay coaches and players. We pay coaches, but no one is paid to play a sport. Maybe we could have professional bigball teams. Would that not be fantastic? There could be games every week. I would go to local games and watch others on computer. Would you not like that also?"

"You know I would. And the coach would be so happy if he no longer had to schedule games and practice around the work schedules of twenty people. It sounds like a wonderful idea, but the fact that it turns the sport into a job could change the nature of the game. It would become more serious. I have watched some professional Earth sports and they are not lighthearted. Much money is paid to the successful athletes, making winning crucial."

"But," Kebeck raised a hand to make a point, "if we were to hire athletes for a twenty-year contract and all players on all the teams were paid the same, then we might have a good system."

"That could work." Yerf's neck began to change color. "I shall ask the coaches' association to research the possibility of such a system." Yerf wiggled with joy on his slantboard.

Two females entered the room, each wearing bright yellow and red clothing, clothing that could have no practical use. Both Yerf and Kebeck turned to look. The fabric was draped on their bodies in such a way that it would neither keep them warm nor protect them against sparks from machinery.

Yerf looked at Kebeck. "What is the purpose of that clothing?"

Kebeck was still looking at the females. His head turned to face Yerf. "It certainly got our attention. I think that is the reason they are wearing it."

"Why would they go to all that effort to get people to notice them? How does the fact that I recognize that they are wearing unusual attire benefit them?"

"It is possible that they are doing so to further their Earth-dining experience."

"Yes, that seems logical; it is just an exercise in Earth imitation." Yerf squirmed around on his slantboard. "Might our food come soon?"

The female in pink who had greeted them walked over and handed them a stiff piece of paper. "What would you like to order?" she asked in English.

"So I suppose you want me to speak English to further the experience?" Yerf said sarcastically.

Kebeck replied, also in English: "That would be nice."

They scanned the list of possibilities. The selections were written in English, but fortunately Yerf had learned to read the language so he could learn more about Earth engineering and building methods. Both opted for the fish and vegetable dish at the top of the list. The female left and they sat, silent, staring into space.

A quizzical look appeared on Yerf's face. "Kebeck, as we came in you mentioned that some of the beings living in the area that they call America are referred to as Native Americans. Is that not also a misnomer? From my studies, those beings are not native to that area, but rather they emigrated to that land from the Asian continent. Why did they substitute one incorrect name with another?"

Kebeck thought for a moment. "Who knows."

"This 'Who' person: where can I find him? That question bothers me and I would like to hear the answer."

Kebeck took a deep breath. "There is no such person named Who. 'Who knows' is an Earth expression that means I do not know the answer and I know of no one else who does."

"Oh."

Silence reigned again.

As they sat, staring ahead, Kebeck recognized a familiar odor. He turned just as his old friend Karna entered the room. Both Kebeck and Yerf stood up to greet him. Kebeck had known Karna since he was a child. Even though he lived only three houses away, Kebeck did not see him often. For the last twenty-five years, Karna had kept to himself and was rarely seen in public. Karna did not feel comfortable in a crowd because he feared that someone would mention how he disgraced himself all those years ago. No one spoke of the matter any longer, but Karna said he could see it in people's eyes. He said the cautious tone of people's voices chilled his blood.

Twenty-nine years earlier, Karna had joined in a union with a female named Graloe in order to raise a child. Karna was young (merely forty Palalan years old) and had signed the union contract within half a year after meeting Graloe. He liked children and was anxious to have one of his own. The union, however, turned out to be a mistake. Karna loved his child but he found Graloe difficult to live with. Karna described her as a trim, active female who had to have everything done right—meaning, her way! Moreover, everything had to be done immediately. Even Kebeck, as an occasional visitor, could see that she was not a patient person. When the child was only four years of age, Karna broke the contract and moved to a village that literally was on the other side of the planet. His actions shocked the community. Breaking a child-raising contract was unheard of. Kebeck knew of people who resorted to keeping two houses next to each other and others who spent many hours at their workplace when their mate became difficult to live with, but to move so far away was most uncommon and viewed as abhorrent behavior. Fortunately, Graloe was able to relocate into a village where she had many friends and neighbors nearby to help her raise the child. Karna stayed in contact with the child by computer but did not return until the child's maturity ceremony. Because he did not fulfill the contract with Graloe, there will always be a blot on Karna's name and he will feel shame for the rest of his life. He now shares his house with a female friend but she will not contract with him to have a child. No one blames her; he is disgraced, after all. Similarly, no one will sign a contract with him in any business affairs. Contracts are the basis of almost all retail activities. When Palalans want to purchase any sort of commodity, be it a computer or a bowl or virtually any item whatsoever, they must first contract with someone who will make and then sell the item. Before his scandal, Karna contracted with builders to make environmental body waste systems for new buildings. Sadly, those activities ceased when he voided his child-raising contract. Since then, he has worked carving shelves that he stores in his home and sells to builders.

Karna turned his body to face Kebeck, avoiding eye contact with Yerf.

"So, you have also come to try the restaurant?" Kebeck queried.

"No, this restaurant thing is silly. I saw your bicycle outside and stopped to talk with you."

"See, he agrees with me. Let us leave at once," Yerf growled.

Karna shyly glanced at Yerf but remained silent.

"No, you agreed to the experience. We must complete the whole process," Kebeck replied. He moved closer to Karna. "Your face shows no happiness. Do you wish to speak privately?"

"I would."

"Yerf, Karna and I wish to step outside to talk. Do I have your permission to leave you for a blip or two?"

"Go. I will be fine."

As soon as they got outside, the words spilled out of Karna: "I need to talk to somebody and I knew you would understand. I apologize for interrupting your restaurant experience, but I am much troubled. Much troubled indeed. In the past we have spoken of the Earth family that I watch. I have watched them for ten years and I have much affection for them all. But bad things are happening to the family. The middle child, Brian, he is now sixteen years old and very accomplished at the sport of basketball. Brian has a disease, cancer they call it, and he is going to die. I wish that he were here on Palala. It would be a simple thing to grow new cells to replace the diseased ones. But the Earth doctors have no cure for this cancer. It is in his brain, and they say he will die soon and in a great deal of pain. This upsets me much. Also, it has made other members of the family do odd things. The older sister, Cindy, is taking into her body a variety of drugs and liquid chemicals that make her feel good for short periods of time, but these are harmful to her health. Brian's mother spends her time each day on their computer searching for someplace or something to cure her son. His father was a talkative, good-humored person. Now, he communicates very little and just sits in his office staring at the wall. It pains me to watch them, but I feel compelled to do so. Somehow, I feel that it would be wrong to stop watching. They say Brian gradually will weaken and die. I do not want to see this, but I feel I must." Karna took a breath. "What should I do?"

Kebeck leaned back against the building and pondered the question. "I do not know. Maybe you should speak with a mind counselor. What do you want to do?"

"I do not know. I would not expect a counselor to understand the emotion involved, as it concerns my feelings toward Earth beings. I knew you would understand because of our conversations about your own Earth favorite, Adeline. You expressed much affection for her."

"I offer my sympathy. This is most unpleasant." Kebeck leaned forward and put his upper hands on Karna's shoulders and looked him in the eyes. "If I were in your situation I would continue to watch, but only for brief periods once a day. Also, try to do many pleasurable things for yourself." Kebeck leaned back and paused. "And after he dies, go to grief counseling."

A glazed look came into Karna's eyes. He sighed. "That is what I shall do. I cannot just stop watching them, as my house mate advised." He motioned toward the door. "Yerf is waiting for you. I thank you for your advice and advise you to not let my troubles be your troubles. Thank you. Go enjoy this restaurant thing you do. Be in the moment and thank Yerf for his patience." Karna turned and walked away.

Kebeck felt sorry for Karna. He felt the social punishment he had endured was too harsh, and now this. Kebeck watched him walk down the road, then turned and went inside. Yerf was where he had left him. With his head back and his eyes closed, Yerf was moving one digit to the music.

"I am back. Karna said to thank you for your patience. I too thank you."

Yerf blinked his eyes open. "The music was pleasant. It is a good thing that you have remained friends with Karna. I respect you for doing so, but I find that I cannot forgive his odious behavior. You are a better person than me."

Kebeck smiled. "Yes, I know."

Yerf growled. "But not that much better, because you are too accepting of irresponsibility. He committed a serious wrong."

"I know." As Kebeck got on his slantboard he reflected on his conversation with Karna. *He is right. I will remain his friend, but I should not adopt his pain. I should talk of nice things now.* "Yerf, I was thinking, when is your next vacation? Are you not near the end of an eight-week cycle of work?"

"Yes, I am free after next eight-day."

"You said something about your waterball team vacationing together. Are all team members going? And where are you going to spend your two weeks off?"

Yerf smiled and leaned back against his slantboard. "Did I forget to tell you? I have reserved a large house on Barha Island. It is going to be much fun, and well worth the credits. The entire waterball team will be there. It was not easy to find a house that could sleep twelve and almost impossible to coordinate all our vacations, but I did it." Yerf sighed. "We will catch our own fish and the house has a grill built into the outside wall. The area is planted with vegetables and fruits that we may pick as we need them. Have you been to Barha?"

"No, but I have heard that it is exceptionally beautiful and the water is clear as air. I would like to go there someday."

"I think not. It would not suit you."

Kebeck was puzzled by Yerf's comment. "Why do you say that?"

"Computers and communication devices are not allowed on the island. No Earth-Watching. Barha is supposed to be a place where one goes to be part of the sand and water. It is a place to stretch your body with physical games and then bask in the sun while you enjoy the company of your friends."

Kebeck straightened his shoulders. "I can do that."

"I have doubts that you ever will. Do you realize that you have spent your last seven vacations, a total of 112 days, entirely in the house ... Earth-Watching? I know you have many credits saved up. You could have gone anywhere, done anything."

Kebeck was taken aback. "You have been counting?"

"Yes, as a concerned friend I have meant to talk to you about your lack of exercise and obsession with..."

Kebeck interrupted his friend: "Ah, look, here comes the dinner server with our plates!"

Chapter 10

Earth

Erwin looked in the mirror and examined his face carefully. Even though he had had this face for more than thirteen years, he still wasn't completely used to it. The plastic surgeon in Hong Kong had given him the face he had wanted, and he liked it. He had said to the man, "I want to be handsome, but not pretty. I should look a bit rugged but not rough." It was a fine-looking face. It was different just enough from his other two faces so that no one would ever connect them. His present face had more of a classic Roman look than the face he was born with or the one he had during his twelve years working as a professional killer. Yes, he definitely liked this one better than his last mug. *Attractive features gets you into places, opens some doors ... and people treat you better.* His last face was designed to blend in; it was a dull, common mask. When he was twenty-seven, just two weeks after his release from jail, he had gone to a plastic surgeon in Taiwan with photos of three rather plain-looking men and said, "Make me look like them." He wore that bland visage for twelve years, making his money killing people whom others paid him, quite generously, to quietly and efficiently dispatch.

Erwin turned his head to the side to see his profile. *Still nice features, even at my age. And what do you know; it's the face of the next Mayor.*

Erwin's administrative assistant rushed into the room.

"Sir, I think I've got all the papers you asked for. Here are the notes from the Parks Committee and a copy of the proposed sign bylaw and a transcript of the interview you did with that reporter who was killed. What's her name again? Carol … something?"

Erwin turned away from the mirror and walked over to his desk. "Thank you, Charles. The reporter's name was Carol Stafford. Let's not refer to the poor woman as 'whatsername.' It's disrespectful of the dead."

"Sorry, sir. Where do you want these papers?"

"Just put them on the desk. I'll look them over later," Erwin answered. "Now you get back to your office and get cracking on my mayoral campaign."

"Yes sir. Which reminds me, if you have a few minutes later today we need to write up a more detailed biographical release for the press. They want to know a few things about you, like where you went to high school, what sports you played, who were your childhood influences, things like that."

"Right, they want some background on me, of course." Erwin glanced over at the mirror, then turned back to face Charles. "Hmm, yes. I'll write something up tonight and give it to you tomorrow."

"Very good, sir," Charles said as he hurried out the door.

Charles seemed to live his life in fourth gear, Erwin thought. Certainly a good attribute for any employee. And Charles was truly the biggest Boy Scout Erwin had ever met: polite, efficient, neat, and honest. Charles looked up to his boss because he thought Erwin was just like him. It amused Erwin that Charles was so utterly fooled. *If the kid only knew who I really am, it would blow his mind.*

Erwin had been very careful to patch together a plausible history before he had started in politics. He had covered his tracks well. No one would ever be able to trace him to the sixteen-year-old who tortured and killed a wealthy elderly couple in British Columbia almost forty years ago. At the time, he had been smart enough to hide the money but not smart enough to avoid getting caught. He only received a ten-year sentence because he was so young, not to mention the fact that he had testified against his rather gullible and relatively innocent partner. His time in prison had given Erwin (or rather Newt Clark, as he was called then) the opportunity to think more about his future and to select a profession worthy of his skills. So he simply chose a profession that seemed to come easy to him: killing!

He hadn't planned on killing anyone that first time when he was sixteen. It was supposed to have been just a robbery, but things had gone wrong. Erwin had intended to just break in and take the old couple's money. But they had been home when, according to his numbskull partner, they were supposed to be out. And then they refused to say where the money was hidden. As he tortured them for the information, he found it easy to see them merely as obstacles that were preventing him from getting what he wanted. His partner left when he first saw blood, but Erwin just kept on slashing them with the knife until they talked. The screams and all the blood didn't bother him, either. He was too desperately in need of money. He had to leave town, he had to leave soon, and he needed that money to get far, far away.

The problem was Erwin's father. His mother had left when Erwin was five, and as he grew up he realized why she had left. The problem was his father, aka Coach Charlie. That was the man's title and life: the high school football coach. Charlie Clark was a thick short man with arms that were the size of most people's thighs. He maintained his military brush cut with a weekly visit to the barber. He demanded obedience and perfection. Yes indeed, Newt Charles Clark Senior was a brutal man. He taught woodworking and coached basketball and football at the town's only high school. He was a better-than-average basketball coach, but he was a fantastic football coach. He pushed his boys to win the state football championship seven times in a row. Coach Charlie was a god in that little town. The townspeople scheduled their lives around the games (the town barber had even delayed his gall bladder operation by two days so he could see a play-off game). Naturally, because Erwin, or Newt Junior as he was called then, was a strong and fit fourteen-year-old kid, his father and most of the town wanted him to play football.

But Newt Junior hated the game. He hated his father; he even hated his name, Newt Junior. Since his mother had left them, Newt Junior was spending a lot of his young life sitting in the bleachers, coloring, reading, putting together model kits and listening to his father yell at the players. The coach's taunts were crude and cruel: "You should be wearing pink, you candy ass pussy. Move those legs; it's not like that little dick of yours is in the way!"

There was no way he was going to get on a basketball court or a football field and have his father yell insults at him in front of other people. It was enough that he had to live with the constant teasing and ridicule at home. Plus, when no one was around, his dad's verbal abuse was usually accompanied by a few smacks to the body. Never hit him in the face, though. It was always jabs to the chest or stomach or a stomp on his foot. No visible bruises, but it sure did hurt.

To Erwin, therefore, money was the only way to put plenty of much-needed distance between him and his father. But instead of flying away to South America, Erwin landed in jail.

And so life carried on and Erwin spent his ten years in jail training to be a professional killer. He took correspondence courses in psychology, physiology, forensics, and criminology. He studied insurance actuary reports to learn more about accidental deaths. He exercised four hours a day and learned six different types of martial arts.

After he was released, his first victim was—not so surprisingly—his father. The old man fell down a flight of stairs. Erwin attended the funeral and then boarded a plane to Taiwan to get his new face, a new identity, and to start his new profession. There's a lot of hate in the world and Erwin had had no difficulty finding people who were willing to pay for the sudden death of a spouse, a relative, or a business associate.

But that's ancient history. Now he was busy playing his new role as businessman and politician extraordinaire.

Erwin picked up the papers that Charles had left on the corner of the desk. He shuffled through them until he found the transcript of his interview with Carol Stafford. He slid into his big leather chair and put his feet up on the edge of his desk. He wanted to read through the transcript very carefully. He couldn't remember saying anything that could possibly give him away, but somehow Stafford had found out something that she shouldn't have. He didn't know what she had discovered, but she had signed her own death certificate when she looked him in the face after the interview and said, "You're not who you seem to be, are you?" He would have thought that line was just a reporter's trick meant to throw him off if it hadn't been for the hard look in her eyes. *Yeah, she knew something.*

Chapter 11

Palala

Yerf was patting his stomach as they walked out of the restaurant. "This custom of making eating into a special occasion is not good for the digestion. I consumed too much food."

"Did you enjoy the experience?" asked Kebeck.

"I enjoyed the experience of having a quiet conversation with a good friend in a pleasant location."

"But did you like the food?" asked Kebeck.

"The flavor was pleasant, but I found that after the third or fourth bite I did not enjoy the sensation of taste as much as usual. There was too much food, and I do not like this bloated feeling from having consumed so much."

"No one forced you to eat so much," said Kebeck.

"Were we not given a normal portion that would be served in an Earth restaurant and were we not expected to eat it all?"

"The one performing the role of waitress said that the portions were like those on Earth," Kebeck replied. "We are uncomfortably full because we are used to only eating two or three bites at one time. I too feel unwell."

"So now, will you admit that this Earth custom is foolish?"

"I will only admit that I have no desire to change the eating habits that are normal for our people. I had intended to rush home to watch Adeline before it gets dark at her location on Earth, but this full belly makes my legs slow and my head sleepy," said Kebeck.

Yerf was just getting on his bicycle when he stopped and looked at Kebeck. "You have a son and a daughter but I rarely hear you say their names. Adeline seems to be the center of your life. Why is this?"

Kebeck paused. "My son Prigo is now fifty years old and has not needed my help or approval for many years. He has chosen to live on the other side of the village, so we do not visit often. But, we remain friends and I have great affection for him. He is very happy with his profession and quite accomplished in his field. Every year he is recognized by the science academy for his discoveries related to new uses for plant-derived chemicals. And as for my wonderful daughter, you know Lios will turn twenty-five next week as you have already received your invitation to her celebration of adulthood. Even though she will not officially become an adult until next week, she has made her own decisions since she was fifteen and chose to live at school. She has always thought it unfair that she could not vote on eight-day. I am glad that now she will be able to vote for herself instead of trying to influence my vote. I will help her with the celebration next week, if she needs me, but otherwise she is quite independent and would not appreciate my attention or any meddling in her affairs.

"I watch Adeline with fascination and love," Kebeck continued. Her world has dangers and deceptions that we have never experienced. On some parts of Earth, populations continue to experience warfare, starvation, extreme weather, and seismic tremors that kill untold thousands. It is so different from our well-regulated world. And while it is morbidly riveting to simply watch how the planet functions and malfunctions, it is even more interesting to follow the life of one individual. Because you have not chosen to Earth-Watch on a regular basis, you have not formed an attachment with any Earth beings. However, allowing yourself to become attached to an Earth being allows you to live in their world through that person."

"You would want to live on that world with its guns and lies and pollution?" asked Yerf.

"Sometimes, I think I might like to. There is almost no danger on our planet. Because of our physiology we developed a social system without deception. Because we have always limited the number of births and emphasized science and logic over superstition, we have had no wars in the last three-thousand years. And we would never pollute our planet. Our water is precious to us; swimming has always been our favorite mode of getting around. After watching Earth it is easy to see that we have a wonderful planet. But, it is not as exciting as Earth. Simply put, Yerf, we are dull."

"We are not dull!" Yerf shot back. "We are sane, intelligent, and logical. Not only are most of you Earth-Watchers behaving as voyeurs, but some of you are also making negative changes to our world. This restaurant may be a harmless diversion, but some of our people are adopting other Earth customs that are hindering our society."

"My logic leads me to believe we could both be right. My logic also suggests we need to study this further and discuss it at a later date. At the same time, my emotions urge me to rush home and check up on Adeline. When I last saw her she was at her late friend Carol's apartment, and she was upset and scared."

"Go then. Hurry home to see your Adeline," Yerf said. "I understand that she is important to you. I will proceed at a more leisurely pace. I have not had such a full belly since my 125th birthday party.

Chapter 12

Earth

Adeline wanted to stop by the office just long enough to pick up her messages, but as she stepped into the newsroom she was approached by her fellow workers. Everyone's face took on a sad expression as soon as they looked at her. She could see their eyes shift as they thought about what to say to a grieving person. Then, when they had the right phrase composed in their minds, they would start toward her. She wanted to turn and run, but she knew she had to stand there and let them say their bit.

As she crossed the room, zigzagging from person to person, she saw Dot standing in profile. Her distinct hawk-like nose left no doubt that it could be none but the oldest living news reporter on the planet, Dorothy Paul. Adeline lowered her head and increased her pace a bit in hopes of getting out of the room before Dot looked up from the copy she was reading.

"Adie!" Dot's clear loud voice rang out.

Adeline froze in mid step. She heard that distinct clacking of the cane and looked up to see Dot heading towards her. *How many times have I asked her not to call me Adie?* A little sigh escaped Adeline's lips. She felt that she should admire the woman; Dot was eighty-two years old, after all. Years in the sun made her face look like a big prune surrounded by short gray hair. Her bad knee was the result of a mine in Vietnam, aggravated no less by a bullet wound or two from her time in South America. Yes, Dot was and even continued to be an amazing reporter, but she was irritating because she would ask anybody anything, at any time. And she expected an answer. Most people have a self-censor switch in their brains that stops them from saying every thought that pops into their heads. Not Dot. Many politicians tried to avoid Dot; some went so far as to hide from her. As Dot approached, Adeline made a conscious effort to make the corners of her mouth turn up a bit. "Hi Dot. How are you?"

"You don't wanna know, 'cause let me tell you this old age thing's hell on Earth. So don't get me started. You know when I was younger, joints were a good thing. They were either where you went for a beer with the gang or things you smoked to get a little high. Now I curse my joints, and pain's my middle name," she said, grimacing.

"But how are you?" she went on. "This death thing's a bitch, isn't it? If you want a shoulder to cry on, just call me. Do you regret anything you said to her? That's a common reaction when friends die suddenly. In Vietnam, I was in the middle of telling a sergeant what an ass he was when he took a bullet and died right in front of me. But you can't let that stuff get to you. He was an ass, and he knew it. I heard about her desk being cleaned out. What's up with that?" Dot paused and leaned in a little while looking directly into Adeline's eyes.

"Uh … I'm all right, thank you, and … the police have checked Carol's desk here and her apartment for fingerprints and stuff, but they seem to have found nothing yet."

"You know, you've got to stay on those people to get results. Who's the cop in charge? I'll check into it."

"His name's Hawes. Nick Hawes. He seems competent enough and I think he really wants to find the killer. Do you know him?"

"Yeah, he was in charge of the case where two little Chinese girls went missing.

He's not bad, but not exactly a go-getter. I'll light a fire under him. So, could Carol have been having an affair with someone big enough to do her in and dump her computers?" Dot moved her face an inch closer and again stared into Adeline's eyes.

Adeline stepped back. She did that a lot around Dot. "No, she wasn't dating any gangsters or politicians or anyone like that. That wasn't her style."

Dot glanced down at the papers in her hands. "Well, I've got to wrap up this story. But I'm here for you. Maybe a good old-fashioned drinking binge would help? Yeah, call me. We'll go out and get plastered."

Dot hobbled back over to her desk and Adeline looked up to see that everyone had been watching the exchange. They quickly looked away, burying their noses in their work. None of them had known Carol very well, but they knew that she had been Adeline's best friend for many years. Carol had just started at the paper nine months ago. Adeline and Carol had led separate lives after university. Carol got a great job in Vancouver working for *Time* magazine. Adeline found a job in Toronto working on one of the city's daily newspapers. Their friendship continued through letters, phone calls, visits, and email. When one of the paper's reporters decided to retire to write his novel, Adeline talked Carol into coming east to take his place. It had been great having her friend alongside her. The people in Adeline's office had heard about Carol for years but unfortunately they only had a few months to actually get to know her.

Adeline smiled weakly and nodded as more people came up to give their mini-eulogies. She tried blocking out the words they were saying. She was not going to allow herself to cry in the office. After everyone had had their say she looked up to see Dalton Clark motioning to her to come to his office.

"That was tough," she said to Dalton as he led her in.

"Yeah, death's a bummer."

She looked up at him, somewhat annoyed with his comment. "What?"

"Uh, I'm not good at this. Sorry, I don't mean to be inconsiderate. But, I try to ignore the concept of mortality. I've almost convinced myself that it'll never happen to me or anyone I care for. I just try to get on with life." He paused and pushed back his thinning gray hair. "Are you ready to ... uh ... get on with life? Are you up to working?"

Adeline thought for a minute. "Well, I guess ...."

"It's all right if you need a few more days off."

"No, you're right. Enough of this dragging my ass around. I'll start back tomorrow morning. No problem. Back to normal."

"Good," he said, looking relieved. "First, I want you to finish the piece on how much corporations pay to put their name on public buildings. Then, I want you to start on your research for a three-part piece on that coffee shop guy who's running for mayor. People need to know who this man is. Do you know anything about him?"

"Just his name ... Erwin Bercic, and also that he owns a few donut places, and that he has served two terms as councilor from one of the districts on the north side of town," she replied. "And Carol said he had a huge ego."

"Yeah, Carol interviewed him, but of course her notes are gone. So, interview him again. Interview his employees. Dig into his history." He paused and shook his head. "What am I telling you your job for? You know what to do. Now, get out of here before one of these sad-faced, well-meaning idiots makes you cry." Dalton touched her shoulder gently. That was a big show of affection for Dalton.

Adeline lowered her head and quickly made her way through the newsroom. She didn't dare look at anyone. Dalton was right; she couldn't take any more of their sympathy. *Thank goodness for the Internet*, she thought. She planned to do a lot of her work from home for the next few days.

Working from home would also give her more time to get better acquainted with Roger. Adeline had never had a cat; her mother had been allergic to them. Now she was going to have Carol's cat Roger living with her. Roger had been put in a kennel the day after Carol was killed. The kennel only charged eleven dollars a day, so Adeline hadn't been in a hurry to collect him and start her new life with her first real four-legged pet. As a child she was only allowed to have a bird and fish. Carol had loved Roger; it was time to pick him up and take him to his new home.

Chapter 13

Palala

Yerf slowly walked down the road, pushing his bicycle beside him. The cool sand felt good on his bare feet. He could not remember when he had felt so bloated. He ran his hand over the little scales of his protruding light green belly and burped. As he trudged along the odor of a female tickled his nose. Before he could put a name to the scent he looked up and saw Sheme coming down the road toward him. It was definitely Sheme; no one else had such a bouncing walk. Joy and optimism radiated from her. Most people have both good days and bad days but Sheme, however, seemed to have only good ones.

"Yerf, what is with pushing that bicycle instead of riding it? Is it broken?"

"No, but I am broken." Yerf laid the bike on the ground, stepped toward Sheme and extended his palms toward her.

"Are you injured? Can I help?" Sheme asked as she put down the cloth bag she was carrying and touched her palms to his.

Yerf smiled. "No, I am just uncomfortable because my belly is too full. And it is all the fault of our friend, Kebeck."

"Did he hold you down and force food into your mouth?"

"No, worse still. He made me go to a restaurant with him. Did you know that we now have an Earth-style restaurant here in our little town?"

"Yes, I saw it on the news. Was it not a pleasant experience?"

"No, never again will I agree to go to a restaurant. The whole concept is ridiculous. To eat at specified times, to wait for people to bring it to you instead of just grabbing what you want, to eat so much at one time … it's simply ridiculous. And then to pay credits for what is already ours? Ridiculous!" Yerf's neck was glowing.

"I would think that it would have been a harmless experiment that allowed you to experience a different way of doing things. Why have you allowed this to upset you so?" she asked.

"I do not know."

Sheme motioned toward a patch of grass beside the road. "I am in no hurry. Let us sit and talk." She leaned down and picked up the bag she had placed on the road. "I have finished making a drinking cup for Kebeck's daughter, Lios. As she is the second born, she does not get the family water cup. I must get it to her mother before tomorrow's Day of Majority celebration."

Yerf followed Sheme over to the grass and they both lay on their sides, propped on their arms.

Yerf glanced at the bag that Sheme had placed between them. "May I see it? Your work is always splendid."

Sheme took the ceramic cup out of the bag and placed it on the grass. The outside of the cup was a sculpted swirl of leaves and flowers and the handle looked like a gnarled root. Yerf ran his fingers over the bumps and valleys of the big earth-red vessel.

Yerf smiled. "Such beauty calms me." Yerf lay back on the grass, using his upper hands as a pillow, with his elbows pointing toward the sky. He sighed. "I have been thinking much about beauty lately. I have been comparing our ideas of beauty with those held by Earth beings. You remember that I occasionally watch a Shopping Mall? But just occasionally. I am not a regular watcher like Kebeck."

He turned his head toward Sheme.

She nodded.

"The Earth beings seem to place far too much importance on the appearance of their bodies and faces. They spend both time and work credits on clothing. And the females paint their faces. It puzzles me that appearances mean so much to them and so very little to us. What is most important to them is the configuration and dimension of the face. They value faces that fit criteria that assign desirability based on a certain size of nose and lips and as well as eye placement. They also value specific body shapes. We have different body shapes and our faces vary. I have larger lips than most people but that is neither an asset nor a deterrent in how others regard me. Your scales have a gray tone and mine are greener than yours, but the color difference does not affect my attitude toward you. Our differences allow us to identify specific people, but otherwise they are of no importance."

"Yes," Sheme sighed. "I am aware of their odd fascination with the appearance of their bodies. I think it to be a sign of their immaturity as a race. But what has appearance to do with watching an Earth Shopping Mall?"

"Everything. The main purpose of a Shopping Mall is to sell. That is, exchange credits for clothing, ornaments, creams, and dyes for the fur on their heads and paint for their faces. I watch them at the Mall. The very young ones and the old ones alike want to look like they are twenty or thirty years old. The females put much more effort into it than the males, but neither sex wants to look younger than twenty or older than thirty-five. It both fascinates me and irritates me."

Sheme shifted her position on the grass. "Explain please."

"There are places on Earth where beings die because they lack credits to purchase food. You are aware of the fact that all on Earth must purchase food? It is not supplied by the government."

Sheme nodded.

"I am much annoyed by the fact that the credits spent on body decorations are more than enough to buy food for those who have none. It is just a matter of will and redistribution of credits. I am also bothered by the time and effort wasted in the pursuit of a specific appearance. But, at the same time, I perceive a beauty in the clothing and body decorations. I enjoy watching Earth fashion shows, but feel very guilty when doing so."

"How is there beauty in clothing? What do you see?"

"I see colors combined in patterns that please me. I see geometric shapes and curves that blend into things that attract my attention and please me. I know of no word to describe it except pretty."

"Pretty is good. Pretty makes life better."

"Perhaps better for us here on Palala, but not on Earth. I do not think I have ever felt of such two minds about anything."

"Could that be the reason that you reacted with such anger when discussing the restaurant?" Sheme asked.

"Yes, I think so. You are perceptive. Even though I disliked most aspects of the restaurant, and please do not mention this to Kebeck, I did enjoy the atmosphere provided by the decorating. I found it pretty."

"We were taught to look for and appreciate the beauty in nature, not in the decorating of bodies and buildings. This is foreign to us, but there is no reason why we should not expand our definition of beauty. How could this harm us?" she asked.

"It may harm us in that if we change what we value, we will act differently. Because the Earth beings put so much value on specific appearances and decorations, they treat individuals differently according to how they look and what they own, and..."

"We would never do that!" Sheme cut in as she quickly sat up. "All people are esteemed and should only be judged by their behavior."

"Yes, that is what we believe now, but would we not change if we acquired unnecessary possessions and body decorations?"

"I do not know. Have you asked Kebeck about this? He is one of the Earth experts."

"No, he has been very busy lately. I enjoy his company and we have had a pleasant time living together, but I am thinking about moving back to my own house."

Sheme smiled and cocked her head to one side. "Are you moving out because you think I might be moving in?"

"No, no. This is just coincidence. I just want to be on my own for now. Kebeck and I have been friends since we were in school together. We were study partners until we reached the age where our professions sent us to different schools to study. I missed him more than I missed my parents when I went away to the island of Hara to study construction. We liked to play tricks on each other. More than once he put rotten Taka fruit in the trough of my slantboard. It takes weeks for the bright red stains to wear off of your feet. But I also did my own share of mischief. Once, I took his computer apart a few hours before an exam and installed the keyboard upside down. He had no time to repair it so he had to write the test that way. He complained of a sore neck for days. Five years ago we found that we were both at a time when neither of us shared a home with spouses or children, so I moved in with him. He is good company. Kebeck is cheerful and shares interesting ideas with me, but he is still sensitive to feelings. It has been good to share time with him. And I will continue to do things with him, but now I find that I desire to live alone for a while."

Yerf looked at Sheme as he continued. "I want to hear silence and be the one to choose when to break that silence. I now find that I like to work at night drawing up plans and to sleep part of the day. In the night our world is a different place. When most people are asleep you are able to hear the insects and animals in the bush. I feel I flow with the fabric of the planet at night. I enjoy swimming down the river with only a few lights in the distance. It is what I want for now. Nevertheless, Kebeck would make a wonderful father if you chose to have another child and I hope you two do decide to parent together. My house is just down the river and I would very much like to assist with the child care."

"Thank you, I will remember that." Sheme stood up, brushing off the loose bits of grass. "I should go."

"I too. I wish you clear water." Yerf stood up, picked up the bicycle, and headed down the road. *I would parent a child with her if she asked me. Why does she not ask me?*

Chapter 14

Earth

"OK cat. Mi casa es su casa," Adeline said to the big black-and-white cat as she opened his cage.

Roger slowly came out of the cage, sniffing the air and moving his head from one side to the other. He looked up at Adeline before proceeding with his careful inspection of the room. Adeline stood and watched.

"Well I hope the place is to your satisfaction, you spoiled cat," she said as she walked into the kitchen to get a bottle of water out of the fridge. When Adeline returned to the living room Roger was already curled up on the couch on her best pillow. "Sure, just make yourself comfortable. You cats have it made. People feed you, pet you, pay the vet bills, and all you have to do is listen to us talk. And you aren't even good listeners. You always listen with this look of disdain. You could even give teenagers lessons on how to look disinterested."

Just as she finished lecturing the cat, Roger looked toward the living room window. He cocked his head to one side, his attention drawn to something. Adeline looked over at the window to see what had caught his eye. He was watching the curtains blowing in the wind.

The window is open. But I know I closed all the windows before leaving the house. Like I always do.

Adeline slowly turned around, scanning every object in the room.

Everything looks normal.

When she looked again at Roger, he had turned his head in the opposite direction and was now staring at her bedroom door.

Oh my god, somebody could be in here!

Adeline quickly moved to the front door, threw it open, and ran towards the street in front of the house. She stood at the edge of the sidewalk and looked back at her house and the houses next door. No one was out, no neighbors to help her. Some birds were chirping and in the distance a dog was barking.

Maybe I did leave a window open.

She crept up toward the house and looked carefully at the window. The screen was missing, and as she got closer she saw a corner of it sticking out of the bushes just below the window.

Got to go next door; got to call the police.

Then she saw something move in the window. She gasped and jumped back. Then she saw it was Roger, who had moved to the open window. *Oh you friggin' cat!* She knew she couldn't let him get loose. *He's a house cat; Carol said he's never been outside.*

"Here, kitty kitty."

Roger looked at her briefly then looked around for the best way down from the window.

"Roger, come to me baby; come on, come over here," Adeline cooed. *Stupid cat!*

Roger moved to the left and hunched his back, preparing to jump. Adeline moved a bit closer to the window and stopped to think. *Maybe there's somebody in there. Maybe they broke in and left already. Damn cat, I can't let it run off and get killed.*

"This is for Carol," she said out loud to herself as she shot up to the window, grabbed the cat, and ran back towards the street. Roger scratched and howled, but she paid him no attention. Holding him tightly in her arms, she walked quickly over to old Mrs. Thompson's house next door and used an elbow to ring the bell.

Two police cars arrived 10 minutes later. The investigating officers found nothing. Accompanied by a rather tall, nice-looking policeman, she carefully examined the entire house. Everything was where she had left it. Nothing appeared to be disturbed. The cop in charge said it looked like someone might have started to break in but he or they probably didn't get inside before something or someone scared them off. The police helped Adeline put the screen back on the window and then filled out their report.

Chapter 15

Palala

Kebeck had watched as Adeline had run out of the house. He saw the policemen prowl through her house with guns in their hands and he watched as she came back inside. *That was exciting, but I am upset that something scared my Adeline.* He continued to watch as she locked the doors and went into the bathroom. He heard water flowing. She had gone to take a shower. *The Earth beings spend too much time washing their bodies.* Kebeck could not remember the last time he had washed his body. It was unnecessary, as he, like most people, swam at least two or three times every day. He thought it funny that Earth beings should only swim for recreation. *It gets you from one place to another, cleans you, and exercises your body.* He could understand why swimming was not used for transportation on the cold parts of Earth, but the fact that they did not swim from one place to another in the areas near the planet's equator baffled him. The Earth beings, he felt, exhibited such a backward way of dealing with transportation. Though he was sometimes amused by the customs of these Earth beings, just as often he was saddened by many of the things they did to their planet. He was shocked when he discovered they had dug the coal and oil out of the soil and spread it all over the planet; they used the dirty stuff to cover the land with roads and parking lots and they pumped it into the air by burning it to operate their vehicles and heat their buildings. Worse still, it got in their water. They had done many awful things to their world, but surely the most heinous planetary offence committed by the Earth beings was to pollute their own water. How could they not understand that water is so precious, the very essence of life? It is to be respected and cherished. It makes up the majority of their bodies, and the water in one's body is the water that we share with those who came before us and those who will come after us. Abusing water harms the planet and the beings on it; it is disrespecting the past and disabling the future. All sentient beings should take care of the water on their planet; it gives life. The soil and plants clean the water, but they cannot remove all of the contaminants introduced by such wasteful beings. Do these self-centered Earth beings not see that by polluting their water they pollute their own bodies? But as he reflected on the question, he realized he could think of many other ways in which the Earth beings disrespected and abused these very same bodies.

"Greetings," came the voice from the doorway.

Kebeck turned with a start. Standing in the door was Jarrell, a friend and one of the five other people on the committee commissioned to study the effects of Earth-Watching. Kebeck had been so involved in his thoughts that he had not heard or smelled his friend approach the house. Kebeck stood up and extended his palms toward Jarrell. "Please pardon that I failed to notice your presence. What did you say? My mind had wandered to other places and I was not here with my body."

"I simply greeted you.

Kebeck looked closely at Jarrell. "Your face shows sadness. Come, sit. Relax and eat. What is the cause of such melancholy?"

Jarrell trudged across the room and perched on the corner of the sleeping platform. "I did not realize that my mood was so clearly displayed on my face. I have just spent two hours watching Earth TV news. The wars, the overpopulation, the areas of starving beings, those things make me sad. I watch reports of the beings who kill strangers and themselves as a means of making a political statement and I glow with anger. I see different news interpretations of the same situation and I shudder at the Earth beings' subtle ways of lying. I see the ways they abuse their planet and I both rage and mourn for the Earth."

"Yes, I have had similar thoughts. I did not detect you as you approached my house because I was deep in thought about the pollution on the Earth. I have been thinking that religion is a factor, possibly a major factor, of why the Earth beings do not see their pollution as a problem," said Kebeck.

"Please explain."

"I am still formulating my ideas," Kebeck said. "But, consider this. Most of their civilizations' religions view the time spent on Earth as but a preparation for a better, long-term life somewhere else; they call it heaven, or paradise. The Earth is not important to them. They see it as something that is at their disposal; something to simply use and forget. They see their planet as they would view a paper cup. You are familiar with their paper cups, are you not?"

"Yes, I see them using and throwing away paper and oil-based cups each day. When I first saw how they manufacture, use, and dispose of such items, I was shocked. My water cup has been passed down for so many generations that I am not sure of its age."

"How fortunate to have one so old; my own cup is only about six-hundred years old," Kebeck noted. "I do not understand the Earth beings' relationship with objects, with things. They desire them and work much to get them, yet they do not value the objects once they obtain them. Things of nature should be respected because they are the product of millions of years of evolution. And things made by people should be respected because of the mental and physical effort that went into making them. My father, he was a wise man, respected by many; hundreds attended his last-day ceremony. He said that that we should appreciate objects created by people for two reasons. First, because some plant or mineral was destroyed or altered in order to make it. And second, because someone had to use part of his lifespan to make the object."

He paused. "But we were talking about religion and pollution. The so-called Christian religion definitely promotes disdain for things of the earth. I have not studied all of the Earth religions in detail, but in none do I detect much respect for the planet."

"Yes, that is quite a contrast to what we were taught. Indeed, I recall that the first thing I ever memorized in school was the Five Methods of Planetary Respect*."

A beeping sound came from Kebeck's computer.

"Excuse me for a second." Kebeck turned and looked at his computer just in time to see Adeline come out of the bathroom wearing a white cotton robe. She sat down at her computer and opened up her email.

"That will keep her busy for a while," said Kebeck. "Now, how might I aid you or do you come seeking my company?"

"The gift of your company is always appreciated, but I have come at this time to discuss a problem with our work."

"As you wish. Shall we recline on the relaxation platform? Let me get a tray of fruits."

"No, stay as you are," replied Jarrell. "I will be brief."

"What is the problem?"

"I am disturbed about the effects of Earth-Watching, and I could not wait until our next scheduled meeting to discuss this matter with you."

"And what disturbs you so?" asked Kebeck.

---

*   (1) Take from Palala only that which you need.

    (2) Water is most valued and shall never be touched by waste.

    (3) Objects of no further use shall be used in the manufacture of any new objects.

    (4) When possible, transplant aggressive animals instead of killing them.

    (5) When possible, transplant plants instead of killing them.

"Our society, the very fabric of our social system and of our planet is in danger of changing because of Earth-Watching. I fear that you and other members of our committee are not aware of many of the changes because you are spending so much time in your research projects."

"What do you suggest?" asked Kebeck.

"We need a new deadline, a definite time within the next thirty-two days, at which time we will release our findings to the public and call a vote."

"But there is so much to study. That is not time enough," countered Kebeck.

"We could study Earth forever and a few of us scientist may do that. But the general public is being influenced by Earth-Watching in many negative ways. We need to vote. And we need to vote soon."

"Our original commission was to study the influences of Earth-Watching for forty years, publish the study to the public, and have a vote on whether to continue to Earth-Watch or to cut off communication entirely with the planet. The study period has almost ten more years before completion. What has changed?" asked Kebeck.

"That is the problem. Things are changing. I see people decorating themselves with unnecessary clothing. There have been incidents of violence. Some people are imitating the Earth religions."

"I agree that there have been some negative effects. A few children have got into fights at school, but that could be solved by allowing only adults to Earth-Watch. But the news reports that I have viewed spoke of people adopting and believing in Earth religions, and that disturbs me."

"They cannot truly believe those Earth-based religious fictions." Jarrell shook his head in disgust. "No, I think they are just playing with the religions. They are just trying on the religious customs to see how they feel. The rituals, the décor of the worship buildings, the costumes, they are different and interesting. One religion claims its planet is carried on the back of round sea creature called a turtle. Another religion encourages its adherents to unquestioningly kill their own child if their god commands them to do so. And yet another tells its believers that after death they return repeatedly to life, in the shape and form of any number of creatures. Surely our people cannot believe such fanciful tales; we are, after all, a scientific, reality-based society."

"I hope you are right. But let us return to the idea of changing the deadline for our reports and calling for a quick vote. Because Earth-Watching has become such a popular amusement, many of our people may not vote in favor of ceasing the activity," said Kebeck.

"Some will not, but we are a logical people and they should be presented with the facts and given the opportunity to vote as soon as possible. Will you make yourself available for a computer-linked group meeting next fourth-day?"

"As you wish. That will be year-day 412. Then, we will discuss this as a group."

Jarrell stood up. "I will depart now."

"Before you go, I must ask you if you are also opposed to more visits to Earth," Kebeck inquired.

"I can offer no definite answer to your query. The yearly visit of two or three scientists does no harm. But I think that we should no longer publicize to the general public any record of those visits. We as scientists should be able to study anything and everything in order to learn more, but the general public should be protected from viewing any phenomena that change their nature in negative ways. I fear that our people are starting to enjoy the excitement of the Earth violence, and some enjoy the escape from reality that religion provides."

"And who is to say what is good for us, for the people of Palala?" asked Kebeck.

Jarrell ignored the question as he continued on. "Earth-Watching started out as nothing but an amusement, a past-time, like the fiction stories that we read as children. When we read fiction we played with fantasies in our minds. But this Earth-Watching has gone far beyond that. It is changing the nature of what is acceptable behavior."

Jarrell looked around the room until he found a time indicator. He looked confused for an instant because there were two time indicators on the wall, one for Palala and one for Earth. "I must depart now. I have to stop by my house before I go to your daughter's Majority celebration. I congratulate you on raising such a competent child and suggest that you savor this special day. We can continue this discussion at the meeting."

"Would you desire some food before the swim back to your home?" asked Kebeck.

"That is a good idea." Jarrell walked over to the refrigerated container on the wall and took out a handful of vegetables. He munched on the green stems as he walked out the door.

Kebeck followed him to the door; he stood in the doorway and watched him walk down the path toward the river.

I do not want to stop watching my Adeline, he thought. *Life would be very dull without her. But, I do want whatever is best for my Palala.* Kebeck strolled back into the house and looked up at the two time indicators on the wall next to the door. One was set to Earth time in what was referred to as the Eastern Zone of North America, while the other was set to local Palalan time. It had taken many hours for Kebeck's friend Tela, a brilliant mathematician, to devise a formula that could easily determine Earth time. The odd numbers had mystified her. It was no mystery where they got the 365 periods of light and darkness, but she could not understand why they chose to divide their year into twelve groups of twenty-eight to thirty-one days. Similarly, the sixty minutes comprising an Earth hour made no sense to her.

As with Earth, a Palalan year denotes the length of time it takes that planet to rotate around its sun. There are 480 days in the Palalan year and twenty-four hours in each of its days—virtually twelve hours of light and twelve of darkness, as almost every Palalan lives near the planet's equator. On Palala, an hour consists of sixty-four ticks. The number four underlies most calculation systems developed over millennia on Palala, evolving primarily because of the four digits on each Palalan's hands. The days are also categorized in groups of eight, and every eight-day is marked as a public holiday when no one works and all adults are required to vote. It is a much better, simpler system than that used on Earth.

Looking at the time indicators, Kebeck realized that he had better leave soon. As the father of the new adult he should arrive a bit early for his daughter's Day of Majority celebration.

Chapter 16

Earth

Erwin lay across the king-sized bed staring at the ceiling as he waited for his newfound friend to finish whatever she was doing in the bathroom and join him in bed. She was probably donning some fluffy bit of silk and lace to hide the rolls of her middle-aged belly. He closed his eyes and let his head sink into the satin-covered feather pillow. It was Mrs. Hugo's second visit. He liked to screw married women. *They don't tell ... too much to lose, and they don't expect anything to come of the sex, except just maybe more sex.* He never paid much attention to their first names. First names would make them seem like real people, and Erwin didn't want to fuck real people; he wanted to fuck his banker's wife, his lawyer's wife. Really, any lonely, lovely wife would do. Seducing wives was his most thrilling amusement since he had given up murder.

He hadn't killed anyone in six or seven years when the problem with that reporter Carol Stafford came along. In the past, he had killed without hesitation. Life had been simple: when a problem arose, he killed the source of the problem. But that was before he got into politics. When you're a city councilor, you can't just run around knocking people off; too many witnesses who might recognize your face. So he was a little out of practice. It surprised him that he hesitated after realizing that Stafford could be a problem and needed to be killed. For the first time, he reflected on his chances of landing in jail. *I'm too old for prison. I wouldn't have the strength to face down the toughs. This life of business and politics has made me soft.* He had spent a whole ten minutes thinking it over before he came to the conclusion that she, and anyone else who threatened to expose his secret, simply had to die. But this time, he was going to be extra careful.

Erwin opened his eyes as he felt a finger trace a line up his naked thigh.

Chapter 17

Palala

As Kebeck entered his daughter's house the smell of flowers overwhelmed him. Kebeck appreciated the custom of decorating the house of the person being honored with hundreds of fresh flowers, but the overpoweringly sweet smell suffocated him. He would have to just do his best to ignore the smell today. It was after all the day of his daughter's majority. She had become an adult, and he was there to honor her and be a part of her majority ceremony. He looked around her circular house and noticed that her possessions had been removed from the shelves that hung on the walls and replaced with trays full of sweet fruits. He looked forward to munching on the tangas and caca melons that had been shipped many miles for this special occasion.

"Greetings, Kebeck," called the voice behind him. He turned to see Leto, one of his fellow Earth-Watching analysis committee members. Leto was a tall gray person, thinner than most. His lower hands were extended, palm up, in greeting. His upper hands held bits of sweet fruits. Though Leto had a reputation for constantly stuffing his face with all manner of foods, it never showed on his slender form.

"Greetings Leto. I thank you for coming to honor my daughter."

"It is I who is honored. Your daughter was a wonderful student; it was my pleasure to be her teacher. I see that we seem to have a few ticks before the ceremony will start. Would you consider it impolite to discuss committee business at this time?" asked Leto.

"No, that would be a good use of our time. Speaking of such matters, I recently referred an ardent Earth-Watching fan to you. He wanted me to explain the logic in religion. I am sure you can do a better job of that than I ever could. Now that I think of it, I would like a copy of what you say to him. It should be most interesting. How goes in fact your study of the Earth's Catholic religion?"

"It is most interesting indeed. Did you know that many of the Earth beings who adhere to Catholic doctrines lack sufficient habitats and food, while the religion's administrative organization called the Vatican has an abundant supply of both? But they share little. They do not help the millions of beings who need food in the lands known as Haiti, Mexico, Brazil, and Ecuador, among others. The Vatican administrators merely send clerics known as priests to talk to them. And while these priests talk much about love, they nonetheless wear metal or wooden representations of torture around their necks or on the lapels of their garments. It is difficult to understand. Also, they encourage their believers to have many children, but do not provide food or homes for these offspring. It is both amazing and depressing to watch. And I could speak at length about their symbolic cannibalism ceremony, which is particularly dramatic among the Catholics." Leto paused to take a breath. "But, we should talk of that later. What I want to discuss right now is Jarrell's proposal about cutting our studies short and calling for a vote in the near future. What do you think of this proposal?" he asked.

Kebeck opened his mouth to reply when he caught sight of something happening behind Leto. His daughter Lios was now standing on her relaxation platform and getting ready to begin her majority speech.

"I think I do not agree with his proposal, but we shall have to discuss it at another time. The ceremony begins," said Kebeck, pointing towards his daughter.

The crowd became quiet as Lios slowly turned around three times. She then leaned down and picked up one of the colorful flower leis that were stacked on the platform beside her.

"Today, I am an adult," she said. "It is my pleasure to thank all the people who have helped me as I have matured. First, I would like to thank my mother."

Kebeck and the rest of the crowd let out a long hum of approval. A female approached the platform and bowed her neck toward Lios. Kebeck had not seen his second wife for at least a year. *I wonder if she is still angry with me for moving back to my house just one day after our contract ended. But surely the move was not a surprise to her.*

Lios placed the lei around her mother's neck and said, "I thank you for your patience, intelligence, and care."

Kebeck looked more closely at his former wife. *She was never patient with me.*

Lios's mother raised her upper hands high and presented a new water cup to her daughter as she pronounced the customary words, "You are an adult. You will now drink from your own cup. You will now make your own decisions. You will now live your own life. We hope that your life will be as pure as the water from our mountains and flow smoothly over the rocks of reality."

The crowd hummed approval as Lios's mother backed away from the platform.

"Next, I would like to thank my father."

Kebeck quickly walked up to the side of the platform and bowed his head.

"I thank you for laughter, love, and the sharing of knowledge," Lios said as she placed a lei around Kebeck's neck.

Kebeck bowed a bit lower, then straightened up and smiled up at his daughter. He was glad that no speech was expected of him, as it was the custom that only the mother should speak at such an occasion. Emotion made his neck glow red. Lios smiled back and then looked around for the next person on her list. Kebeck eased back into the crowd as the assembly hummed. He spent the rest of the ceremony watching his daughter with his mind wandering through memories of her childhood. *I am proud of her. She has become an intelligent and thoughtful person.*

As soon as Lios had presented the last lei, the crowd gravitated toward the trays of sweet foods. Kebeck was quickly surrounded by people congratulating him on raising such a clever and considerate daughter. Kebeck tried to have at least a word or two with everyone in attendance.

A familiar smell tickled his nose before he saw her.

"Where have you been hiding? I have not seen you lately."

Kebeck smiled and extended all four hands to touch hers. "I have been very busy, Sheme. I must apologize for missing our usual Jamjam game. I sent a message to your computer. I enjoy your company and delight in playing Jamjam with you, but it seems both my mind and my schedule have been saturated lately."

Sheme stepped back, removing her hands from his. "I understand. You are preparing for your visit to Earth. I am sure there is much to do. Have you taken even a tick to consider my proposal?"

"Yes, I am honored that you asked me to be a husband-mate for a child, but I need more time to reach a decision. My mind is too crowded at this time. We must talk after I return from Earth."

Sheme smiled. "I like that you deliberate carefully before making a big decision. It is a good thing. We will talk when you return. And on the subject of the trip, I have just discovered that I will be one of the engineers overseeing the launch of your vessel to Earth. I will see you there." She lightly touched his hands and blended into the crowd.

The evening grew late and the crowd had already thinned when Kebeck congratulated Lios once more and took his leave. As he walked toward the river, Kebeck thought about Adeline, or as he sometimes thought of her, his Earth daughter. *I have also watched her grow up. And even though I had no influence in her childhood, I also feel proud of how she has turned out. It is unfortunate that she lives in such a dangerous world.*

Chapter 18

Earth

Adeline walked completely through her house one more time. She inspected each of the beautifully framed canvases hanging on the white walls. Adeline liked to collect art when she traveled; each piece had its own story and memories connected to it. The red and yellow Picasso-like painting of two nude women was especially arresting. When she was in Guadalavaca a year earlier, she had walked past the painting every single day of her stay until she decided that she simply had to have it. It reminded her of Cuban music: hot, fast, and wild. She noticed that the little watercolor of the Charles Bridge in Prague was hanging crookedly. She straightened it.

Adeline listened as she walked, but the only noise she heard was the sound of her own shoes tapping on the hardwood floors. The police and neighbors had left hours ago, but she still didn't feel relaxed in her own home. *I wish Jim were here*, she thought to herself. His last email and her half-written reply stared at her from the computer screen. *I don't want to worry him. What good will it do anyway if I tell him that someone sort-of broke into my house? He'll be here soon; maybe I'll tell him then.* Adeline smiled at the thought of having her wonderful man back in her arms for three days; they were going to have a great weekend together. *Well, better get to work.* She turned and took a step toward the computer. It seemed to have grown fur.

"Roger, get down!" The cat looked at her before slowly easing up off the keypad, his paws typing the letters ooollllllkkkkknnnn while doing so. "Oh would you please get down?" she yelled. The cat jumped off the desk and landed gracefully on the floor. He gave Adeline another look of disdain and headed into the kitchen.

As soon as she sat down in front of the computer the doorbell rang, startling her. *Whew! Am I jumpy or what?* She headed toward the door but then paused for a moment and went over to the window instead. Looking out, she saw Mr. Stafford, Carol's father, standing in front of her door. She had always liked Mr. Stafford. His British accent and his manner of speaking had made her laugh when she was a kid. Like when she and Carol got into trouble and he would say, "Quit playing silly buggers." Or when he would finish giving them instructions of some sort by saying, "And then Bob's your uncle." There he stood with his dyed dark-brown hair neatly parted on the side, a pair of gold-rimmed glasses resting atop the man's rather large nose. Adeline always thought poor Mr. Stafford's nose was a striking contrast to his virtually chinless features, though this was compensated by his small and always neatly trimmed beard. Fortunately, Carol had inherited her mother's nose and chin. He also seemed to have had grown a bit of a paunch, but he still presented himself, as always, like the proper British gentleman.

"Mr. Stafford, how nice to see you," Adeline said after opening the door. "Please come in." Adeline didn't feel up to speaking with Carol's father today. She thought he was a lovely man, but just seeing his face brought her down. He made her think of Carol and all the good times at the Stafford house. Seeing him standing there reminded her of all the times he had greeted her at his door. Mr. Stafford stepped inside and gave Adeline a big hug. As he released her she could see his eyes welling up. Adeline quickly dabbed at her own eyes to keep the tears from running down her face. "Come in, please, sit down. Can I get you anything? Some tea?"

"No thanks, luv, I'm fine. I just want to talk." He slowly eased himself onto the green wing chair beside the couch.

Adeline sat on the blue and green couch and turned toward him. His head was turned toward her but his eyes were looking over her shoulder, off into space. A single tear made its way down his leathery face; he made no effort to wipe it away. The silence felt awkward. She had to say something. "I thought the funeral was nice; lovely music."

He looked directly at her. "I went over to Carol's apartment to start on the job of dealing with her possessions and there was yellow police tape across the door and a sign that identified it as a crime scene."

"I'm sorry, yes, I should have called you and told you … but I didn't want to bother you … and … I'm so sorry. I should have called."

Mr. Stafford adjusted his glasses and sighed. "It's all right luv, Carol's leaving us so suddenly has thrown us all for a loop. Anyway, I called the name on the door, a police detective, Nick somebody, and he said that now the police think Carol's death was perhaps more than just a random mugging."

"They told you about the missing papers and computers?" she asked.

"Yes. Somehow, that makes it both worse and better. Worse because someone actually planned to kill my baby girl and did it on purpose. But somehow better, because now at least … well, there might be a chance of catching that bastard." His voice became rough as he said the words. His eyes welled up again behind his glasses. "Do you have any idea, luv, any idea at all, about why someone would have wanted to kill my Carol?"

Adeline shook her head. "I've racked my brain. It doesn't make sense. She hadn't made any enemies here, or anywhere as far as I know. She hardly even knew anybody around here. All the stories she'd written after coming to Toronto were just about regular, everyday people, not gangsters or criminals or anything like that. She was the last one hired at the paper, so she didn't know the city very well. She got the light, soft pieces. Dan Stevens or Dorothy Paul usually cover the hard-crime cases. I do some of the white-collar crime. As far as I know, no one in the city had any reason to hurt her. And when she was in Vancouver she did mostly fashion stuff. Those designers can be real bitches and they hate critics, but they don't kill them. No, it makes no sense."

Mr. Stafford looked around the room. "You've got Roger?"

"Yeah. He's around here somewhere." Adeline was relieved by the change of topic. "You sure you don't want to take him home with you?"

"No, my wife's allergies couldn't handle a cat in the house. But Carol loved that cat, so I'm glad to see him with you. Thank you for taking him." Mr. Stafford was trying hard to keep a stiff upper lip, but his pale face was lined with sorrow. "Adeline, if Carol's death is somehow related to her job and you feel in any way threatened, please call us or just come down and stay with us."

"Oh, thank you Mr. Stafford. I'll keep that in mind."

He straightened up and looked her directly in the eyes. "Adeline, I know you probably grew up thinking of me as that silly old Brit who happens to be your best friend's father. Well … I just want you to know that I'm a bit more than that. I'm … well, I'm … someone you can call if you need help." He took off his glasses and wiped at the damp spot on his right cheek. "Adeline, before I retired, I didn't really work for an insurance company. I was with the military. When you kids were young and I spent months away, I wasn't really on any run-of-the- mill business trip. I had a very … unique government job." He hesitated and glanced around the room before looking at her again. "It involved security … top-secret security, in fact." He took her hand. "I tell you this because with both your parents having passed on, you might need me someday. You're like a daughter to me. The only daughter I have left now. So please don't hesitate to call if anything doesn't seem right."

Adeline was trying hard to suppress a look of amazement. *Mr. Stafford had been some kind of secret agent or James Bond or something. Wow!*

"I assume Carol didn't know about your real job?" Adeline asked him, still trying to wrap her mind around this new piece of information. "She couldn't have known. Carol couldn't keep a secret about anything; she would have told me for sure."

"No, she certainly was a bit chatty at that. Only my wife knows."

"I guess you don't want me to tell anyone, right?"

"Yes, I'm afraid no one must know. Not even Jim."

Adeline now noticed that Mr. Stafford's accent had almost disappeared. "Okay, not even Jim." She smiled at him. "And thank you for the offer."

Mr. Stafford put his glasses back on. "I'll be going now, luv. Mrs. Stafford likes me to get home before dark, you know."

As they both stood up, the thoughts ran through Adeline's mind. *Should I tell him about the window? Yes. No. I don't know. No, come on, it was nothing.* He gave her a hug. "I'm serious. Call me if you notice anything unusual." He walked out, closing the door behind him and leaving Adeline standing in the middle of her living room reevaluating the lanky, big-nosed man she had known for more than twenty-five years. *I should just tell him about the break-in.* She went over to the window beside the door and looked out. Mr. Stafford was just getting into his car. *It's okay. I'll tell him next time we talk.*

The phone rang somewhere in the room. Adeline gathered her thoughts and looked around for the portable phone. *Where did I put it?* After the fourth ring she found it under a cushion on the couch.

"Hello? Oh, Dalton, yes, hello, how are you?" She listened to her editor's questions before responding. "Yes, I'm almost finished the 'who-rides-the-bus' story and I've started the research on Erwin Bercic. Not really finding a lot on him, though. I thought I would call his office today and set up a face-to-face interview. I'm sure he'll be happy to meet with me; he is running for Mayor, you know. I'll email you the bus story so that you'll have it by nine tomorrow, okay? Okay then, talk to you later. Bye."

Chapter 19

Palala

A white ball splashed down beside Kebeck's head. He quickly turned and grabbed the ball. Kicking his feet and lower hands together under the water to get some height, he held the ball in one hand and then hit it with the other, sending it toward the point circle. A player on the opposing team leaped up and deflected the ball so that it shot out of the playing area. Kebeck heard a noise behind him and turned to see a black ball floating nearby. He slammed it with his fist, sending it splashing out of the playing area. Players from both teams swam out to retrieve the balls and the game continued. As a white ball flew through the air toward him, Kebeck looked around to find another player wearing a piece of white fabric around his neck. He was surrounded by players sporting black neck pieces; the other team had him cornered. The only way he could possibly score a point in this last eighth was to send the ball high in the air hoping it would reach someone on his team. He struck the ball upwards and watched it come down next to Prigo, his son and teammate. Prigo smacked the ball dead on, driving it straight through the curved goal markers on the shore to score a point. Everyone on the white team splashed their hands in the water and yelled Prigo's name four times. The timer then rang. The game was over and the white team had won. Kebeck, Prigo, and the other team members swam to shore and handed their white neck pieces to their coach. He reminded them all to be on time for practice next third-day. Most of the team then headed off to work or home.

Prigo and Kebeck got out of the water and stretched out on the thick blue grass. Both sides of the river had been planted with this particular vegetation because of its very soft, somewhat spongy texture. Fifteen or twenty steps further inland was a forest of yellow-leaved Yepa trees that shaded the area.

"A good game," said Kebeck. "You play well."

"Thank you, my father."

Kebeck noticed that his son was rubbing his upper hands together. "Is there a problem with your hands?"

"There is a pain in the third digit on this hand." He held up the hand. "I think I may have hurt it when I hit that last ball."

Kebeck held his son's injured hand in his own upper hands and examined it. "The skin is not broken, but we should go to the medical facility and have someone look at the digit," said Kebeck.

"That may be the proper and logical thing to do, but that is not what I want to do. If I am injured then they will require that I stay at the medical facility until the damage is healed. There is work that I must do. I do not want to spend days or even weeks idle because of one injured digit."

"Prigo," said an exasperated Kebeck. "I am aware that you have always resented inactivity. Rarely do you stand still. But it is our custom to rest the whole body when one part is injured. Your body can not be isolated into separate components. The whole body must be at rest for any one section to heal. It is a custom that is backed up by logic and science."

"They do not rest the whole body on Earth. I have watched their television programs and they just medicate and bandage the injured limb and get on with their lives," said Prigo. "Why would this not work with our bodies?"

"Earth beings have a different physiology. I may not know the exact details of how their bodies work, but I do know they need to keep their bodies at a constant temperature. Also, they require greater quantities of food than we do. Much of the food they eat is converted to energy to keep their bodies at a specific temperature. They refer to themselves as being warm-blooded. And they would think of us as being cold-blooded. We simply are very different."

"But we are not cold," countered Prigo.

"That is the Earth term for animals that adjust to the ambient temperature rather than maintaining their own constant temperature. I am sure you are aware of the fact that Earth beings often live in frigid areas of their planet. Because their bodies actually produce heat, they are able to live in cold places; they can live in places that would be much too cold for us."

"But this is odd terminology; how could we who cannot live in cold places be called cold-blooded?" complained Prigo.

"I think that is enough talk about Earth for now. I will accompany you to the medical facility and we can see about your injured digit."

"As you wish," sighed Prigo. "I do have two other topics I need to discuss with you in private. We can talk as we walk. Which do you wish to hear first, the pleasant or the unpleasant?"

Kebeck stood up and looked around. "It is a beautiful morning. Let us start with the pleasant."

As Prigo stood up a big smile stretched across his face and his neck reddened. He blurted out, "I want to have a child!"

Kebeck reached out and took his son's four hands in his own, being careful not to squeeze the injured digit. "It is time. In a few eight-days you will be fifty-one years old. This makes me very happy." Kebeck was beaming; like Prigo, his neck now turned red with excitement. "Am I correct in thinking that the female you have chosen is Parda?"

"You are indeed. She has been my friend for many years. She will make a good mother. You do give your permission?" asked Prigo.

"Of course! Parda is strong and intelligent. She will lay good eggs. When do you intend to sign a contract with her?" Kebeck's enthusiasm was evident.

"I wish to sign it on my birth anniversary. That way we can celebrate both occasions together." Prigo excitedly rushed his words out: "Then we can retain her next cycle of eggs and after eight days the eggs will be ready for the selection."

"I remember your selection ceremony like it was yesterday. Your mother brought in a big blue bowl filled with her eggs. Your grandfather and I inspected each one to determine the biggest and healthiest. It seemed like your grandfather was going to take forever. Finally, we placed your egg in the red bowl and first your grandfather and then I squeezed the essential fluids out of our bodies and into the red bowl. Your mother and I had spent much time discussing which sex we wanted you to be. I wanted a male and she wanted a female. We finally had to settle it with a game of digit matching. Only my good luck made you male."

"Thank you, father, I am glad for it. I think I like being male," Prigo said with a mischievous smile.

"Did you know there is an animal on Earth whose sex is determined, like ours, by the temperature at which its eggs are kept?" Kebeck paused.

"No, no I did not."

Kebeck continued on. "The sex of a large, green primitive reptile called alligator is determined by the temperature at which the creature's eggs are kept. Like with us, the males are developed at a higher temperature. But that is not relevant; I am silly with excitement. Have you told your mother? She will want to reserve a hall for the selection ceremony."

"I will tell her tomorrow. First I wanted to get your permission and cooperation," said Prigo.

"As it should be. I am very happy."

"I must ask you: could part of your happiness be because you are also going to father a child?"

"No! Where did you get this idea?"

"I heard that your friend Sheme was planning to have her second child, so I assumed …."

"Do not assume," Kebeck growled. "Now, let us walk toward the medical facility as you tell me of the unpleasant topic you mentioned earlier, though I think nothing could cast a shadow on your wonderful news."

The path wound its way through the green and gray foliage. Spots of yellow, red, pink, and orange highlighted the lush greenery; the flowers aimed their faces at the sun. Kebeck's friend Lona once said she can tell time by the angle of the flowers as they follow the sun across the sky. Kebeck and his son walked in silence a bit longer before Prigo broached the next subject.

"It is about Earth-Watching," Prigo began. "Yesterday afternoon I was in the room of rest in the Hall of Science. I was tired from many hours of working on my plant growth experiments so I opted for an eight-minute nap. As you know, it has been my custom since childhood to cover my head while sleeping. I simply cannot sleep with any light in my face. I was alone in the rest room and I quickly fell asleep under a pile of covers in a corner of the room. I had finished my nap and was still lying quietly under the covers thinking about my experiments when I heard a voice. I recognized Jarrell's voice; he is one of the members of your Earth-Watch study, is he not? He said, 'Kebeck must be removed from the project. His emotion has compromised his logic.' I then heard another voice saying, 'Yes, I agree.' Jarrell then said, 'Will you go with me to the Assignment Committee to petition to have him removed?' The other person answered, 'Yes, I will.' Then Jarrell said, 'Good! We must stop the Earth-Watching. It is most important that we do so.' Then the voices faded as the two walked out of the room. I did not recognize the other voice. I did not intend to listen in on a private conversation but after I heard your name mentioned, I was not going to reveal myself."

Kebeck stopped walking. With a surprised look on his face, he turned toward his son. "This news causes me great sorrow and infuriates me. I thought Jarrell to be my friend. He spoke kindly to me yesterday and now he plots behind my back. What could have caused his strong dislike of Earth-Watching? Has something happened that has affected his thinking? He should have discussed this with me instead of plotting to have me dismissed from the committee." Kebeck's voice grew louder: "To disparage my logic in public would ruin my reputation! I might not be able to continue my work as a scientist!" Kebeck's neck had turned a deep red. He clapped his upper hands together in rage.

"You must find him and resolve this problem," said Prigo.

"First, I must conquer my anger. Let us walk on. I will meditate as we walk. I will not allow myself to think of it until my color fades. Logical thinking is difficult in the presence of anger."

They walked in silence. Kebeck no longer saw the bright colors of the flowers or felt the warm breeze that rustled the trees. His neck faded slightly to a pinkish shade of gray. When they reached the medical facility, Kebeck turned to his son and said, "If you do not mind I will leave you here. The medical experts can examine your digit; I can be of no further aid. I would like to go home and think on how to proceed with the problem of Jarrell. But know that I am happy about your decision to become a father."

"Thank you. If I can be of assistance, call me."

Kebeck watched Prigo open the door to the building and go in. Then he walked over to the river that flowed alongside the building and jumped in. The swim home would stretch out his muscles and release the tension built up from his anger.

Chapter 20

Earth

Erwin was just sitting there, staring into space. Three stacks of folders sat on the desk in front him. One pile was all coffee-shop business, important matters that supposedly only he could handle. The next pile was city business, those endless memos and letters that he must read and reply to in his capacity as Councilor. The third consisted of campaign material that he needed to read, edit, and send back to his minions. Erwin felt overwhelmed.

He leaned his head back, closed his eyes, and took a deep breath. *My feet are relaxed and limp ... my feet are relaxed and limp ... my legs are relaxed and limp ... my legs are relaxed and limp.* He continued upward until he reached the very top of his head. It was his method of dealing with life when it knocked him around and stuffed him down a toilet.

He had first read about self-hypnosis when he was twelve and trying to survive the experience of having to live with his father in their little hometown outside Vancouver. Newt Junior's only escape was to go into his room and close his eyes, relax his body, and let his imagination take him to the warm peaceful islands he had seen so often in National Geographic. His favorite photo was of a long white curving beach in Belize. In his mind he would watch the palm fronds swaying in the wind as he swam in the gentle blue water. He loved that beach.

Erwin opened his eyes. *How did my life get so complicated.* A light on his desk phone turned on as he was reaching for the folder sitting atop the city pile. *Good, a distraction.* He picked up the phone to find out what Charles wanted.

"Mr. Bercic, I know you said not to disturb you, but I have a reporter from the Globe on the phone right now who's asking to speak with you. What should I tell her?"

"Put her through. But after this, no more calls for the next two hours. If you call me, the building had better be on fire. I have to get through some of these papers. Got that? No flames, no interruption!" Erwin hung up before Charles could answer him. *Idiot. But I guess if I hired a Mensa candidate I'd have to pay him a decent wage.* He looked down and tried to remember from which stack he had taken the file in his hand. Just as the phone rang some of the papers slid out of the folder and fanned out onto the floor.

"Erwin Bercic here. How can I help you?"

"Hello Mr. Bercic. This is Adeline Morgan from the Toronto Globe. I'm working on some candidate profiles for the upcoming election and I wonder if we might set up a time for an interview."

"Sure. You must be replacing Carol Stafford?"

Adeline paused for a minute, then said, "Yes, you probably heard about her case."

"Yes, I read that she was killed. How unfortunate. Did you know her very well?"

"Yes, we were very good friends."

"I'm sorry for your loss," he said, sounding like he meant it. In a way he did mean it. Mostly though, he was sorry that this Stafford broad had found out something that had forced him to kill her.

"Do you have her notes or will we need to start over?" he asked. *Shit. This bitch had better not have any of Stafford's notes.*

"I'm sorry for the trouble but we can't seem to find her notes anywhere. But I've done some of my own research, so I think we can wrap this up in about half an hour max. How about tomorrow? Could you fit me into your schedule tomorrow morning?"

"Sure, no problem." Erwin paused for a moment. *She doesn't really sound like the type who's impressed by fancy furniture and designer decor. So we shouldn't meet at either of my offices. I want her to feel comfortable. I need to find out if Stafford told her anything about me. I'll meet her somewhere familiar… maybe near her house.*

"I've got a meeting over on Jarvis St. tomorrow. I also wanted to check out what my competitors are up to in the coffee-shop biz, so how about if we do the interview at the Tim's at Jarvis and Gerrard, right by your place? How about eleven?"

There was silence on the phone. "You know where I live?"

Erwin couldn't believe he had let that slip. *Fuck!* He quickly replied, "I think Carol Stafford had mentioned in one of our conversations that her best friend lived in that part of town. So I, well I mean, because of what you just said … I assumed that was you."

"Well … yeah," Adeline said hesitantly. "That was me … the best friend."

"Well, okay then, I'll see you at the Tim's at around eleven. Oh, wait! What do you look like? How will I recognize you?"

"I'll be the one with a cup of coffee in my hand." She paused, waiting for Erwin to laugh at the joke. He didn't. "No, really now, look for a blonde with a briefcase that says *Toronto Globe* in big blue letters. That'll be me."

There was more dead air as Erwin collected his thoughts, trying to sound nonchalant. "And … uh … don't worry if I'm a bit late. The traffic is brutal with all the road construction this time of year, but I'll be there as close to eleven as I can."

"No problem. That's actually one of the things we can talk about in the interview. People are going to want to know what you would do about our traffic problems if you get elected."

"Of course it is. We'll talk about that tomorrow. Ok, I've got to let you go, then; there's someone standing here waiting to talk to me. Bye for now." Erwin hung up the phone. He sat there alone, thinking about his predicament.

Chapter 21

Palala

Kebeck wobbled a bit as he entered his house. He was physically exhausted. In an attempt to get over his anger, he had swum all the way from town in record time. But though his body was tired, his mind was still racing. As he dried himself off he reviewed everything he knew about Jarrell. *Jarrell is one year older than me. He has two mature sons. He extended the marriage contract with the mother of his second son and they still live together. He is generally quite logical, but sometimes a little more emotional than most people.*

Kebeck thought he had known Jarrell quite well because they had attended the same common school, sometimes even swimming there together from home. They had spent their first eight years of schooling in a four-room building, with one teacher looking after the class of eight students. They had remained friends even after Kebeck moved on to Ecology School while Jarrell pursued his studies in psychology and sociology elsewhere. Though they continued to meet and speak with each other fairly regularly during their first fifty years, they had drifted somewhat apart as they got older.

Kebeck took two pieces of fruit from the bowl in the refrigeration unit and then stepped outside to rinse them off using the hose that hung on the wall just next to the back door. There was no inside water faucet. Many of the houses built during the previous hundred years had inside sinks. Kebeck's house, however, was five- or six-hundred years old. It had been passed on to him at the time of a distant relative's last-day. He had never felt the need to install an indoor sink; he liked to step outside to admire the view and enjoy the smells. He chomped into the fruit, watching as the water from the hose flowed along the cement troughs toward the Kala fruit trees that grew behind his house. He had spent many hours working on those trees, but that was before he began Earth-Watching. He felt a twinge of remorse over the fact that he had stopped his experiments soon after starting his Earth-Watching activities. As a hobby, experimenting with tree sap had been a sedate but satisfying use of his spare time. He had even discovered that Kala sap contained proteins that likely would make it a good food for fish. His problem was determining how much sap one could remove from a given tree without harming the plant in any way. Lately he had been thinking of sending his data to a friend at the local biology station to see if he wanted to take over his project. He certainly didn't want all his work to go to waste. But now, with Jarrell trying to prohibit Earth-Watching, Kebeck thought that maybe he should just put that idea on hold for the next four or eight years.

As Kebeck turned to go back inside, he heard his computer chime. The sound brought him out of his thoughts. He had set his computer up to chime with a distinct three-note tone whenever anyone entered Adeline's house. Adeline had a visitor. Kebeck plodded over to the computer. He recognized the visitor; it was the policeman investigating Carol's death.

Chapter 22

Earth

"Well well, look who's finally here. I've been waiting for your call, Detective Hawes." Adeline gave Hawes a big fake smile. She was feeling quite irritated, as he hadn't contacted her since they parted ways at Carol's apartment two days earlier. She realized though that it would be unwise to chastise the man. Legally speaking, he didn't have to tell her anything. As she wasn't related to Carol, she could not simply expect a full disclosure. Still, though she had to treat him with courtesy, she really wanted to just yell and rant. "Please, come in. Would you like a cup of tea or coffee?" Adeline backed up and gestured in the direction of the living room chairs.

"I appreciate the offer but I'm trying to cut back on the caffeine. The wife says it's bad for me." He didn't move from the doorway.

She couldn't imagine how this monk-like man could actually have a wife. Once again he was wearing brown, and his gray halo of hair almost glowed in the sunlight. The only thing missing was the big cross hanging over his monk's chest. It bothered Adeline that Hawes would not come away from the door and sit down with her. "I have herbal teas. Please, come in. I'd like to talk."

"Well, that's the thing. I'm only here for a minute because, well, we really won't have much to talk about."

"What?" Adeline said, a little louder than she meant to. "What do you mean?"

"I've got nothing. No fingerprints, no hair, no DNA, no evidence at all. Nothing. The only thing we found was some black plastic hair, from a wig, and that leads nowhere."

"But why can't you trace the plastic hair?" she asked.

"The stuff's just too common. It's the hair they use in all those cheap Halloween wigs. Those wigs are made in China and distributed all over the world. I'm sorry. I want you to know that I'm a good cop, and I won't let this case die, but I've got no leads. Except that ... well ... the fact that whoever stole her computer and papers really knows what they're doing."

Adeline glared at him.

"I mean, whoever stole her stuff is really a pro to be able to do it without leaving any evidence."

Adeline was not pleased and it was showing on her face.

"Did Carol have a man in her life? Either here or back in Vancouver?" he asked.

"No, there wasn't anyone. I mean, the guy she seeing in Vancouver was killed in a car accident about a year and a half ago. That was one of the reasons for moving here. She just wanted to get away from the bad memories and start fresh."

"So, it wasn't love gone wrong; that's a dead end." He blanched. "Sorry. Bad choice of words."

Hawes looked lost in thought for a few seconds. Suddenly his eyes widened and he looked straight at Adeline. "Listen, I've got an idea. This might point me in the right direction. But I'll need your help."

"Well sure, whatever you need, I'll do it."

"This could be difficult for you, and a lot of work." he said. "But it really might help me a lot."

"Yes, yes, what do you want me to do?" Adeline realized she was sounding impatient again.

"I want you to write out everything Carol said to you during the last two weeks before she died, every word you can remember. And write out the names and phone numbers of everybody she spoke to during that time ... everyone you know of, you know, anyone she mentioned talking to. Then email me the list so I can go over it and make some calls."

"You think I haven't already thought about this a thousand times? I've been racking my brain trying to think of something ... of anything that would lead us to her killer?"

"Please, just humor me. You never know. Some little phrase that was just chatter to you at the time could be an important clue for me at this point. Look, I've got nothing else to go on right now. If this doesn't work, I don't know what else we can do."

"All right, is tomorrow soon enough?"

"That's fine. And before I forget, could you please tell Dorothy Paul to quit calling me. I know she's well-loved as Toronto's oldest living reporter, but can you please get her off of my back. I mean she calls me all day, almost on the hour. She's one of those people who thinks she can say anything to anyone because she's old. And I can't believe the language she uses; she says things that would embarrass a porn star."

"She's just looking for a story," Adeline said with an innocent little smile.

"No, really, I mean it. I can't work when I have to talk to her for ten minutes every single hour of the day."

"All right, I can't stop her, but I can tell you how to do it. If you promise to keep it to yourself."

Hawes nodded.

"The trick is to put her on to somebody else. Pick some detective you don't especially like. Try to let it accidentally slip out to Dot that he's working on a big case and ...."

"Gosh, I hate to do that to anyone, but I'm desperate." He scrunched his eyebrows together, then a sly smile appeared on his face. "I know just the guy. So, I'll be expecting to hear from you tomorrow?"

"Yes, I'll send it tomorrow ... right after I finish an interview with one of the guys running for Mayor. I'll sit down with a box of Kleenex, take the phone off the hook, and write out every word that I can remember." She paused. "This is not going to be easy."

"I realize that, and you know I can't guarantee that it'll work, but it's worth trying. My email address is on my card."

He handed her a card and then headed towards his car.

Chapter 23

Palala

A good night's sleep was just what Kebeck had needed. He threw the covers back, climbed down from the resting platform, stretched all four arms, and meandered over to his computer. As he read over his schedule for the day, he gently cursed under his breath. He had forgotten that he was supposed to spend the morning working at the Earth Museum. Usually he enjoyed the curiosity of the young ones who came through and found it challenging to try to explain Earth behaviors to the visitors, but he had other things on his mind today. *Why is Jarrell so opposed to Earth-Watching, and why is he trying to ruin me?* Kebeck's mind churned as he mulled over the situation.

As he headed out the back door of his house and down the walkway to the body waste area (commonly referred to as the "b-wah" by most Palalans), Kebeck considered several options for handling the problem. It was on days like this that he regretted selecting a house that was so close to the river. If he had chosen a house in town, he could have simply used the dwelling's interior b-wah. But, in the country, all b-wahs needed to be at least a thousand feet from any waterway. So, Kebeck usually started his day with the long walk—or at times a brisk run—down this path. Still, at least he was able to enjoy the smell and sight of the flowering wetland plants that surrounded his b-wah. It amazed him that such beautiful plants were so efficient at turning body waste into nutrients for the soil and purifying his wastewater before it seeped back into the water table.

Maybe I should talk with Jarrell, he thought as he headed back toward his house. *No, from what my son heard, Jarrell will not be reasoned with.* He picked up the hose next to the back door and rinsed his face and hands. *Perhaps I should speak with someone else on the committee.* Kebeck adjusted the water to a pulsing jet and rinsed his teeth. Then he took a towel off of the rack above the hose as he entered his house. As he dried his face he noticed that the towel smelled a little off. He walked over to a nearby shelf, grabbed the laundry bag embroidered with a large number three, and stuffed the towel and two others into it. He then tossed the bag onto the floor beside the refrigeration unit so that Dar, his local supply agent, would see it when he came to deliver more food.

Dar would leave three clean towels and another laundry bag when he came to pick up the others. He always brought a fresh supply of food, clean towels, and sleeping-platform covers on the odd days during eight-day cycle. Sometimes Kebeck envied Dar's simple job. There were times when he would rather not have to deal with all the complexities and responsibilities involved in his work as a research scientist. Dar was over two hundred and fifty years old but still enjoyed his work. Dar had delivered supplies with his father from the time he was a child. Dar's children had tried to talk him into retiring and giving the route to someone else. He refused. He said he could not imagine a more pleasant task than driving a supply cart from house to house, talking with the people, and enjoying the scenery.

Kebeck selected a piece of fish and a quado fruit to munch on as he headed toward the river. If he swam fast, he would get to the Earth Museum just as they were opening the doors for the day.

Chapter 24

Earth

Morning was usually a quiet time for Adeline. She liked to get up early, make a breakfast that normally consisted of an egg, some toast, and tea and then sit listening to the CBC radio news as she ate. As soon as she found out the world had not been destroyed overnight she turned off the radio and quietly put herself together for the day. The morning routine was different when Jim was home. They had spent two months living together before Jim left for his three month stint in England. In the mornings he sang, made jokes, and hugged her almost every time she stood still. He was certainly a morning person, whereas she woke up slowly and liked to coast through that first hour of the day. It was going to be an interesting life with her Jim, that was for sure, but she was ready to leave her solitude. Having Carol die suddenly made her want to embrace her life all the more, to experience everything it had to offer. Though a few doubts had lingered in the back of her mind about sharing her life with her gregarious fiancé, she now decided that he was just what she needed. *We'll travel everywhere, and we'll have children and bring them too! We'll make lots of mad passionate love. And enjoy every one of the remaining hours we have on this earth.*

Adeline looked at her watch. It was already nine. *Better get my email done so I'm on time for my meeting with that donut guy.* Then she stopped. *First things first.* She went over to her music system, selected a CD, and put it on. Jefferson Airplane blared through the house.

Chapter 25

Palala

A warm breeze blew over the skin on Kebeck's face and the scales on his body, drying him as he walked from the river toward the museum. The Earth-Museum had been established only two years earlier. The large half-sphere structure had been built in the same design as most houses, only bigger. Yerf had managed the construction project and had invited Kebeck to watch the enormous underlying plastic bubble being sprayed with layer upon layer of cement until the structure was strong enough to stand without the bubble. Eight days later, the workmen deflated the bubble, folded it, and put it away until it was needed again. Then, they cut the openings for doors and windows. Kebeck always enjoyed watching as buildings were formed in this usual manner.

When he first started Earth-Watching, Kebeck was surprised by the shape and structure of the Earth beings' dwellings and other public buildings. Earth engineers and builders seemed to erect angular buildings that were subject to damage and destruction by windstorms, tornadoes, and hurricanes that were much more frequent and severe than any experienced on Palala. Kebeck was also puzzled by how the buildings' door and window openings often did not face the direction of the wind, and by how the Earth scientists had yet to develop a precise method of watching and predicting the weather. Palalans, on the other hand, were always notified via computer of any forthcoming severe weather activity. After receiving such notification, they simply would gather their possessions and move to the underground rooms that are part of all homes in storm prone areas. Storms were but a temporary inconvenience on Palala and it saddened Kebeck to see the destruction they caused on Earth.

The museum was quite busy when he arrived, as usual. He made a few adjustments to the computer behind the museum's information desk, connecting it to his home computer. As soon as he looked up from the computer, the questions began.

"I have a question about the age of maturity for Earth beings," asked an older fellow. "I have accessed studies of the human brain that show it does not reach full, physical maturity until after age twenty. According to my research, the judgment section of their brains is the last area to develop. Knowing this, why do they allow their young to enter into coupling contracts, have children, or join armies to fight and die in battle? Why are they allowed to make such major decisions before the reasoning section of their brain is fully developed?"

Kebeck softly sighed. *I have just arrived and already I must answer such a difficult question.* "I do not really know. But I think many of the laws concerning maturity perhaps were made because the Earth beings' physical bodies seem to be fully developed by age sixteen to eighteen."

"But why would they not change the laws now that they know the true age of maturity of their kind?"

"From what I have observed, the lawmakers do not always respect science."

The old one huffed. "It pains me to see their wars being fought by these young immature ones. Of course the older ones make the decisions and give the orders, but it is cruel to send young ones to their death before their brain is fully developed." He stomped off toward the door.

Not even a moment passed before the next question. "Why do Earth beings seem to need so many more objects than the thirty or so we have in each of our houses?" asked a forty-year-old youngster.

"They do seem to have many more objects than they need," Kebeck answered. "But remember that they wear clothing all the time, and it is their custom to have a variety of clothes. Also, they manipulate their food so they have many implements, containers, and appliances for this purpose. Furthermore, many of them live in cold places where they spend much time indoors. So they have disproportionately large homes filled with such items as games and exercise equipment in order to pass the time.

You have to realize that they come from a different historical tradition. Possessions were considered good things by primitive Earth cultures. The early Earth beings decorated their bodies with metal and shells. Our reticence to acquire possessions came into being thousands of years ago when the majority of our ancestors were followers of the Oswa religion who believed that owning more possessions than necessary was a sin. They believed disrupting nature to make anything that was not essential was wrong. The very strict Oswans even refused to build houses and only ate fruit that they found lying on the ground; they considered it a violation of their relationship with nature to pull fruit from bushes or to break the branches of any tree. Even though we have matured past the need for religion, a part of these ancient philosophies has stayed with us."

"But as you have noticed," Kebeck continued, "the Earth beings appear to very much enjoy their objects. From our observations, it seems that many of them base their whole lives around the goal of obtaining as many objects as possible. We have even heard of an odd expression used by some of the Earth beings: *he who has the most toys, wins.*"

"But wins what?"

"Unfortunately, we're not sure," answered Kebeck.

"About the clothing," a tall dark green person asked, "why do some Earth beings spend much time pursuing and purchasing clothing? I see them express great pleasure during this activity. They fill their storage units with the clothing, but after a few years they give the clothing to beings who have earned fewer credits before going out to acquire yet more clothing. Though this system does supply clothing to poor people, it does not seem very efficient. It puzzles me. Also, why do certain bits of clothing cost so many more credits than other garments of a similar size and texture?"

Kebeck racked his brain for an answer he felt would satisfy the visitor. "I suggest that you research a concept that is called 'fashion' to get a better understanding of this behavior. It is illogical, but so too is much other of the Earth beings' behavior."

Another person piped up. "Why do the ones who live in the warmer areas of the planet wear clothes?"

Kebeck paused before answering. "It is a custom that is related to their religions. Essentially, they believe it is inappropriate to see other Earth beings' bodies."

"But many of them do not believe in a religion," interjected a tall light gray fellow. "Why do those who believe in reality, the non-deists, not go without clothes?"

"It is a custom of most beings on Earth to wear clothes all of the time. Although the custom seems to have religious roots, it evolved into a convention that most beings accepted. Also, the non-deists do not want to be treated badly by the religious majority."

"You are saying that the majority of Earth beings, not just a few, really think that there is a very powerful being controlling their planet?"

"Yes."

The tall fellow shook his head and wandered off toward the Earth home-furnishings exhibit.

"I have a theory," said a short smiling female. "I think the Earth beings have been so slow to develop because they have been handicapped by having only two hands."

"No, it is their short life span that has held them back," suggested someone else in the crowd. "How can anyone get anything done when they only have fifty to seventy-five years to devote to a project?"

Kebeck was about to explain some of ways the religions had held back Earth sciences when he heard the computer chime a three-tone sound. He had set the museum computer to view Adeline's house when he had arrived. Glancing at the screen, he noticed someone he had never seen before entering the back door of her home. It was an Earth male who looked somewhat like one of the actors on the daytime Earth TV dramas, someone who oddly enough was wearing both a business suit and what appeared to be rubber surgical gloves. The visitor went straight to Adeline's desk and started searching through her papers. Kebeck ignored the crowd of visitors in the museum and continued to stare at the computer screen. The Earth male was now accessing Adeline's computer.

"Excuse me. I have more questions," said one of the visitors.

He looked up to see about a dozen people waiting to talk to him.

"I have a question about what Earth beings do to produce offspring, the actions they call sex." It was the short female again.

Kebeck glanced down and saw that the Earth male was still working on Adeline's computer.

"What is the purpose of the elaborate rules that determine how Earth beings choose the other beings they wish to have sex with? If their so-called sex activity is pleasurable and not harmful, why do they not practice it more routinely with anyone, and at anytime?"

Kebeck looked back at the female who asked the question and he tried to think of an answer. "Many of the rules related to their sex conduct were religious edicts, and some evolved as a method of determining who fathered the child …," Kebeck's voice trailed off. "It is complicated." He looked back at the computer screen. The Earth male was wandering around Adeline's living room. He went over to a bookshelf and looked at the books for a moment before pulling one off the shelf. He flipped through it. There was a pile of paper money in the book. The man paused, counted the money, then put it in the outside pocket of his jacket. He put the book back on the shelf. The title on its spine was "Marx." Kebeck wondered why the man had selected that particular book; perhaps it caught his attention because it was more worn looking than the others.

A loud voice brought his attention back to the group in front of him. "Tell us about the Earth visits. I understand there is another one scheduled in the near future. Will you go on this one?"

"And have you been before?" asked the short female.

"No … I mean yes." Kebeck glanced back at the computer screen just in time to see the Earth male leave the house through the back door. He turned his attention back to the museum visitors. "I have never been to Earth and I am excited to see it in person. I will be going to the North American region and, as others have done before us, we will time our visit to coincide with the holiday known to some Earth beings as Halloween so that we can wear disguises and move about freely." Speaking of the planned expedition to Earth reminded him of his worries about Jarrell. If Jarrell did get him dismissed from the committee, he obviously would not be allowed to go along on the journey.

"What costume will you wear?" asked someone behind the short female.

"I do not know yet; but it will be made by one of our clothing manufacturers." Kebeck's head was reeling from all the questions and his concern for Adeline. He looked up at the time device on the wall. He was relieved to see that it was nearly time for his replacement to arrive.

As soon as his colleague took his place behind the information desk, Kebeck moved towards the exit as quickly as possible through the crowd. "Thank you. Excuse me. Thank you. Excuse me ...."

As he swam back to his house, thoughts rushed through his head. *Who was that male sneaking through Adeline's house? Is she in any danger? Could that male be the Earth being who killed Carol?*

Chapter 26

Earth

The hard seat of the red metal chair was beginning to feel uncomfortable. As usual, two cops were sitting at a table over in the corner. As she waited, she looked at the brown and tan uniforms worn by the women behind the counter; they were so totally unsexy. *No chance of any of the employees doing it in the storeroom at this coffee shop.* Adeline looked at her watch. She had already been waiting for about twenty minutes when Erwin Bercic walked in.

"I was beginning to wonder," Adeline said as he walked up to her table. "You know how it is when you're supposed to meet someone at a restaurant, and if they're just a bit late you start to worry if you've got the time or place right."

"I must apologize," Erwin offered. He tilted his head to one side and smiled. Adeline felt like she was watching an actor on stage in a mediocre play. "All the traffic and not being able to get off the phone made me a little late. I'm sorry about that. Can I get you another cup of coffee? I see you've almost finished that one," he nodded towards her cup.

"No thanks, but please get one for yourself and we can start the interview."

Erwin smiled and turned to go the counter. She watched him carefully. *He has the perfect soap opera face.* She continued to look at him as he ordered his coffee. He was wearing tan slacks and a dark green blazer over a black turtleneck sweater. As he reached into an outside pocket and took out a wad of money, something white dropped to the floor. He quickly bent down, scooped it up, and put it back in his pocket. *Looked like a surgical glove, but it was probably just a Kleenex.* Someone at a table near the counter spoke to him. Erwin turned towards the table, coffee in hand, and exchanged a few words with the man. *He has the posture of a confident person. He seems to pause and think before speaking. I know I should like those characteristics but I don't like them on him. He's too smooth. I don't like this guy, but I can't let that show as I do this interview.*

Erwin placed his cup on the table as he eased into the chair opposite Adeline. "First, let me tell you again how sorry I was to hear about Carol Stafford."

"Thank you. Like I had told you, we were the best of friends and I really miss her." Adeline suddenly was on the verge of tears, but she refused to let herself cry in front of this man. She straightened up and looked over his shoulder to avoid direct eye contact. In a weak voice she said, "so ... let's do this interview, shall we?"

"Are you all right? We can put this off, you know; maybe 'til tomorrow."

Adeline looked him square in the face. "No, I'm fine. Let's do it now. Tomorrow I pick up my fiancé at the airport at noon." She smiled. "I have to say I'm really looking forward to tomorrow."

He lifted his cup in a toast. "To happiness tomorrow! Now, what would you like to know?"

"Let's start with your childhood. Where did you grow up? Do you have brothers and sisters? What were your parents like?"

"Well, simply put, my childhood was a bit tragic. I was an only child. My mother died with cancer and soon after my father died in a car accident; it was probably suicide. But, who knows. I was only four. After that I was raised in an orphanage in Edmonton."

"What was the name of the orphanage?" She scribbled in her notebook.

"It was simply called the Edmonton Orphanage," he said. "But I can save you some time if you're planning to call there. It burned down not long after I left."

"That's too bad. It would have been nice to speak with someone who knew you when you were just a kid. So, how old were you when you left the orphanage?"

"At sixteen I left the orphanage and went to work. I traveled around the country and found work doing all sorts of odd jobs."

"How did you go from that to being a millionaire?"

"One of the skills I picked up after I left the orphanage was small-motor repair. I started making some real money when I worked down in Belize and in Honduras repairing outboard motors for boats."

"Hold on, I'm trying to visualize where Belize and Honduras are on a map." Adeline tilted her head up slightly. "Oh yes, I remember now; they're down in Central America, just below Mexico. What made you go there?"

"I met an old guy who had spent years in the South Pacific repairing outboard motors. It seems that there were lots of isolated islands where the natives had bought outboards for their boats but they had no one to fix them. He said the natives would give you anything, even their daughters for a night, if you could get their boat engines working," he said with a smirk.

"Well," he continued, "that sounded good to me. I knew small engines. So I thought maybe Belize and Honduras would have the same problem. Plus, I didn't have enough money for a ticket to the South Pacific. So I packed my tool kit and went to Belize. And it worked. Lots of outboards and almost no one else there who could fix them. It was good money. I had a buddy who was good with the stock market so I kept investing the cash that I was making. I also set up a touring business in Belize, and then later on I bought and expanded a small company that manufactured furniture. I was lucky to sell all my businesses down there just before Hurricane Kate wiped out a lot of the area."

"So, disasters follow in your wake," Adeline said, raising one eyebrow.

"Well, I wouldn't say that. Hurricanes are common in that part of the world. It was love that saved me from that hurricane. I met a woman named Susan who was traveling down there, and suddenly Toronto looked like a good place to live."

"Sounds like an interesting life. So when did you come to Toronto?" Adeline finished the last of her coffee and placed the empty paper cup on the table a few inches from Erwin's elbow.

"I've lived here about twenty years now."

"I heard somewhere that you have a son," Adeline queried. She watched to see how he would react to her subtle invasion of his privacy.

"Yes, I married Susan the year after I moved up here and we had Jeff the next year." He kept looking at her as he pushed the empty cup over to Adeline's side of the table. "Unfortunately, Susan and I discovered that we didn't really enjoy living together, so we divorced. Jeff's in university now. He's spent most of his life with his mother. But still, he's turned out to be a son that I can be proud of."

"Which school is he attending? Is he here in Toronto?"

"No, he wanted to live in New York and go to Columbia. I wish he were here though; then I wouldn't worry about him so much."

Adeline looked down at the list of questions in her notebook. Most of the information had already been disclosed in the press release that Bercic had faxed to the Globe. *How can I get him to come out of his shell and get him to be real with me?* When she looked up she noticed that he had quietly crushed her empty cup.

"You said you worked all across Canada. Whereabouts?"

"Gosh, that was so many years ago." He stared off in space. "I remember working at a filling station in Red Deer for four or five months. I worked as a dishwasher in a restaurant in Vancouver for a few months; I think it was called Fran's Place. Last year, when I was in Vancouver, I drove by where it had been, and noticed it had been torn down and replaced by a condo." He smiled. "Let's see ... I learned to ski when I worked for a while at Grouse Mountain, near Vancouver. Hmm, what else? Oh yes, I did the bike messenger thing in Montreal." He shook his head. "In retrospect, that was the most dangerous job. Have you ever driven in Montreal? I should be dead." He took a deep breath and slowly let it out. "You know, I wouldn't say I was wild, but basically I drank a lot of beer, chased a lot of girls, and changed jobs every few months. Let's just say I was immature. What do you expect from a sixteen-year-old, out there on his own. But I guess I grew up after I moved to Belize."

"So Belize was good for you?"

"Yep. There I learned to start putting business before pleasure ... most of the time. I became a businessman."

Adeline looked at her notes again.

Erwin flashed a tight little smile. "I think you're looking for something more exciting to write about me. Unfortunately for you, I've become a little dull in my old age. I'm now just the owner of a couple of coffee shops who wants to be mayor. But I tell you that I'll make a good mayor because I can use my business sense to make the city prosper." He put both elbows on the table, placed his chin in his hands, and broadened the smile so it almost looked real.

Adeline decided to go at him from a different direction. "What political party do you support?"

"None, of course. Working with a party would make it more difficult to run the city."

Adeline was running out of ideas. "Read any good book lately?"

"*Guns, Germs, and Steel.* It's the best thing I've read in years. The author did an incredible amount of research to show how we developed on this planet. Really amazing stuff. Have you read it?"

"Uh ... no, but I've heard good things about it." Adeline was getting frustrated. She flipped through her notes once more before flopping the pad onto the table. "Well, I guess that's all for now. May I call you later if I think of any other questions?" she asked.

"Of course you can. Call me anytime. I love the press."

Adeline left the coffee shop feeling that her interview was incomplete. She had asked the right questions. He had answered them. But something was missing, though she didn't know what.

Chapter 27

Palala

The sun that warmed his back made the water seem cool as Kebeck swam down the river. He stopped to watch three children playing at the water's edge. Kebeck recognized one of the young ones as the daughter of his friend and colleague, Agara. He floated for a while, looking at the house on the shore behind the children. He remembered hearing someone mention that Agara had recently moved to a house along this river. An adult male came out of the house, looked out toward the river and waved. *There's Agara now. I should talk to him. I wonder how he feels about Jarrell's ideas.* He swam over to the shore.

"I am so happy to see you," Agara said as he extended a hand to help Kebeck out of the water. "I am getting so excited about our trip to Earth. My mate and daughter are irritated by my constant chatter about Earth. Please, come in and relax. My mate is at work and I am watching our daughter and two of her friends."

"Greetings, Kebeck Warnon." Kebeck turned around to see Agara's daughter Marfu addressing him. He liked that Agara had taught her to call adults by their first two names, according to Palalan tradition.

"Marfu, I am delighted to see you. Your father tells me good things about your schooling. We are proud of you."

Marfu's neck beamed a light pink and she smiled. "Thank you. I wish you enjoyment and learning on your trip to Earth." She leaned a bit closer to Kebeck and whispered. "Please take care of my father. I love him, but his enthusiasm sometimes interferes with his wisdom."

"I heard that," Agara grumbled. "I appreciate your concern, but it could be phrased with more respect." Agara pointed toward the two children sitting on the riverbank. "Your friends are waiting. You should join them."

"I bow to the sage advice given by my father." Marfu smiled, laughed, and ran off to join her friends.

Agara shook his head. "An intelligent child can be a difficult thing to live with. Come into the house and we will share our joys and woes. Your face tells me that something is churning in your mind today." Agara motioned toward the house.

As they entered the house Kebeck heard the sounds of Earth TV coming from a computer. Kebeck paused just inside the door. "I do not wish to interrupt your work."

Agara went over to the computer and muted the sound. "You do not interrupt. I had recorded twenty hours of what they call a 'soap opera.' I am watching bits of it. It is of such a nature that it is not necessary to watch all of it. It concerns itself with lies and secrets, with much emotion. I understand wanting to visit a fantasy world to escape reality, as there is much harsh reality on Earth, but the world of this soap opera is not a pleasant place. Ah, but that is Earth. Let us talk of your reality. Sit. Eat. Tell me, what troubles you?"

Kebeck took a piece of green fruit out of a bowl on a shelf, reclined on the resting platform, and took a big bite of the fruit. Agara turned a slantboard to face him. He climbed on to it and sat, smiling at his friend.

Kebeck propped up on one arm. "You know I watch a female Earth being named Adeline?"

"Yes, of course, you have talked much about her over the years. I hope there is nothing wrong with her?"

"There are odd things happening in her life and it gives me concern."

"You take the Earth beings too seriously, Kebeck. Worrying about an Earth being is like worrying about which way a wave will fall. You have no control and ultimately it is of no consequence."

Upon hearing that, Kebeck decided Agara might not be the right person with whom to discuss his Adeline. "You are right. I should dismiss it from my mind." Kebeck swatted his hand in front of his face. "There, it is gone."

Agara cocked his head to one side. "And what else troubles you this day?"

"Have you seen Jarrell recently?"

"Yes, he came by yesterday. He expressed strong negative feelings about Earth-Watching and he wants it stopped. He was quite aggressive in his insistence that it was harming Palala. This puzzles me, because in the past he had a more balanced attitude toward Earth-Watching. Do you know of any reason for his sudden change?"

"No. But I also had such a visit. Did he mention the possibility of having me removed from the committee?" Kebeck took another bite of the fruit and sat upright.

"He said nothing of that, but he may have suspected that because we are friends, I would not agree to that course of action. Also, you are a brilliant researcher who is quite valuable to the project. What is he thinking?"

"I believe he is thinking of doing almost anything to stop Earth-Watching as soon as possible."

"How do you know that he is trying to have you removed from the project? Did he discuss it with you? Did he ask you to resign?"

"No, it was overheard by someone who later told me about it."

Agara's neck reddened as he stood up and waved his upper arms in the air. "This sounds like an Earth soap opera in itself. This one tells that one, and that one tells another. There are misunderstandings and things left unsaid. We do not live that way. We do not do such things. If we have a problem, we discuss it. And if it cannot be settled between two people using the mediation methods we were taught as children, then we call in an arbitrator."

"But, I do not want to go through all that just before our trip to Earth. I am thinking that I might prefer to deal with Jarrell when we come back."

"That is reasonable. If changes in the Earth-Watch project are discussed at our upcoming computer-linked meeting, whether these are related to the duration of the trip or to the personnel involved, I will propose that nothing be done too hastily. After all, what is another eight days this way or that?"

Kebeck felt an internal sigh of relief. *If Agara can delay Jarrell's proposals, I can spend more time watching Adeline. I cannot intervene in her affairs, but I must know what happens to her.* "Excuse me for a moment." Kebeck got up, went over to the hose hanging just outside the back door, rinsed his fruit-stained hands, then turned to his friend. "Agara, between you and me, I want your opinion as our specialist in Earth TV and movies. You surely view more of those media than anyone on Palala. Tell me. Is watching such programming harmful to our people?"

Agara shook his head. "I think not. The so-called situation comedy TV shows and movies are usually based on lies or misunderstandings. Some have physical humor and even though it is often of an adolescent nature, it makes me smile nonetheless. The dramas and crime shows are of deception and violence. They are interesting to watch, but do not relate to our way of life. I like the reality shows because they seem to give us true insight into how the Earth beings think. And the nature programs are great studies of the creatures of Earth; they are similar to our educational programs. But, all in all, it is just innocuous entertainment.

Ah, wait, I almost forgot about the religious-preacher shows." Agara paused. "They are interesting in that the preachers seem to sincerely believe the incredible things they are saying. On occasion I have found their enthusiasm and earnestness to be mesmerizing. But, I would think that no one could be persuaded to believe their rantings."

"So we agree," Kebeck said. "It is all but mere entertainment. I should go now. I thank you for sharing your time and thoughts with me. I will probably next see you on the day of our trip to Earth."

Agara bounced up from the slantboard. "I am most anxious to go. Understandably I am also a bit frightened. I have never left our planet. You have. What is it like?"

"There is nothing to fear. It feels like flying from one city to another, only longer." Kebeck moved toward the front door. *Yes, soon I will fly to Earth, home of my Adeline.* A mental image of the unknown Earth male he had viewed in Adeline's home played in his mind. He extended his palms, said a quick "clear water," and moved rapidly toward the river.

Chapter 28

Earth

Adeline wandered through the house straightening up papers and pulling dead leaves off the houseplants. As she passed the big bookcase in the living room, she noticed that the Marx volume was sticking out a bit. Her father had been talked into buying the Great Books Collection when he was in university. Those red, green, and tan hardbacks with the names of Freud, Darwin, Chaucer, Pascal, and about forty other great authors embossed in gold on their spines had always been a part of her life. When Adeline had entered high school her father had insisted on moving the books into her room, "so they would be handy," he said. For years she avoided opening the books just to spite her father. The Marx was the only one she had ever opened. It was the family tradition to keep a bit of cash in Marx in case someone needed it. Her father had been fond of quoting Marx's "to each according to his need," and so anyone in the family would borrow from Marx when they needed cash. But anyone taking some money was required to leave a note and repay it. It was only after her father's death that she started to read the books. They were a part of her life now. She had lugged them from home to the dorm, and then to her first apartment. Wherever she lived, she felt like she was at home when she saw those books lined up on a shelf. And she still kept a stash of spare cash in Marx.

She pushed Marx back into place and sighed. Now, she remembered why she didn't like working at home. *Too damn quiet.* Roger was turning out to be a nice cat, but he only communicated with her when he wanted food. In those cases, he would sit by his empty food bowl and meow loudly until she put something in it. Adeline knew she needed human interaction with live people, but it was still too soon to go back to the office. She didn't want to be pitied and consoled. *By next week they will have almost forgotten about Carol; newspaper people don't care much about the past. News is what's happening now.*

She spent hours searching through sites on the Internet, made a zillion calls, and finished two new pieces. By four o'clock she was done for the day. Done physically and done mentally. And it was time for Jim's weekly call; she knew that would energize her. She and her fiancé emailed each other almost every day, and she liked that. But she looked forward to hearing his voice each week at their prearranged time. She wished she could tell him about Mr. Stafford's secret life. But she knew she couldn't. She was sure Jim would keep the secret, but she had given her word. *Best to just bury that little bit of information in some back corner of my brain and leave it there.*

When the phone rang she was so preoccupied thinking about Mr. Stafford that she forgot that she was holding a handful of dead leaves and dropped them on the floor as she reached for the phone. "Yes, Jim, hello."

"Hi! Hey, are you all right? You sound a bit discombobulated."

"Sorry, yeah I'm fine. I just dropped something. No big deal." Adeline plopped back in a chair and put her feet up on the coffee table. "How is my man?"

"Well, pretty busy. Pretty horny too, hearing your voice. I've been working long hours every day, going to the gym in the evening, and collapsing into bed every night. It's sort of a dull existence, really. If the research wasn't so interesting, I'd fly home to you in a minute."

"I wish you were here."

"Me too! I can't wait to see you tomorrow. I'll come straight there from the airport. We'll have a wonderful weekend. Stock up on junk food and rent some movies. And you're not leaving my arms all weekend."

"That's exactly what I need; lots of hugging."

"Just hugging?"

"No, and lots of good loving too." Adeline's smile faded. "But I'm warning you, I think I've still got some crying to do."

"You cry all you want, ok? I'll bring Kleenex and wear wash-and-wear shirts." She could hear him take a big breath. "Any news about Carol?"

"Not really. This afternoon I've got to try to write out everything Carol said to me during the two weeks before her death. The detective wants me to write it all out so he can read through it for clues."

"I guess that makes sense. But it's not going to be easy on you."

"Yeah, I'm starting to tear up already. You know, believe it or not, I don't feel like talking right now. If you don't mind, babe, I think I'd like to say bye now and get on with writing this stuff about Carol."

Jim's voice mellowed. "Of course, Adeline. Best to do it now; just get it over with. I'll see you tomorrow at the airport. I've sent you a copy of my flight schedule. Don't be late; we only have a couple of days together. I don't want to waste a minute of it. And … I love you."

Adeline told him she loved him too and then hung up the phone. She grabbed a box of Kleenex and sat down to write.

Chapter 29

Palala

Kebeck was lying on the sleeping platform staring at the ceiling when he smelled Yerf approach. He sat up and greeted his friend in the traditional way as Yerf entered the room. Kebeck stretched his four hands out in front with his palms toward the sky. Yerf returned the greeting. Yerf had been away visiting his second son in Ronlyn that day.

"It makes me glad to see your face," Kebeck said. How lives your son and his family?"

"Wisdom and chance have served them well enough, but there was an incident with my son's mate." Yerf sat on the edge of the sleeping platform.

"What is the matter? Tell me."

"Do you remember his egg-hatching mate, Mutect?" asked Yerf.

"I know her. What happened to her?"

"She was gathering fresh lecalm leaves and accidentally put her hand in a poxal nest. We had to take her to a medical facility. She will need to stay in a healing facility for ten to fifteen days."

Kebeck looked off into space and said, "Most unfortunate. And I hear their bite is very painful."

"Yes, but she will recover. Now that you are done with the courtesy of asking about my visit, tell me why I read unhappiness in your face," said Yerf.

"I have two sources of woe; both disturb me." Kebeck put his upper two hands on the sides of his face while he propped his body up with his other two hands.

"I am a friend who is here to listen," said Yerf.

"Problem one: Jarrell wants to cease Earth-Watching. He is campaigning to have me removed from the Earth Analysis Committee and he wants to call a vote to totally outlaw all Earth-Watching activities. I get the impression that even scientists would not be exempt from this prohibition. I do not know why he is now so negative about these matters related to Earth."

Kebeck realized that he was getting loud so he lowered his voice and continued on. "And also, I think that my Adeline is in danger."

"What is happening to Adeline that would lead you to that conclusion?"

"I saw an Earth male enter Adeline's house in her absence and look through her papers. Then I saw that same male meet with her at a coffee shop. I had not seen this male before. I could not hear their conversation because my only method of viewing them was via a computer screen with no microphone. I need to find out more about that strange man."

"Why?"

"He might be the one who killed Carol and he could be planning to kill Adeline." Kebeck found himself waving his upper hands in exasperation at Yerf.

"He could be a friend you are not familiar with, or perhaps a being from her workplace. It could be that he was in her house retrieving something for her."

"No. I am aware of all her friends and her work companions. That male was not in Adeline's house with her permission. He entered surreptitiously, wearing thin, nonporous gloves." Kebeck realized that he now had clasped his upper hands on top of his head in the traditional sign of worry and concern. He put his arms back down by his side and tried to calm down.

"I do not understand the significance of the man's gloves."

"It is the nature of the gloves that matters here. He was wearing special gloves that criminals often wear so that they do not leave evidence that they commit crimes."

"They make many products on Earth, but it surprises me that they make special gloves for criminals that allow them to commit crimes without getting caught." Yerf shook his head.

"Sometimes I think your brain is full of water," Kebeck sighed. "Of course the gloves are not made especially for criminals. They are made for doctors and others who wish to work without getting moisture or germs on their hands."

"So, you have determined that the male who was in her house is a criminal and thus you think Adeline is in danger. Is it possible that the male in her house was a physician?"

"No. It is not possible." Kebeck puffed out his cheeks in frustration. "Is it so complicated? Why would a doctor wish to touch her computer, her papers, or her books while wearing gloves? This male was not wearing gloves to protect his hands from germs. He wore them to prevent a transfer of the unique designs on his fingertips."

"I did not mean to upset you. Calm yourself. Red is not a good color for you. Not a good color for anyone, really. Of course I bow to your knowledge and wisdom in these matters. So from your experience, you think this male could be someone who might harm or kill your Adeline?"

"Yes."

"That is unfortunate, but you cannot do anything about it. The problem you have with Jarrell is nothing compared to the problems you would have if you broke the Earth communication ban and sent a message to your Earth pet. I suggest that you forget about Adeline and concentrate instead on your problem with Jarrell." Yerf stood up and strolled over to the refrigeration unit.

"No, I must find out if this Earth being is a threat to Adeline. Please help me. Who do we know that can find out more about this male?"

Yerf turned toward him with a piece of smoked fish in one hand, a yellow vegetable in another, along with a towel and a green vegetable in his other hands. "If you must do this, I will tell you a name. But then I will have nothing more to do with it. Agreed?" Yerf bit off the top of the yellow vegetable.

"Agreed," said Kebeck.

Yerf chewed quickly then said, "Do you remember Namucal Dulmal? He has adopted a police station in the city where Adeline lives. He accesses the police records as part of his fun. He spends much time following the life of a male who works in what is referred to as the homicide department. Namucal is familiar with how they search for the irrational ones who kill their fellow Earth beings. I am sure he would enjoy helping you solve your mystery."

"I apologize for saying your brain was full of water," Kebeck smiled sheepishly. "Obviously there is also some useful knowledge sloshing around in there."

Chapter 30

Earth

"Mr. Bercic? Excuse me. Mr. Bercic?"

Erwin roused himself out of his stupor to find his City Council assistant, Zoey Fraser, calling his name. His mind had wandered. He was thinking about the Adeline Morgan situation. He sat up in his big leather chair and placed his hands on the desk in front of him. Zoey was wearing a tan suit that complemented her red hair and showed just enough of her nice figure. Erwin was glad that he had hired such a pretty assistant; she sure was easier on the eyes, he thought to himself, than his other assistant Charles.

"Yes, sorry about that. Just doing a little daydreaming. What's up?"

"You asked me to give you a rundown of what we'll be dealing with at the next Council meeting?"

"Yes, yes, of course." He studied Zoey's face as she started to chatter on about zoning changes, parking regulations, and heritage designations. *She's about the same age as Adeline Morgan*, he thought. *And they're both well-educated and single.* "Ah, Zoey..." he interrupted.

Yes?" She looked up from her papers. "I'm sorry, do you want more details on the parking regulations?"

"No, your explanations of the proposed bylaws are great, right on. I appreciate all the work you've put into it. Remind me to give you a raise after I'm elected." He pursed his lips and paused. "I'd just like to ask you some questions that are, well, a little on the personal side. Not that I'm trying to get personal with you."

Zoey's eyebrows had moved up at least an inch.

"You see, I'm trying to understand someone about your age a little better. It would be helpful to me if you, uh, if you just let me ask a few questions and only answer if you're comfortable with it. How about it?"

"Sure. I certainly don't mind, if you think it will be helpful."

"Great! So, let's see. Do you have a female best friend?"

"Yes."

"How often do you two talk?"

"Well," she tilted her head in thought, "almost every day."

"What do you talk about?"

Zoey blushed a little. Her perfect teeth gleamed. "Everything, really."

"Do you talk about work?"

"Oh yeah, we dump our work problems on each other all the time." Zoey hesitated and her face froze. "Should I not be talking about work? Is that what this is about? Am I in trouble? But I've been careful not to ... well, say anything that would make you look bad in the papers."

"No, no. Relax. I have no secrets in this office. I mean, don't go to the press and tell them every word I've ever said, but no problem with you talking things over with a friend." Erwin thought for a second. "And this is common practice among women?"

"So what you really want to know is if women talk about things that happen at work and stuff they are working on? Well, yeah, big time. But if you think we spend all our time talking about men, no way! Most men aren't that interesting. But yes, we do talk about work all the time. Does that answer your question?" She tilted her head again.

"Yes, thank you. That does answer my question. So! Back to work! Tell me more about the new parking regulations that are being proposed."

Chapter 31

Palala

Kebeck was just entering the house by the back door when he noticed Yerf sitting on a slantboard in front of the house computer. "Ah ha! I see that you are Earth-Watching."

"No, not really."

"Well, the computer screen is displaying an Earth Internet site, and you seem to be viewing the screen. Does that not suggest that you are Earth-Watching?"

"Again, no," Yerf shook his head. "I am simply researching Earth building methods. As a builder, I find that observing construction techniques of other cultures adds to my knowledge. I see that the Earth beings are not good builders. Their methods are wasteful. They use wood and metal, materials that rot and deteriorate when exposed to water. They do not build structures that will last. I find it odd that hundreds of years ago some of the Earth beings built thick-walled cement and rock structures that still stand to this day, but now no one appears to erect any structures that will endure more than one or two hundred years. I know their own life span is less than one hundred years, but it is odd that they no longer build for their children and grandchildren. They used to do so."

"So you find nothing of value in their methods?"

Yerf perked up. "There is one thing I have seen that inspires me. They use many windows, these sections of clear glass in the walls. Our houses have few and usually they are up high so that we can let in light. The ability to view more of the outdoors from inside the house would be pleasant. I will even look into the possibility of using more glass in my buildings."

"Yes, that would be nice. Might I have one of these window devices on the wall, next to the computer? It would be pleasant to view the trees in back as I work. But did you not tell me that you build with a set ratio of glass to cement in order to keep the buildings at a desired temperature?"

Yerf looked down at the floor. He was thinking. He looked back up at Kebeck. "Yes, and I think I have found a way to deal with that in new buildings, but I am not sure about how I can insert a window into an existing structure. I will have to work on that."

Yerf stiffened noticeably. "But about your claim that I was Earth-Watching. I did watch a mall for a while, but I have come to the conclusion that Earth-Watching is a voyeuristic amusement that removes one from reality. So I do not wish to watch the activities of the Earth beings. I do not care about their governments or their customs or their personal lives. They are merely creatures with different brains and bodies that live on a planet far away. My only interest in that planet is the structures that they have built and the methods used to build them. I do not disparage you and others who wish to watch the antics of these creatures. We are all free to chose the nature of our work and our amusements. Nonetheless, Earth-Watching is not something I choose to participate in and I view it as a waste of time. Life is long and we should use every one of our hours for either achievement or enjoyment."

"And Earth-Watching is what I enjoy."

"So be it. Enjoy what you will. I need to be on my way now."

Yerf was halfway out the door when Kebeck called to him, "Wait, before you swim back to your lab, please tell me the name and contact number for this Namencal or Numancal person you had mentioned."

Yerf turned to face Kebeck. "You are talking about my friend who watches an Earth police station, are you not? As I have told you, his name is Namucal. You met him some time ago at my office."

"Yes, him. What is his number? I must find out more about the male Earth being who had entered Adeline's house illegally."

"I urge you to turn your energies to your problems here on Palala and forget about Earth. Even if you saw this Earth male hold a knife at Adeline's vital organs, there is nothing you could do about it." Yerf turned to go out the door.

"That is the truth, but you promised me the name of your police-watching friend."

Yerf turned and glared at Kebeck, then walked over to the computer and typed in a contact number. "There. Go ahead and pursue this criminal like a detective in an Earth movie, but remember that you cannot save the girl. You can only watch."

"So ... you have watched Earth movies."

"Yes, yes, but only a few. I once was stuck out at a remote building site for a few days, and it was better than watching the cement dry. I have an appointment. I must go." Yerf flashed his palms at Kebeck and turned to go.

As Yerf finally walked out the door, Kebeck threw himself down onto the sleeping platform. *What will I do if I discover that this male plans to harm my Adeline?*

Chapter 32

Palala

Yerf sniffed the air as he walked down the path that curved through the trees and approached the round little house where Kebeck's daughter Lios lived. Like most houses on the planet this one had the usual shape of a half sphere, but the long covered porch along the side of Lios's house made it somewhat unique. This is where he usually found Lios; she liked to work on a small sleeping platform that was set against the wall. Today he could neither smell nor see her. *I must talk to her*, he thought. He walked around to the other side of the house and sniffed the air again. He then noticed the red rocks that marked a path of contemplation. *That is probably where I will find her.*

In more primitive times, the people of Palala had made paths in the woods that ended at beautiful sites where the trees and flowers blended together with the streams and rocks to form outstanding vistas of beauty. These sites were called prayer sanctuaries. Ancient Palalans would go to these spots in the woods and worship the water, the soil, and the plants. Today, few Palalans continued to worship such things, but some people still liked to go to such places to relax and think. They are now referred to as paths of contemplation.

I am reluctant to disturb her, but it is important that we talk. He walked down the path marked by the red rocks very slowly so that she might smell him before he got to her.

"Who approaches?" Lios called out.

"It is Yerf," he said as he rounded a bend in the trees and saw her. He extended all four hands, palms up, as a greeting and she replied in a like manner. "I ask pardon for disturbing you here, but it is urgent that we talk." Yerf paused for a moment to take in the scene in front of him. He had never been down this path before and the loveliness of the place was breathtaking.

Lios got up off of the mossy ground. "I prefer not to talk here. This is a place for silence. Come. We will talk at my house."

Yerf was a little reluctant to leave. The area was so perfect, so relaxing. A little stream bubbled over the rocks beside red and yellow flowers and tall, dark green grasses. *I must come here again.* He then followed Lios back up the path to her house.

As they entered the house, Lios motioned toward the sleeping platform that stood in the center of the room. They both reclined on the platform. "What is so urgent?" she asked.

"I have concerns about your father."

"Is he ill?" A look of distress came across her face.

"No, no. His health is good. What disquiets me is his Earth-Watching. He is ...."

"But that is his job," Lios interrupted while letting out a sigh of relief.

"Yes it is, but he is too involved and attached to his pet Earth being, the one named Adeline."

"Yes, I am aware of his affection for her. But what harm can it do? Many people watch the life of a single Earth being and feel much devotion for them. You call them pets?"

"Yes, they are just pets; they are just amusements. But I am concerned that his devotion to his pet may lead him to break the rule of non-communication and ruin both his career and his life," said Yerf.

Lios quickly sat up. "I cannot imagine my father breaking the rule of non-communication. What makes you think that he would do so?"

"He has much anxiety about the physical safety of the Earth being Adeline, and his anxiety may be justified. Her friend was murdered and it appears that an unknown male has illegally entered her home. He fears that she too might be killed and he has expressed extreme frustration that he is not able to prevent it."

"I understand having affection for a real pet," Lios answered. "I had a promgo for many years. It was comforting to have his fuzzy body snuggle up to me on the sleeping platform. He made happy sounds when I came in the door. But surely my father has learned to distance himself from these barbarous and somewhat silly and stupid beings that he studies. I am sure he has seen many of them die. They have short life spans and they even seem to enjoy violence."

"Yes, I am sure that he has watched them die from war, starvation, murder, and old age. But though they do not possess our intelligence or value for life, even I find sorrow in their dying. And because your father has watched this particular pet from the time of her birth, he has developed a strong fondness for her and it has affected his reasoning. I therefore have come to ask you to speak with him."

Lios put her upper two hands on the sides of her head and clapped her lower hands together in frustration. "Very well. I will go and speak with him. But never did I think that I, the daughter, would be required to counsel the father."

Chapter 33

Palala

The sun was starting to go down and the photocell power system had already activated the lights in Kebeck's house. He was leaning back on the slantboard in front of his computer. "I am grateful that you are willing to help me with this problem," Kebeck said to the face on the screen. He had been relieved that Namucal Dulmal was quite excited about the project Kebeck proposed to him. He said he would be delighted to help Kebeck identify and investigate the male Earth being who had been trespassing in and around Adeline's house. Namucal was a chemist by profession but his hobby and passion was Earth crime. He had selected a police station in Toronto for his case studies and he watched it on a daily basis. "At first I was watching a police station in the large urban area known as New York City," Namucal told Kebeck, "but it was overwhelming. My first problem was merely trying to understand the police personnel; they talked quickly and used many terms unknown to me. For instance, 'buzz' means to display a badge, and 'on the box' refers to the administration of a lie detector test. These and other words are not defined in any Earth dictionary. Also, there was so much happening at any given time; it was difficult to follow a specific case. So, I switched to a police station in Toronto, in the northern area known as Canada. There are fewer murder cases in this district, and much effort and publicity is devoted to each one."

"That is all very interesting. For now, I am sending you a photo of the man I am inquiring about," said Kebeck as his hands clicked over the keyboard.

"I will start on this as soon as we end our present communication. I can easily look through the Earth police computers. I must say this is rather enjoyable; it seems to me much like an Earth police TV show."

A light flashed on the corner of Kebeck's computer screen. "Again, I thank you," he interrupted. "Now I must receive a communication. Clear water," he added quickly before switching to a screen showing Adeline's kitchen. The very same Earth male he had just spoken about was entering Adeline's house. And once more he was wearing the thin gloves that indicated he was doing something illegal.

"NO!" Kebeck yelled aloud as his upper hands shot up in exasperation. "What is that Earth being doing in Adeline's house again?" He watched as the man crossed in front of the little TV in Adeline's kitchen and walked over to her electric stove. He was carrying a rectangular container similar to the ones in which Adeline placed her shoes. He put it on the floor by the stove. Kebeck watched intensely as the Earth male pulled the stove away from the wall. The man then removed some tools from his pocket, bent down on his knees, and placed the tools on the floor. He opened the rectangular container and took out a gray-colored animal that was twice the size of the Earth man's hand. He held it by the tail; it was limp, as if dead. He placed the animal by the stove and then stood up and crossed the kitchen to the door that led to the basement.

"Oh, no," Kebeck said softly as the male disappeared down the stairs. Kebeck knew that he wouldn't be able to see or hear the male in the basement. He remembered hearing Adeline say that it was just an empty storage space. There did not seem to be any TVs or phones or computers in that part of the house. Suddenly, Kebeck's computer screen went blank. He ran his hands across the keyboard trying to reconnect with any of the transmission devices in Adeline's house. Nothing worked. *This only happens when the electricity in her house is cut off by some power failure. He has turned off the power source.* Kebeck sat with his hands poised over the keyboard, trying to think of some other way to view the inside of Adeline's house.

What kind of animal was that? he wondered. With a few clicks of his keyboard he identified the animal as a rat; an Earth dictionary indicated that it was a destructive and injurious rodent of worldwide distribution, larger and more aggressive than the Earth creature known as a mouse.

What is happening? Kebeck impatiently accessed TVs and computers in neighboring homes, trying to get a view out their windows of Adeline's house. Nothing. He even linked up with the satellites circling the Earth, but that only showed him the house's exterior. He tried connecting into the local traffic cameras, but again to no avail.

Without warning, the computer reconnected to Adeline's house. The screen displayed an empty kitchen with the stove replaced to its original position against the wall. The Earth male came through the basement door, paused in the middle of the kitchen, and looked at the time-telling device on his arm. As Kebeck watched, the man went through the house and adjusted all of Adeline's own electric time-telling devices. Then, he returned to the kitchen. Standing five hands from the front of stove, the man took a small metal tool from his pocket and tossed it at the stove. Kebeck could see sparks fly as the object bounced off the stove. The Earth male smiled, picked up the little tool, and put it back in his pocket. He then turned and went out the back door.

Chapter 34

Earth

Adeline looked around at the fifty or so people standing around the airport arrival area. She heard Chinese, Italian, and Greek being spoken by the families waiting for their loved ones to arrive. The woman beside her was wearing a lovely light blue sari, while the man standing on her other side had on a black suit and a large black hat under which braids of hair curled down by the man's ears. Anyone at the Toronto airport could instantly see that this was truly a multicultural city. She liked that about Toronto. It made her feel like she wasn't just a citizen of Canada; she was a citizen of the world. *I wish more people could think of themselves not just as Americans or Palestinians or Italians or what have you, but as living beings on this planet of ours.* As she looked back toward the gate, Jim rounded the corner and stopped. She was so happy to see him that she found herself bouncing from side to side on her feet. She waved as he scanned the room. Their eyes met and they both smiled.

They found it difficult to hug, talk, kiss, and drag Jim's suitcase all at the same time, but they still managed to get to Adeline's car in the airport parking lot. They thought it best that she drive.

Jim had gotten used to driving on the left side of the road in England and the airport exit wasn't the best place to switch back to right-lane thinking. As they made their way through the maze of highways surrounding the airport, Adeline and Jim discussed wedding plans, his research, traffic, everything and anything except Carol's death. But as soon as they stepped into Adeline's house, she was in his arms crying.

"I needed that," Adeline sighed as she backed out of his arms and took out another tissue to wipe her eyes and cheeks. "Thank you." She ran her hand through his thick brown hair before sitting down on the couch. *I am so lucky,* she thought to herself.

"Hey, I bought a new outfit ... just for you." She smiled mischievously, trying to change the subject.

"So, let's see it." Jim raised his eyebrows and smiled back.

"Why don't you take a quick shower while I go put it on?" Adeline pulled him up and gently pushed him toward the bathroom.

Chapter 35

Palala

Yerf let out a deep breath as he sat down on the slantboard beside Kebeck. "That was fun. There is no better game than Jamjam. I defeated that fellow by six points. Are you ready to play or are you going to just sit here and stare out the window at the river?"

Kebeck turned in his seat to look at Yerf and the room behind him. This was his favorite game room. It was located on a hill overlooking the town and the river; the builders had put big windows across one side of the building to take advantage of the view. It had every indoor game that a person could want and it was just a short swim from his house. He was at home here and though he should have felt relaxed, he was worried about Adeline. The image of that male Earth being sneaking around inside Adeline's house kept playing in his mind. "Yes, yes, let us begin."

Kebeck walked over to a rectangular table that measured about six hands by twelve hands and picked up the four paddles laying on the edge of the table. Yerf collected his own paddles and when they were both in position at opposite ends of the table, Kebeck pushed the button to activate the air walls that kept the ball in the playing field above the table. The electronic score boards beside the hand-sized goal holes on the ceiling changed quickly as both Kebeck and Yerf racked up points. Several people stopped their games to watch the two friends play. Yerf was skilled at bouncing the ball off the walls at impossible angles, but Kebeck's straight shots went into the goal more often. Kebeck was in the lead as the time clock winded down but Yerf bested him with a last shot off of two air walls to win the game.

"Ha! See, I am the better player." Yerf dropped his paddles on the table and rushed over to hug Kebeck.

Kebeck reluctantly hugged Yerf. "You are the better player today. But that is only because my mind is heavy and distracted by serious thoughts. Remember that last week I won, and I will win again next week. Yes, enjoy this win for it is a rare occasion."

"It is indeed because of its rarity that I am celebrating. Come, you must be thirsty." Yerf pulled Kebeck in the direction of the back wall. Hanging from the ceiling were a series of finger-sized clear tubes. Yerf grabbed one of the tubes, detached the plastic clip from its end, and let the water flow into his mouth. Kebeck did the same. ThenYerf walked over to a shelf beside the tubes and took two pieces of yellow fruit out of a large bowl. He tossed one to Kebeck and started to munch on the other. Yerf glanced toward the windows. "It grows late and I told someone ... the tall fellow who lives beside the lab, and whose name escapes me ... that I would look over his building site today. I must go." Yerf picked up his satchel, snatched another piece of fruit, and flashed two palms at Kebeck as he rushed out the door.

Kebeck wandered back over to the slantboards by the window and was about to sit down when he heard shouting from the other side of the room where several people were gathered around a computer screen. Kebeck approached the group and peered over someone's shoulder to see what had got their attention. They were watching an Earth game called football that was being broadcasted on Earth TV. Chabar, a short light-gray fellow, was explaining the game. "It is a well-regulated little war in which the participants fight without weapons. They struggle to possess that awkwardly shaped ball and deposit it in their opponents' end of the rectangular playing field. They wear body armor and there are specific rules on where and how they are allowed to hit one another. Many of the players display admirable throwing and catching skills while running."

"Are any of the participants killed in these battles?" asked someone in the crowd.

"No, there are injuries, but they are not allowed to kill each other."

Kebeck watched. "There appears to be a third team on the edges of the field who wear striped black-and-white clothing and do not participate in the fighting. What is their purpose?"

"They are the administrators," replied Chabar.

"And how is dancing involved in this war? I see drums and horns, and Earth females moving about as if they are dancing," Kebeck asked.

"The music and dancing females are present at all of the games, but I have yet to determine how they relate to the fighting on the field," Chabar admitted.

"Why do they start each section of the game by bending over and throwing the ball backward between their legs?" someone asked?

"I do not know," answered Chabar. "It would seem more logical to stand up and look in the direction where one was throwing, would it not?"

"It most definitely is not a logical game," Kebeck mumbled to himself as he meandered back to the slantboards. He settled onto one and picked up the satchel he had left on a small shelf by the windows. With the touch of a button, his communicator connected to his home computer, allowing him to watch Adeline.

She was wearing a thin black dress that Kebeck had never seen before, and Jim was nude lying alongside her on Adeline's bed. The lights were dim and soft instrumental music played in the background. Kebeck watched as Adeline wrapped a leg around Jim and ran her hands up and down his bare back and buttocks.

Jim reached down and untangled her leg and gently pushed her away from him. He opened the top of her dress and moved his face down to her breasts. She smiled and moaned as he licked one of her nipples.

It pleased Kebeck to watch Adeline perform the sex act with Jim. It seemed to make her happy and she appeared to enjoy it very much. He liked to see her experience such pleasure. He had viewed Earth beings' sexual habits a number of times and thought he understood the ritual, though at times its underlying violence still perplexed him. He felt somewhat uncomfortable when they yelled and jerked their bodies quickly during their sex activity.

On Palala, sexual stimulation simply constituted a quiet rubbing together of the upper bodies that produced a pleasant sensation which relaxed the female and induced her to drop her eggs. Though it also provided a pleasant sensation for the male, there was no climactic moment for either partner. There was no shudder or collapse at the end of the sexual activity as seemed to be the norm with the Earth beings. It was merely an enjoyable, peaceful interaction performed between any two people who intended to raise a child.

Kebeck watched, feeling strangely envious of the animated excitement that seemed to be a part of this Earth sex. It appeared to be as much fun as a game of Jamjam. But Kebeck knew also from his Earth-Watching activities that the Earth beings' desire for this spirited form of sex often resulted in much mayhem, sometimes even murder. He knew too that most Earth beings thought that sex was something that should be experienced privately, so out of consideration for Adeline he turned off the connection and headed for home. He suspected they would have completed their activity by the time he got home, at which point he would again access Adeline's home.

Chapter 36

Earth

Jim was wrapped in a sarong, standing in the doorway to Adeline's bedroom. "No, there will be no cooking this weekend, my dear."

Adeline stood up and slipped into a red silk robe. "Why not? Are you saying I'm not a good cook?"

"No, I would never say that. You're a great cook. But then again, even if you were a bad cook, I'd never be stupid enough to say it."

"So how do I know that you're not lying when you say I'm a great cook?"

"Because you are an exceptional cook, and you know it."

"Right then, so I'm cooking tonight. Besides, ordering out is a waste of money."

As she came up to him he kissed her forehead. "But that's why I make the big bucks, Adeline," he smiled, "so we could spend it. Plus, I want you to save all your energy for the bedroom."

"There is a perfectly good kitchen in there that I hardly ever use when you're not here. And I intend to cook supper for you tonight, mister." Adeline brushed past him, gathering her clothes off of the living room floor on her way to the kitchen.

"Knowing you, I'll bet there's nothing in the fridge to cook."

Jim zipped through the living room and headed toward the kitchen. Adeline reached for him as he went by but he ducked away from her and rushed to the refrigerator. He grabbed the handle and in his excitement pulled open the fridge door a little too hard; it swung open and banged against the stove. An explosion that sounded like gunfire made them both jump back as arcs of light crackled and flashed at the point where the fridge door touched the stove!

"What the hell's going on!?!" Jim yelled as he stepped in front of Adeline, shielding her as the appliances continued to spark.

Chapter 37

Palala

Kebeck almost fell off his slantboard. The loud noise and flying sparks had startled him and had turned his neck a bright red. *What was that? The intruder who had tampered with Adeline's stove must have set a trap, intending to kill her. If Jim had not been there to save her...!* Kebeck placed his upper hands on the sides of his head in an attempt to calm himself down. He got up and walked around as he watched Jim take Adeline in his arms and hug her tightly. *She is safe for now.* He quickly ran his fingers over the keyboard, desperately hoping to make contact with Namucal Dulmal to find out if he had uncovered any information on the Earth man. He continued to walk about, waiting for a reply.

Namucal's face appeared in the center of Kebeck's screen. Kebeck paused in his pacing. "Greetings Kebeck, I was just thinking about you and the man you have inquired about."

"Do you know his identity?"

"Yes, that was easy. His name is Erwin Bercic. He is a politician on the City Council of the city of Toronto. He campaigns to be Mayor of that city. He is divorced and lives alone. He has one child; the child lives in another town so that he may attend a particular school. This Bercic is the proprietor of several stores that sell food and beverages. Your pet Earth being Adeline wrote a newspaper article about him. I am sending a copy of the writing to you now.

"Is he not a criminal?" Kebeck asked.

"Apparently not. I find no record of anyone bearing his face or his name having been accused or convicted of doing anything illegal."

"But he tried to kill Adeline!"

"What? How do you know this?" asked Namucal.

"I watched him rig an appliance in Adeline's house so that it would kill any Earth being who touched it." Kebeck again started to pace in front of his computer as he talked.

"How did it happen that she did not die?"

"It was merely by chance that the problem was discovered before she or her mate touched the appliance. Were it not for this mate, whom she calls her fiancé, she would certainly be dead."

Namucal looked puzzled. "What is a fiancé, please?"

"It is the name given to an Earth being that is intending to marry another. This one is a male, named Jim."

"So the Jim fiancé saved her life?"

"Yes, essentially he did."

"I would like to view this event. Would you send me that section of your Earth-Watching record?"

"Yes, I will send it so you may witness what I saw." Kebeck stopped the pacing and moved closer to the screen. "Can you find out more about the Erwin Bercic being?"

"But why? You can do nothing about any such happenings on Earth."

"Yes, I know." Kebeck paused and glanced down at the floor for a moment before looking back at the screen. "But remember, we search for knowledge because understanding allows us to feel complete."

"That is a truth," replied Namucal. "I shall become a detective like those in the Earth TV shows, and attempt to find out why the Erwin being wants to kill your pet Adeline."

"I thank you. I must now end our communication. I need to attend to a meeting of my work committee." Kebeck touched the keyboard and leaned back on his slantboard, sighing.

He looked up at the clock. It was almost time for the computer meeting that he had been dreading for days. *I must compose myself before they see me. I am sure my neck is red.*

Chapter 38

Earth

After Jim had flipped the circuit breaker to shut off the electricity in Adeline's house, he examined both appliances. They found a dead rat behind the stove and it looked like the stove's power cable had been gnawed through. The cable's rubber covering was scratched off, exposing the copper that was now touching the metal panel on the back of the stove. At Adeline's insistence, Jim put the rat in a plastic bag and put it in the trash can that was sitting by the curb, ready for the morning pick-up.

Still shaken up, they dressed by candlelight, stopping occasionally to hug and say how fortunate they were to still be alive. Then they went out to dinner. The restaurant was an Italian place, with panoramic scenes of Venice painted on the walls. Plastic grapes hung above their heads. But, the food was good.

"What do you think the odds are of getting an electrician on a Saturday?" asked Adeline.

"Not so good."

"I've got the number of the fellow who had helped put up the light fixtures. He was friendly enough; he might do it."

"I'll call around in the morning," Jim said as he placed his hand over Adeline's. "We'll be warm enough in bed tonight, but we definitely have to get someone in before we can turn the electricity back on. I'm still amazed at the size of that rat. How did he get in the house? And why would he be so stupid as to gnaw on a live wire?"

Adeline shuffled the pasta around on her plate; she had eaten very little of it. "Maybe some cooking grease sprayed onto it or maybe some food or an old piece of cheese found its way back there. I don't know. I'm just glad I didn't run into that monster when he was alive. I thought having a cat was supposed to prevent mice."

"That was no mouse. That was a big city rat. Roger's no match for him. Tomorrow, I'm going to the hardware store for some rat poison and some caulking and traps."

Adeline said nothing and continued to play with her food.

Jim reached across the table and touched her hand again. "What's wrong, babe? Hey! We're alive! We should be happy about that. So we've got no electricity; so what! That means we'll just have to make love by candlelight. It'll be romantic."

"I've just had so much happening lately. Carol's dead, then her stuff is taken, then the break-in thing, and now this."

Jim let go of her hand. A worried look crossed his face. "What do you mean? What break-in thing?"

"Uh, it's nothing, really. I mean, I couldn't decide if it was anything. So … I, uh, didn't mention it to you."

"So tell me about it now. Obviously it's bothering you." Jim took her hand. "Hey, remember me? I'm the guy who loves you! What break-in are you talking about?"

Adeline told him about the day she had come home to find the front window open and how she had panicked and ran out the door, afraid that there might have been someone in the house. Then she told him about rescuing Roger as he tried to jump out the window and showed him the scratches she still had on her arm.

"Did you call the police?"

"Yes, they came and searched through the whole place. There were no signs of forced entry. Nothing was taken. Everything was where it should be. I had all the neighbors standing on the sidewalk with me. I felt like a fool."

Jim leaned over and kissed her hand as he continued to hold it. "Yeah, but you're my fool. I'm glad that you ran out the door and called the police. With that window open, there could have been someone in the house. It was the right thing to do. I just wish you had told me about it. Are there any more secrets you're keeping from me?"

"No, nothing. That's about it, I'm afraid." Adeline tilted her head and a sly smile lit up her face. "What about you? Anything I should know?" Adeline was joking, so she was quite surprised to see Jim's face suddenly become more serious.

"Well, this seems like an awkward time to let you know," he said, "but I've been meaning to tell you since I got back …."

"What?" Adeline unintentionally pulled her hand back. *Nooo! I knew he was too good to be true!*

"Hey! No, no! It's not that bad. It's just a family issue that you need to know about."

"I'm listening."

"Well, you know when my Mom came to visit, how I said my father couldn't come because he was tied up with business?"

"Yeah?"

"Well …, damn, this is embarrassing. Dad's in jail."

"Jail? What did he do?" Adeline's eyebrows shot up in surprise. *Oh great! What kind of family am I marrying into here?*

"Nothing too bad. Well, relatively speaking. He stole money from the company he worked for. I mean, it was an awful thing to do, but it's not like he really hurt anybody or anything."

Adeline leaned back in her chair. *Well, that's bit of a relief. A thief I can handle, I guess.* "Please, Jim, tell me everything."

"All right, well, this is the way Dad explained it to me. You see, my father only had a high school education, so the best job he could get was with the local newspaper, in the advertising department. He basically started at the bottom and worked his way up until one day he was in charge of the paper's classified ads. You know, taking the orders and collecting the money. He said that one day he was so busy that he had stuck a two hundred dollar payment in his pocket and forgot to put it in the cash register. When he got home that night and discovered the cash, he realized that no one would miss it or even know it was gone. So he kept it. He said he felt underpaid and was tired of living on the edge of bankruptcy, so he started skimming a little more on a regular basis. Some merchants liked to pay cash for their ads, so it was easy to just pocket the money and place their ads. Before he started this scheme, we had lived on a very limited income. Mom worked only part-time at a dress store, and Dad said that between their two salaries they just managed to pay the monthly household bills. He told me that the added income had paid for our two European vacations, our trip to Disney, and it had even put me and my brother through university. Dad said he started taking the money when my older brother Ted was entering junior high school. He said he had come to realize that working at the paper would never be enough to take any trips or to put us through school, and he thought that it was his duty to show us the world and give us an education. He said that earlier in his life, when we were still in elementary school, he had even considered robbing a bank. Luckily, he talked to a friend who worked at a bank and found out that most bank robbers only get a few thousand dollars, ten thousand at most. He said his weekly, uh, as he called it, 'side income' at the paper varied according to how many people paid in cash each week, but it definitely made a difference in our lives. Dad got away with it until he retired about two years ago. As soon as the new person took over his position, things started to look a little fishy. After a team of auditors went through the books, they estimated that he took over a million dollars. The trial was in all the papers. They gave him five years, but at least he's in a minimum security prison, one of those white-collar jails. And if he's lucky, he could be out in three. Mom moved out of town when they took him off to jail. Everybody knew us in Kitchener; it would have been too difficult to stay there. Mom's in an apartment here in Toronto now. She loves Toronto; nobody knows her and there's a lot to do. I send her some money. The courts had some difficulty differentiating between earned money and stolen money, so she was left with little to live on." Jim sighed and slumped back in his chair, letting his hands fall limp on the table.

Adeline reached for his right hand, took it to her lips, and kissed it. "I'm sorry that you had to go through that. Look, you know you're not responsible for what your father's done. But when were you going to tell me about this?"

"I was all set to tell you before my trip to London ... and then I put it off and then, ... well, Carol died. I wanted to tell you in person, Adeline, and as soon as I could. But the time never seemed right. I hope it doesn't change anything?"

"No, I love you. Your father ... well ... he must have some good points or you wouldn't have turned out this nice. So he wanted a good life for his family and broke a few rules to get ahead. I understand what he did. I can't excuse it, but I can understand it. When do I get to meet him?"

Jim let out a long sigh of relief. "I knew you'd understand." He looked up and smiled. "Wow. I feel so much better having that out in the open. He's going to love you, too. He was a great father in spite of all that and he's a really nice person. We can set up a visit next time I get back." Jim reached out and took both her hands. "I love you, Adeline. And to think I could have lost you tonight. If you had grabbed one of your pots and put it on that stove ...." His voice trailed off . "You need someone to take care of you. Looks like I'm going to have to marry you just to keep you out of trouble."

Chapter 39

Palala

Kebeck settled back on his slantboard and sighed. He glanced at the timepiece on the wall. It was almost time for the meeting. *Better early than late.* His fingers scurried across the keyboard. Three squares appeared on the screen, each one showing the face of one of his three co-workers. Each of these colleagues had his own specialty. Leto, who had been at Lios's majority ceremony, studied Earth religions. Samot, probably the smartest and certainly the oldest member of the group, studied politics and how the Earth governments functioned. Laniff's research focused on crime and violence.

Two more squares popped up on screen, displaying the faces of Jarrell and Agara. Jarrell's role was to examine Earth news media and to determine what was happening on the planet. In doing so he had to consider how the Earth beings tended to distort reality and to frequently lie, or what the Earth beings themselves referred to as "spinning the truth." He was fascinated by the untruths he discovered. Agara, on the other hand, studied Earth TV and movies; much more fun, he felt, than those topics examined by his colleagues. And Kebeck, in turn, continued to be in charge of researching the ecology of Earth and observing how Earth beings interacted with their planet.

Samot, as committee leader, started the meeting. "Greetings to all. It is good to see your faces. As you know, we are having this special meeting at the request of Jarrell.

He has said that his concerns cannot wait until the next scheduled meeting." Samot paused and scratched his head, a gesture he was known to do when he was irritated.

"Jarrell, please tell us what disquiets you."

The square displaying Jarrell's face moved to the center of the screen and increased in size, clearly showing the dusky red hue of Jarrell's neck. "I call on you all to save our society from destruction," Jarrell enunciated with icy precision.

Puzzled and questioning looks appeared on the faces of the others on the screen.

Jarrell continued: "We must stop the Earth-Watching before it is too late. We would not expose the people of our planet to polluted water, yet we allow them to watch the mind-pollution of all the Earth violence, and to watch beings that are so primitive that they accept as truth the fantasy of religion. Our people are being harmed by viewing these ridiculous, lesser beings." He went on, raising his voice: "You can see the results of this contamination everywhere. Some people have organized into groups that they refer to as churches, as they are called on Earth. These deluded individuals actually pray to the sky, as if there was something up there powerful enough to change even the way Palala spins on its very axis! Others are wearing clothes when clothing is not necessary, and some people have selected specific times for consuming food. And worst of all, there have been incidents of physical anger and destruction. We simply cannot let Earth-Watching continue. These Earth-like behaviors are unacceptable. It is getting worse every day, and it must all stop immediately."

"You see no worthwhile aspects to Earth-Watching whatsoever?" asked Samot.

"None," replied Jarrell.

"But let us not forget that it is fun," suggested Agara.

Jarrell scowled. "Your notion of so-called fun is changing our society, and we must not ...."

Samot interrupted his colleague. "Society is always in flux. It is not a stagnant thing that you can keep in a container. I realize that there are many negative things about Earth that ...."

Laniff interjected: "I must agree here with Jarrell and say that I also have concerns about the viewing of their brutality and savagery. A number of our people watch wars, beatings, and murders. Some even seem to enjoy watching these things. I even have heard of a group of people, an organized club, who gather together to view such acts of Earth violence."

A terrible worry began to gnaw inside Kebeck. He remained silent, listening. This talk of violence brought back thoughts of the Erwin Bercic being who had apparently tried to kill Adeline. *The Earth beings may at times kill each other in a random manner, but surely this particular man must have some reason for trying to take Adeline's life.*

Agara piped in: "There is even a sport in which the goal is to physically hit a fellow Earth being until the opponent falls down. And they watch this on their televisions."

Laniff spoke up again. "They are cruel and misguided beings. An Earth being who has ample credits will walk directly past another who has insufficient credits to even buy food, and the well-off being will instead purchase an unnecessary piece of clothing or house decoration. They do not see each other as related bodies and minds that share the water of the planet. Each seems to think that his or her own skin is the border that separates them from all else. They do not flow together, but instead operate separately, almost as mindless plants. Their thinking is not for the benefit of all beings on the planet but only for themselves, or for perhaps a few friends and kin. In the more developed areas, they each have a device referred to as a car, a truly air-polluting method of transportation that many of them treat like a second skin. These machines put even more distance between them and their planet.

It is such insensitivity that is destroying their planet. And you, Kebeck, as our ecology expert, should certainly be able to see that. I do not want our people to learn their ways."

Kebeck blurted out, "Yes, of course I …."

Samot interrupted Kebeck: "I agree that the Earth societies have many negative aspects. But they also have their good points. For instance, we have been introduced to new theories in art. Because they can easily deceive, their drama and literature is unlike anything we could write and so it makes us think in different ways. I suggest also that seeing the ways they abuse their ecosystem simply reinforces our policy of caring for our own planet. Similarly, even viewing their violence may be beneficial to us all; we see how awful and foolish it is in relation to logic and negotiation. I see no reason why…."

Jarrell shot back: "You just want to carry on … as is, and let our world deteriorate into a vile imitation of the current mess on Earth."

Leto, who had been silent through all the discussion, finally asked, "Jarrell, how do you suggest that we stop Earth-Watching? The initial proposal for our project called for a vote at the end of the forty-year study. It was agreed that we would examine all aspects of this new form of amusement until the end of the study period, at which point our reports would be on view for another thirty-two days before the votes were cast. That is how the proposal was worded, a proposal that we all voted on. How can we then …."

Jarrell's neck reddened: "We simply cannot allow this to go on for another ten years. We must recommend to the public that all viewing be stopped immediately! We must put forth a formal proposal for a vote next eight-day."

"You think that so much damage will be done in a mere ten years?" asked Laniff.

"Yes, I do. Also, our people are growing attached to the Earth beings. In ten years it could be difficult to get a majority of Palalans to oppose Earth-Watching," Jarrell declared.

Samot was scratching his head again. "I do not agree with this, but the charter for this committee mandates that we may ask for a vote if three members of a five-person committee or four of a six-person committee request us to do so. I tell you now, however, that I will not be one of the four."

"Laniff and I make two," Jarrell stated loudly. "Who else will stand with us?"

Leto huffed, "You expect us to make a decision like this so soon? I will think on it."

"Yes," Agara said, nodding his head. "I will also think on it."

Kebeck, who had stayed almost mute as the words had flown back and forth, finally opened his mouth. "I do not need time to think. I agree that Earth-Watching has had some bad influences on us, but we gain much more than we lose by keeping open this window to another world."

"Kebeck, your vote does not surprise me" said Jarrell. "But Leto, do you not see what that religion nonsense is doing to our people."

"I will think on it," Leto said in a firm voice.

"Then we seem to be done here," said Samot. "I am anxious to watch a British Parliament meeting that is scheduled for this time. Leto, Agara, please contact me when you finish thinking and come to a decision. I wish you all clear water."

The screen went blank. Kebeck leaned his head back on his slantboard. He was glad that the meeting was over. He got up off the slantboard and took a piece of rebo fruit from the bowl on the shelf. *Conflict gives me an appetite.* He walked around the room munching on the rebo and reflecting on what had been said.

Chapter 40

Earth

Erwin threw the newspaper down on the floor on top of the stack already laying there. It was ten o'clock on Monday morning. He had checked both the Sunday and that morning's papers and there was no mention of a dead Adeline Morgan. *Maybe her body hasn't been discovered yet? That's possible; she lives alone. But her boyfriend was going to be with her this weekend. Maybe they're both lying dead in the kitchen. That would be all right; she might have told him something.*

Erwin heard a tap on his door. "Come in, Zoey." His assistant swept into the room. He could see the look of confusion on her flawlessly made-up face. His normally pristine oak- and leather-trimmed office was a bit cluttered this morning. Her eyes glanced down at the pile of papers on the floor.

"Is something wrong?" she asked as she gracefully bent down and started gathering the newspapers.

"No, no, nothing wrong. I'm just, uh … not a hundred percent today. Nothing to be concerned about. Just leave those papers; they're trash. Anyway, did you want to see me about something?"

"I just wanted to remind you that we should leave soon for that press conference at the new school over on Collins. We can't be late for that," she smiled.

Erwin looked at the papers on the floor. "Yes, of course. Just give me a minute to make a quick phone call." He waved her toward the door. "Go on. I'll be down in two shakes."

"Damn, damn, damn," Erwin muttered under his breath as he flipped through his daytimer looking for a number. "Is she or isn't she?" He picked up the phone and punched in the numbers.

"Hi, this is Erwin Bercic. I'm looking for Adeline Morgan. Is she in? No, I'll just wait on the line."

The high-pitched young voice at the front desk of the Toronto Globe informed him that Ms. Morgan had called earlier and said that she would not be in til noon. "I think she's taking her fiancé to the airport." He heard a gasp. "Oh, shoot! I did it again! Sorry, I'm not supposed to tell personal stuff. Please forget I said that. Would you like her cell phone number, or can I take a message?"

"No, thank you, no; I'll try again later." Erwin slowly put the phone down and then pounded his fist onto the desk. *Damn, damn, damn!*

Chapter 41

Palala

As Kebeck walked across the white ceramic floor inside his house his foot touched an orange vegetable leaf. *Who dropped this?* he wondered. He picked it up and threw it out the door into the bushes. *This place is a mess. I know Yerf is a little sloppy at times, but we have really let this place go.* He started toward the back door, intending to get the hose and rinse the floor when his nose detected a smell. *A female approaches.* He sniffed the air. *It is Lios.* He glanced around the house. *I do not want her to see it like this.* He straightened the covers on the sleeping platform, picked up a few bits of paper and other litter from the floor, and used one of the towels hanging by the back door to wipe down a shelf. He was standing by his front door smiling when his daughter reached the front step.

"Father, I greet you." Lios extended all her hands, palms up, and Kebeck touched his four palms to hers.

"I am both surprised and happy to see you," said Kebeck. "I enjoyed your majority ceremony; it went well." He noticed that she had not returned his smile. "Is there a problem that brings you here? I welcome your presence, but it is unusual for you to visit without calling first."

Lios stepped back from her father. "I have concerns that I have come to discuss with you."

"Then come in and be comfortable," said Kebeck as he motioned her toward the sleeping platform.

They moved onto the platform and reclined on their sides, propping themselves up on an arm to face each other. Lios sighed. "Father, I have come for a serious talk."

"What troubles you so? I have not seen you so distressed since the time you lost your mother's ancestral water cup."

Lios nudged her father. "I was seven. I thought we had agreed to forget that incident."

"Your mother may have, but I will always remember it as the first time my little girl found herself in real trouble."

"Father, I am here today to try to keep you out of serious trouble," Lios snapped.

"What? What do you mean?"

"Yerf came by and told me he is concerned that you might break the Earth non-communication rule. I do not want you to become like your friend Karna. I remember you telling me that one of the stipulations of your work contract was that you not communicate with the beings you study. If you break the contract, you will be shunned, like Karna. That would be terrible!"

"But I ... but ..." he sputtered.

She interrupted him: "I understand that you have much affection for your Earth pet, but you cannot let that lead you to do something that can ruin your career here in the real world."

"Their world is real too."

"But they are insignificant, like the small insects that eat the crumbs on our floors. Maybe at some point in the future, if they do not kill themselves first, maybe then they will evolve into thinking, caring people, but until ...."

Lios paused as Kebeck sat up and glared at her; his neck reddened.

"Father," she said gently, "can you not step back from them and observe them as you would any other lab experiment?"

Scenes of Adeline at different stages in her life played through Kebeck's mind as Lios continued to talk. There she was at six years old, playing with dolls; at age fourteen, studying at her desk; and there was seventeen-year-old Adeline, talking on the phone with her friend Carol, the two of them laughing, crying. He realized that in many ways Adeline was as real to him as his own daughter, and maybe just as important. He dared not say that to Lios and chose his words carefully: "No, they are more than mere lab specimens to me, and to many of our people as well."

Lios's face took on an expression he recognized from her childhood. She was thinking.

"But father, before you started this Earth study you were part of a committee doing a twenty-year study of another planet. When I was a child you showed me images of the planet. I remember the images. The beings wore shiny metallic garments on their bodies. You did not have affection for them."

"They were quite different from the Earth beings," Kebeck answered his daughter. Shebor was a planet that had evolved in such a way that there were no surprises. The Shebor beings had a method for doing everything and a prescribed way of expressing their thoughts. Through genetic engineering and elimination of the noncompliant they had become a very homogeneous people and had transformed the planet into an efficient but completely uneventful and bland place. They were tall, thin beings. Because Shebor was a chilly planet, the Sheborians wore polished steel clothing padded with fabric that absorbed their distant sun's heat. Those are the images you remember.

They were so different than Earth beings, and also very different than we Palalans. The Sheborians had no art or creative literature or music. They developed their planet in such a way that every resource was used in a productive way. It was amazing to see such efficiency. They had no interest whatsoever in space travel; they did not see it as a practical use of their time. As such they certainly will not be visiting us, and that is quite fine with me because they are the dullest beings in the universe."

"That might be an overstatement, father. We have only become aware of five planets with sophisticated beings on them thus far. I agree that the Earth beings are the most interesting, but their penchant for violence and illogical thinking patterns make them dangerous. I thus appeal to you to pull back your emotions and to maintain greater objectivity in your study of these beings."

Kebeck reached out and placed a hand on one of her arms. "Lios, please calm yourself. I appreciate your concern, but I will do what I think is best when I come to a decision about what is right. Unlike the Sheborians, we are a people who have emotions and science alike. And contrary to your opinion, the Earth beings are not just animals."

Kebeck slid to the side of the sleeping platform and stood up. "Now, I see a light flashing on my computer. Touch my palms and leave your father to do some work. Please know that I value your thoughts and feel good that you show this love for me, but leave me for now. We will talk more on this subject later."

Lios got up, nodded, and took a step toward the door. Then she turned and said,

"Father, perhaps if you had a child with Sheme you might not feel so strongly about your Earth pet."

"Is there no one on this planet who does not know of this proposed child?" Kebeck's neck glowed red. "I appreciate that you have now reached the age of maturity, but that does not mean that you may counsel your father on whether to enter into a parenting contract."

Lios lowered her head. "I apologize. I only meant it as a suggestion that came out of concern for you." Lios extended her palms toward her father.

Kebeck moved to touch his palms to hers. "Your apology is accepted. Now go help someone who needs your help. Your father can take care of himself."

Lios stepped back, smiled, and moved toward the door. She stopped. "I almost forgot. I will not see you before your trip to Earth. I hope that it will be an enjoyable adventure that brings you no harm."

"Thank you, Lios. And remember: life is long. We must endeavor to enjoy it."

As soon as she was out the door, Kebeck rushed to his computer. With a few clicks on the keys Namucal's face appeared on the screen.

After an exchange of greetings, Namucal filled him in on how he had used the Toronto police computers to research the Earth being Erwin Bercic. "I discovered there is no record of Erwin Bercic before he came to Toronto. I even broadened my search to virtually the entire planet and there is no record of his name or his face in any police files or media records. Though I did find information on some other Erwin Bercics, their faces and ages did not match those of the man you had asked about."

"What now then? How can we find out more?" asked Kebeck.

"What this tells us is that the Erwin being is probably a criminal because he is hiding his past. The history he has told the media cannot be true. There should be some documentation known as a passport or a driver's license or some other form of identification from his past. This man seems to have appeared in Toronto twenty years ago without a past. I think something is amiss."

Namucal continued. "From the way he speaks, his original language seems to be the North American form of the Earth beings' English language; I will therefore search only in the United States and Canada regions of the continent. He cannot, without great difficulty, change his adult height or approximate age. Earth beings sometimes have surgery to change their facial features, so I cannot depend on matching the face. But they cannot so easily change their fingerprints; it looks very suspicious if they mar them in any way. Unfortunately, I find no records of Erwin Bercic's fingerprints. So, I shall search for a male of his age and height. Occasionally, the Earth beings surgically change their sex, but that is rare. As I said, I will search for a male of his age, height, and coloring. These Earth beings do come in a variety of colors and that is difficult to alter. I will seek out those who committed crimes twenty to forty years go. This particular fellow has lived in Toronto with the Erwin Bercic name for approximately twenty years, though his only crimes were inappropriate automobile parking. Therefore, he must have been involved in some crime prior to that time, otherwise he would not be hiding his history of what he did before he relocated to Toronto. I will look for beings that disappeared from the records after being caught for a crime or accused of a crime twenty to forty years ago. I think bank records and drivers licenses will be very helpful in this search. They help me match physical features to names and to financial activity. On Earth, they can do nothing without money and most beings in the North American drive vehicles."

Kebeck was impressed. "You have put a lot of work and thought into this project. For that I thank you. But is it possible that even though this Erwin Bercic is an evil being, he has never committed an illegal deed?"

"I think not. The fact that I can find no history of him simply indicates that there is something in his history that he is hiding."

"Again, thank you," Kebeck said gratefully.

Namucal shook his head. "No, I thank you. This is most interesting. I do not know when I have enjoyed anything more. I will disconnect now. I am anxious to continue on with this. When I know anything, I will contact you." His image faded to black.

Chapter 42

Earth

As Adeline turned into the driveway she scanned the house and yard; she was looking to see if anything looked out of place. The incidents with the window and the stove had scared her a bit; she found herself more alert and cautious than she had ever been before. As she approached her door she checked out the lock to see if there were any signs that it had been picked. After opening the door she stood on the threshold for a few seconds and listened. When Roger came running out of the kitchen, she jumped. *Oh my God! Am I going crazy or what? Scared by a cat.* "Shit!" she said aloud as she threw her bag onto the chair by the door. *I've got to reclaim this house,* she thought to herself. Adeline took off her jacket. She marched over to a shelf and selected a heavy marble sculpture and headed into the kitchen. With weapon in hand she inspected every room and closet in the house. Roger trotted along behind her, probably wondering what this new behavior was all about.

She had intended to go straight to the office after dropping Jim at the airport, but changed her mind when she realized that the papers she needed were still on her desk at home. She could work from home. *No problem.* No problem except the fact that she was now frightened of her own house. She had felt all right while Jim was there, but now Jim was on a plane back to London.

Adeline sat on the couch, clutching the marble statue and thinking. *The rat gnawing the wire behind the stove was a fluke; an accident that couldn't have been prevented. Like a car accident. Just get over it. Get back to normal. And break-ins happen all the time. Just move on with your life, Morgan.*

Adeline exhaled deeply, got up, and put the statue back on the shelf. She turned on the radio and looked over at Roger on the couch. "Cat, we have work to do." Adeline pulled out the chair at her desk, sighed again, and sat down to write.

"I need more details," Adeline murmured to herself. She picked up the phone, ran her finger down the phone list taped to her desk and dialed.

"Hi, this is Adeline Morgan from the Toronto Globe calling. May I speak to Erwin Bercic?" She fiddled with a little box of paper clips until she heard his voice. "Mr. Bercic, hi, this is Adeline Morgan from the Globe. Just a quick follow-up call ...."

Erwin interrupted. "Oh yes, how are you?"

Though it was a perfectly normal greeting, Adeline thought there was something a little odd in Bercic's tone of voice. "I'm fine, thanks," she replied.

"And how was your weekend?"

"Good, thank you." *What do you care?* she thought to herself. *You're just some politician trying to sound like a nice guy. Well, I'm certainly not going to tell you what really happened.* "Mr. Bercic, if you have a minute, I was going over my notes for the second article on you and I need a few more details about your time in Honduras and Belize."

"Sure, what would you like to know?"

"Well, for instance, where were you living exactly? In what towns or villages?" she asked.

"Hmm, let me see ... I was in Placentia for a while; that's in Belize. In Honduras, I worked in West Bay for almost a year. I also spent some time in Ambergris Caye, in Belize. I don't quite remember exact dates. That was a long time ago."

Adeline instantly realized that she had never heard of any of those places. "How big are those towns?"

"Oh, they were just a couple of stores clustered together with a dog sleeping in the middle of a dirt street. Wonderful places back then. I'm sure they've all been turned into busy tourist spots now."

"Uh ... yeah. Probably." She was scrambling to think of some way to check up on that part of Bercic's life. "Any old friends living down there?"

"Not really, at least none that I know of. I've lost touch with everybody. Anyway, my pals were mostly Australians, Americans, some Europeans; you know, scuba divers, just travelers and wanderers. We were so young and carefree. But as we got older most of us went back home to real jobs."

I'm getting nowhere with this, Adeline thought. "Well, thank you for your time, Mr. Bercic. I'd better get on with this. Deadlines and all of that."

"Thank you for calling. By the way, that first article was great. Thanks."

"My pleasure." She put the phone on its base. *Why do I dislike him so much?* Adeline sat back in her chair and stared at the phone she had just hung up. *I feel like he's a fake. But he's a politician; that's to be expected.* She looked over at Roger, who was stretching out and pawing the air. "Must get on with it," she said.

Not five minutes had passed when the doorbell rang.

Adeline hopped up and quickly went over to the window to check out who was at her door. It was the detective, Nick Hawes, wearing his usual monk-brown suit. He was standing on the porch, with a little smile on his face, staring into space.

Adeline unlocked the door and jerked it open. "Hi. Come in. I'm really glad to see you."

Hawes shuffled into the living room. His smile faded as he stepped into the room. "I was in this part of town and thought I'd stop by ...."

"You've got something?" Adeline interrupted.

"No. But I'd like to say that I appreciate all the time and effort you put into the information you emailed me. Thank you for doing that."

"What? You still have no leads? Nothing?" Adeline threw her hands up in the air in exasperation.

"No, not really. Sorry. I have no physical evidence. No suspects."

"But ... when you were standing there on the porch, you were smiling. I thought maybe ...."

"Sorry, I'm just a happy person. And you have a pretty house." He shrugged his shoulders. "I was just enjoying the day. I didn't think you were looking."

Adeline placed her hands on her hips and shook her head in disbelief. "With everything going on I thought you might finally have something on Carol's murder."

Hawes's eyes narrowed. "What do you mean, everything going on?"

"Just some stupid incidents."

"What, something that scared you?"

Adeline nodded yes.

Hawes seated himself in the nearest chair and motioned to Adeline to sit on the couch. "Tell me about it."

They sat there in the living room for about fifteen minutes while Adeline told Hawes all about the window break-in and the rat behind the stove.

"They do sound like coincidences, but maybe they're not. Know anybody who'd want to, uh, hurt you?" he asked.

"No, of course not."

"Know of anyone who'd want to hurt your fiancé?" he asked.

"No! He's a wonderful person, a university professor; everybody just loves him."

"How long have you known him?"

"About a year," Adeline answered, clutching a pillow to her chest. "Look, if you think my Jim has a checkered past, you're wrong. He's a saint. His father had a … well, his father's in jail, for embezzling, but Jim is just …." Adeline's voice trailed off. She felt her stomach churn as a smidgen of doubt entered her mind.

"Tell you what," Hawes said as he stood up to go, "I'll check out this fiancé of yours, just as a precaution. He's probably ok, but I'd like to make sure." He paused as he was about to step out the door. "I just don't buy the idea of a rat gnawing through a major electrical wire; it sounds fishy." He shook his head. "I mean, it's possible, but pretty friggin unusual." Hawes glared at her. "I wish you had called me before you cleaned it up." He turned around to come back inside. "Show me the stove." They went into the kitchen and the detective pulled the stove out from the wall. "So that wire was chewed and the rat was beside it?"

"Yes."

"Was the rat burned? Did he smell like cooked meat?"

"I don't remember any smell, but his fur was singed."

"Where is it now?"

"The rat? Jim put him in the trash. But it's gone. They picked up the trash this morning."

Hawes shook his head, then he waved his forefinger at her. "Look, if there are any more incidents, anything unusual, call me, ok? Back away from it, don't touch it, whatever it is, and call me."

"I will," Adeline promised as she saw him out the door. She was disappointed with him and now he had introduced a new worry. She couldn't imagine her Jim having something to do with anyone who would want to harm him, or her. And if he did, then Jim had lied to her. After things got serious, they had spent countless hours disclosing everything to each other; anything that had ever happened to them. She knew her Jim. Or then again, she thought she did before she found out about his father.

She turned the deadbolt in the lock and started back to her desk. Before she could get her bum in the chair, the phone rang. *Who is it now? I'm not getting any work done*, she thought as she reached for the phone.

"Oh, hi Mr. Stafford. I'm fine, thank you." It took her a moment to mentally switch gears. She still wasn't used to the idea that her friend's father was in fact some kind of secret agent.

"Adeline, I just called to check up on you. The detective who is investigating Carol's murder called me this morning and said they have nothing …."

"Yeah, I know." Adeline interrupted with a sigh of exasperation. "He was just here. It amazes me that with all the new technology they still have no leads about who killed Carol. If this were a TV show, the killer would already be behind bars."

"Yes I know, but this is reality, luv. And in real life, if a murderer is skillful, he will probably avoid being caught."

"Mr. Stafford, am I correct in assuming that because of your background, you know more than the average person about this type of thing?" Adeline asked without any hesitation.

There was silence on the line.

He finally answered. "Adeline, luv, reminding you that we are speaking on a telephone, I will say yes and expect you to leave it at that. Now, tell me the truth. Has anything unusual or frightening happened since we last spoke?"

"Yes." With a feeling of relief, Adeline proceeded to tell Mr. Stafford about the break-in at the front window and the exploding stove.

"Listen my dear, I want you to forget all about the break-in. It's nothing; I'll explain tomorrow. But, the thing with the stove troubles me. I should come up there tomorrow morning. May I show up at your door at nine a.m. tomorrow?"

"Of course. In fact, I'll have breakfast ready and I'll put on a pot of tea. You think somebody rigged the stove, don't you?" Adeline bit her lip.

"No, not to worry, luv. I'm just being extremely cautious. We'll just have a little tea and talk. And, yes, I do want to look at that stove. But as a precaution, it wouldn't hurt to lock up your doors and windows tonight. And a cell phone is a handy thing to keep in your pocket."

"Mr. Stafford, you're scaring me." Adeline glanced around the room, not knowing what she expected to see, but relieved that everything looked normal.

"Not to worry, dear. I'm an old man who just lost a daughter. Of course I'm being overly wary. Don't pay any attention to me." He paused. "But it wouldn't hurt to lock up. I'll see you tomorrow, luv."

Adeline hung up the phone and looked around the room. *It'll take more than a couple of rum and cokes to put me to sleep tonight,* she thought.

Chapter 43

Palala

I have got to get some real work done, Kebeck mused to himself as he leaned back on his slant board. *I would not like to give Jarrell a legitimate reason for having me dismissed from the committee.* Even though he was only expected to put in three or four hours of work each day, he was a bit behind schedule. Still, he enjoyed examining and explaining Earth ecology and observing how the sentient beings related to their planet. It had been so very interesting to discover that the basic flora and fauna of Earth were somewhat similar to those on Palala. The big differences he had found were in how the dominant species, the Earth beings, interacted with their planet. On Palala, water was venerated and protected; on Earth it was defiled and contaminated. It pained him to see how Earth beings abused their planet.

Kebeck was busy reading over a scientific report he retrieved from the Earth Internet discussing the polluted air surrounding the area known as Mexico City when a thought occurred to him. *Of course! I should watch the Erwin Bercic being.* He quickly set up his computer to watch Bercic's house, his business office, and his office at city hall. It was easy to search through tax, cable

TV, and telephone company records to find what he needed. He even patched into the screen on Erwin's cell phone. Soon he had his computer rigged so that half of the screen displayed the pollution research information he had been reading while the other half was dedicated to following Erwin Bercic's activities. He had programmed it so that he would be able to watch or listen to Bercic whenever the Earth being appeared before any of the sixteen devices that Kebeck had accessed.

Kebeck was still studying Mexico City an hour later when a flashing green light in the corner of the screen notified him that someone was requesting a face-to-face computer conversation. He muted the Bercic portion of the screen before receiving the new connection.

Kebeck was surprised to see Leto's face appear before him. "Greetings, my friend," Kebeck exclaimed. Kebeck and Leto had grown up in the same village. As youngsters they had played on the same waterball team. After their school years, they had gone their separate ways and rarely met, except on such occasions as Lios's majority ceremony. Both he and Leto had been pleased when they found that they had been selected for the Earth-Watching committee. It had been a pleasure to resurrect an old friendship at that time and Kebeck was glad that he was seeing more of Leto recently.

"It is my hope that I am not interrupting anything of importance," said Leto.

Kebeck noted that Leto's voice and facial expression were unusually serious. In fact, it was unusual for Leto to be anything near serious. He had always been the joker, usually the funniest person in the room.

"Leto, why the stony face? What troubles you?"

"My friend, my soberness is caused by something I must tell you, something that I know will displease you. I have thought long on this, but I must …."

"You are voting to stop Earth-Watching," interrupted Kebeck.

Leto nodded his head. "Yes. That is so. After listening to Jarrell, I reviewed all of my notes as well as the recent news stories about the development of religions here on Palala. I was shocked to find that so many people are interested in it."

"People have the right to …" Kebeck added.

"Please, let me finish," Leto said in a determined tone. "I then looked over my research notes from my study of Earth religions. Yes, I acknowledge that the religious groups undertake some good work, such as providing food to beings that have none. But far too many beings were killed and continue to die in wars between conflicting religious groups, such as those struggles between their so-called Catholics and Protestants, Muslims and Christians, or their Jews and Muslims. And while I will admit to you that such warfare was merely part of their tribal development and many of them are moving beyond such behaviors, Earth beings to this very day continue to kill each other because of differences in their religious beliefs."

"But they will outgrow that," Kebeck countered.

"Probably, eventually." Leto paused. "But, the part of religion that I find most unacceptable is its rejection of science. The Earth beings' illogical desire to believe that which is not provable fact makes them incapable of functioning in a mature society. I must discourage anything that leads any of our people to adopt the absurd belief that there is a powerful father figure watching over them. This is but a childish illusion. Our people have matured past the need for religion. It was a part of our primitive development, and we grew out of it thousands of years ago. I must deter anyone from wrapping themselves in the warm blanket of this fantasy. It is a mistake I wish to stop them from making."

"So you would restrict their freedom to view whatever they wish in order to keep religion out of our society?" asked Kebeck.

"Yes," Leto said with a solemn nod. "Usually I am opposed to any form of censorship. But in this case I will support any and all methods that Jarrell proposes to stop Earth-Watching as soon as possible."

Kebeck sighed and let his head fall back against the slantboard. "I see that my words would be useless at this time. Your neck is red with passion and your jaw is set. It saddens me that you are willing to sacrifice our right to view because you fear that some people will display immature judgment. You no longer trust people to judge for themselves?"

"No, I do not. For religion fogs judgment. It is more pleasant to believe lovely lies than to face harsh truths. But I do not wish there to be bad feelings between us because of my decision. It is still my desire to remain friends." Leto extended his four hands palm up. "I will cease our communication now. I thought it best to tell you face-to-face before I contact Jarrell and Samot. I wish you clear water." Leto's image faded on the screen.

Kebeck was dumbstruck; he slumped down on his slantboard, feeling like a deflated balloon. He could never have predicted that Leto would utter such an opinion. He felt hurt and betrayed. His good-humored team mate seemingly had changed overnight into someone he hardly knew.

Now, there were three people working against him. Only Agara and Samot appeared to be on his side. Kebeck's hands flew across the keyboard as he punched in the codes to reach Agara. He was convinced more of Samot's than Agara's support. He knew Agara to be an easygoing person who flowed with life, so Kebeck feared he might be persuaded into going along with Jarrell.

Agara's face appeared on the screen; he smiled and blinked. It looked like he had just woken up. "Greetings, Kebeck."

"I do not wish to disturb your routine, but it is urgent that we speak," said Kebeck.

"Not a problem, my friend. Please, speak."

Kebeck noticed then that Agara's neck was very red and his smile was quite broad, almost exaggerated. "Are you all right?" Kebeck asked.

"Well, not really. Two friends and I mixed up a beverage similar to the alcoholic drinks they make on Earth. We wanted to experience the feeling of inebriation that many of the Earth beings find so appealing. It was an interesting experiment. Because our bodies' circulation system allows for variations in temperature, the alcohol probably did not have the same effect on us as it does on Earth beings. But it did have an effect nonetheless. It made us all feel very relaxed and seemed to slow down our thinking."

"Did you enjoy the experience?" Kebeck queried.

Agara thought for a moment. "No. I do not like feeling like there is a cloud in my head. Not to worry, though. I will not become addicted like an Earth alcoholic. The actual experience was not desirable. It had appeared to be so much more pleasant when I saw the Earth beings drinking these concoctions in their TV programs and movies. But the mist is almost clear from my head. Now, what is the urgent matter that you spoke of?"

"Leto has aligned himself with Jarrell and Laniff. Now there are three who want to stop Earth-Watching as soon as possible. Please tell me where you stand."

"With you, my friend. I went for a long swim and thought on it. I wish to uphold the original plan outlined for our committee. We should continue our watching for another ten years, issue our reports, and put it to a vote at that time. I believe in the judgment of the majority and the freedom of the individual."

Kebeck felt relieved. "Thank you. I must ...."

"Sorry, Kebeck," Agara interrupted, his face looking a bit contorted. "My stomach does not feel well. I must end our communication. We will talk again later about our Earth visit." The screen went dark.

Kebeck got up from the slantboard and paced around the room. He went over to the cooling unit and opened the door, looked over the contents, and closed the door. He circled the room again then opened the door and selected a purple and green vegetable. As he sat on the corner of his sleeping platform munching on the vegetable, he detected a faint odor. Someone was approaching his house, a male. He thought he recognized the scent.

Samot's deep voice boomed through the open door. "Kebeck, I greet you."

Kebeck ran to the door and greeted Samot, whose wide body barely fit through the door opening without touching the frame. Samot was an unusual person; he was overweight. Such large people were rare on Palala. "It is a fortunate coincidence that you appear just as I was thinking of you," said Kebeck. "Enter and welcome."

"I think it is no coincidence. From my last conversation with Leto, I have surmised that he will soon ask for a vote to cease Earth-Watching. We need to talk and plan if we want to stop this nonsense. Jarrell is determined to force his will on us and on the people of our planet. I am alarmed at his disregard for procedure and freedom."

"I offer you food and invite you to make yourself comfortable," said Kebeck, motioning toward the sleeping platform.

"Yes, bring food. I did not get to this size by accident. We will talk."

Chapter 44

Earth

The room reflected the owner. Expensive antique furniture sat on polished hardwood floors. A large silver-framed mirror hung over the marble fireplace. Erwin stood in front of the fire, warming himself up after a long day at both offices. He sipped on a bourbon and water as he admired his face in the mirror. *If I had the time I'd go to China and hire someone to give this face a tune-up.* Erwin turned as he heard Sam enter the room. Sam looked up at him with a big, Great Dane smile. There was no doubt that the dog loved Erwin.

Erwin squatted down and rubbed Sam's head. "Sam, old friend, I'm all worn out from dealing with idiots at the stores and fools at city hall, so we're going to just kick back on the couch and watch some TV tonight. Sound good to you?"

Of course, Sam would do whatever Erwin wanted; after all, Erwin was his god. Because Sam was the only being on Earth that Erwin could really talk to, the dog was treated like a prince, a 130-pound black prince with a white chest and white paws. A hired minion took him to the dog park so he could play with his friends every morning and yet another underling was retained to run with Sam in the early evening. But Erwin was the only person allowed to feed him or give him treats.

Sam settled on the floor next to the couch as Erwin sat down and started chatting about his day. He told Sam about the employee who didn't know the difference between a trundle bed and a bunk bed. He verbally ripped apart several of his fellow city councilors and he complained about the waiter at dinner. Sam appeared to be listening attentively as Erwin recounted all the problems of the day. When Erwin finally stopped talking, Sam got up and wagged his tail as he licked Erwin's face. The tail swept across the coffee table, knocking several magazines to the floor. It was time for a treat. After wolfing down his usual bacon and cheese treat, delivered daily from the deli down the street, Sam climbed up beside Erwin on the large couch and laid his head on his master's leg.

Erwin flipped through the channels for a few minutes before he settled on an old black-and-white movie. It was a British film, shot in the 1940s; its gray tones added to the film's atmosphere and the music could only be described as melodramatic. The plot involved a love triangle. Erwin watched as a jealous husband shoved his wife off a crowded London subway platform. A scream was heard as the train zipped by. The husband disappeared into the crowd.

"Damn it, Sam. Here I was, looking for some mindless entertainment, and wouldn't you know this gives me an idea for a simple way to get rid of that pesky reporter." Erwin shook his head. "Just can't seem to get away from business." Sam looked up at him with loving eyes. "I know. I said I was going to retire and never kill again. I admit it; it's my own fault that I had to kill that first reporter. I was so relaxed during her interview that I let a couple of things slip. So, I had to remove her. And now I'm sure, just by the way that Adeline Morgan looks at me, that her friend told her something she shouldn't know. So then, I've got to exterminate her. Simple as that." Sam licked his hand. "Then I quit that part of my life for good. I promise. Well, maybe the boyfriend too. I'm not sure yet." Erwin took a sip from his glass. "And after I'm elected … well, I'll just lie and steal a bit like any other politician. That's all."

Both Erwin and Sam fell asleep long before the murderer in the movie was marched off to prison. The blaring sound of a commercial for some type of automobile woke both of them. Erwin stumbled off to bed, with Sam following close behind.

Chapter 45

Palala

Kebeck's eyes had widened when he heard Erwin say that he planned to exterminate Adeline. He reviewed that section of the Earth-Watching video transcript to make sure he had heard the Bercic being's communication correctly. Yerf was laying on the sleeping platform reading something on his hand computer. "Yerf, please come view this."

"What, now? Tag it to my computer. I will view it tomorrow. I was about to go to sleep."

Kebeck stood up. "Please. It is important to me. View it now."

Yerf glared at him as he got up and came over to the computer in front of Kebeck. "What is it then?"

Kebeck replayed the section for him. "He could be jesting," Yerf said. "They often joke about killing each other, you know."

"No, not this time." Kebeck shook his head. "He truly intends to kill Adeline."

Yerf turned to face Kebeck and put his upper two arms on Kebeck's shoulders. "That is unfortunate, my friend, but you can do nothing about it. Just quit viewing her and concentrate on the ecology of the planet as you are supposed to do."

Kebeck stared at him and said nothing.

"I am going to sleep now. You should do likewise. There is nothing more you can do." Yerf turned and went back to the sleeping platform; he was asleep within a matter of seconds.

Kebeck leaned back on the slantboard and gazed at the computer as he replayed Erwin Bercic's comments over and over. *I'll contact Namucal,* he thought. With a few clicks of the keyboard, Namucal's jovial face appeared on the screen before him.

"Greetings Kebeck. I have been working on the Bercic case and I have narrowed his past identity down to nine Earth beings, but I must do more research to determine which of these correspond to his true identity. I think he may have had a surgeon change his face because he resembles none of these suspects." Kebeck could see by the redness of his neck that Namucal was excited. "And you? Have you any news?"

"Yes, bad news. This Bercic intends to kill my Adeline."

"That is what you suspected previously. What makes you now certain?" asked Namucal.

"He said it aloud to his dog," answered Kebeck.

Namucal looked confused. "I have not studied Earth beings for quite as long as you, my friend. I was not aware that they had conversations with animals of lesser intelligence. Also, it is my understanding that the Earth beings are the only type of animal on Earth with the ability for complex speech. Is that not correct?"

"Yes, but …."

"For what purpose then are these one-sided conversations?"

Kebeck was annoyed to be wasting time on explanations of the Earth beings' relationships with their pets: "Because the Earth beings feed and dominate the animals that they keep in their houses, these pets accept their more powerful owners as alpha leaders of the pack. The Earth beings in turn interpret this acceptance as love and speak to their pets as if they were very good friends. On Earth, they even refer to the dog as being man's best friend."

"There is a chaca who comes to my door every day for food, but I have no delusion that he feels any affection for me. Still, he is interesting to watch. I once saw him ...."

"Namucal!" Kebeck interrupted. "He is going to kill her. What should I do?"

Without hesitation Namucal said, "Observe the event, of course. I have several friends who would like to see it. Do you know when and where it is to happen?"

"No! You don't understand! I do not want it to happen. I want to prevent it. You know much about Earth crime and police. Tell me how I can stop her from being killed." Kebeck was trying to stay calm, but he felt his neck grow red with anger.

Namucal's usually cheerful face took on a serious look. "It is unfortunate that you have affection for the Adeline being, but you cannot change her fate. Centuries ago it was voted that we could observe other planets if we refrained from communicating with them. This policy has served us well. Remember that they are not like us and that the death of one or of many of the Earth beings is of no significance whatsoever. They are like an illusion or a character in one of the fiction books of our childhood; you cannot think of them as real people."

"But ...." Kebeck could think of nothing more to say before Namucal spoke up again.

"Would you send me a copy of the section where the Erwin being says he plans to kill your Adeline? Maybe something in the conversation will give me a clue as to where or when he plans to do it. I want to set up the viewing so that I can see the murder as it happens. I would invite friends to my house and we could watch a life-sized hologram of it happening. If nothing else, it will be most exciting to watch."

Kebeck realized that it was useless to try to reason with Namucal any further. "Yes, I will send a copy of the section. I wish you clear water," he said before ending the connection.

Chapter 46

Earth

"This is really going to be fun. I love Halloween. If we meet at the Lazy Lizzard at nine or ten, then we can go from bar to bar by subway til one or two. I've made a list of the ones that are having the best parties." Adeline was pulling vegetables out of the fridge as she talked to Nina on the phone. "I know the witch costume is just too ordinary for you, but I've made this fantastic hat and you aren't going to believe my make-up. I am going to be the ultimate witch."

For years now, Adeline and a group of four or five other women had enjoyed a tradition of dressing up in elaborate costumes and barhopping on Halloween. It was Adeline's favorite holiday, and though Carol would no longer be joining them, she still wanted to go out and make the most of the night. She wanted to see what weird creatures would show up at the bars tonight. More than ever, she wanted to be in disguise so she could feel silly and free, if only for one night, from the recent events in her life.

Nina said, "I'm looking forward to seeing what Shirley shows up in. It's already Monday, and Halloween is on Thursday, and she says she hasn't even started on her costume. This should be interesting."

Nina could be a bit catty, but Adeline had known her since high school and didn't take her digs seriously. Nina had had the parents from hell, so she had developed a toughness that helped her survive and get ahead. She was now one of the leading divorce lawyers in Toronto.

Adeline took a wok out of the drawer. "Hey, I've got to go now. I'm starving. I haven't had supper yet. We'll talk later, ok? All right, bye for now." Adeline hung up the phone, washed her hands, and started cutting up vegetables for a stir-fry.

Later, Adeline was just taking her last bite of the supper when the phone rang. She almost choked on a piece of asparagus as she struggled to say hello.

"Are you all right?" asked Nick Hawes.

"Yeah," she said, coughing. "I was just eating when you called; think I swallowed the wrong way. I'm fine. You've got news? Tell me that you found Carol's murderer and he pulled a gun and got himself killed. Tell me he died in a hail of bullets."

"I'm afraid not. Unfortunately this isn't a TV show. The reason I called was to tell you that … well, because of the recent gang killings, my Captain took me off the case, and, uh, it's been put on the back burner."

"You're kidding me. And exactly how far back is this back burner?"

"Look, try and understand. We have no evidence to follow. The bullet led us nowhere. So many people come and go from the newsroom where Carol's papers were taken that we have no real suspects. We questioned everyone who works there. There were no surveillance cameras at the office or in her apartment. Really, it seems like a professional job. And with those kinds of hits, well, if you know why the person was whacked, then it might lead somewhere. But no one knows why she was killed. We've got nothing … so the boss said to move on to other cases. And by the way, your boyfriend is all right ... I checked. I checked on that rat, too. And rats do chew wires."

Adeline slammed her fist down on the table, making her plate and utensils clatter. "NO! You can't just quit! That's not fair! That's not fair to Carol!"

"Look, I'm really sorry. But that's the way it is."

"Have you told Carol's parents?"

"Yes, I talked to Mr. Stafford a few minutes ago. He said he understood."

"Well, I don't. Who can I call to get the case reopened?"

"Really, there's nobody. But if it'll make you feel better, my captain's name is Michael Corbin. He's left for the day but you can catch him here tomorrow. Anyway, it was nice meeting you Miss Morgan. Sorry I couldn't do more."

Adeline made the dishes clatter again as she slammed the phone down on the table. "Shit!" she yelled out. "Shit, shit, damn shit!" Roger ran from the room. She pushed the dishes to one side and laid her forehead on the cold table. Minutes passed before she raised her head and took a deep breath. *I've got to calm down.* Roger stood peering at her from the edge of the kitchen doorway. *I'll deal with this tomorrow.*

After clearing away the supper dishes she grabbed the remote and the TV schedule and stretched out on her couch. Roger wandered into the room, looked over the situation, and leaped up on one arm of the couch.

"Ok Roger, here's an old movie I've always meant to see. *Cape Fear. Nina mentioned this one; said it scared her. About a convicted rapist, released after serving his sentence. He stalks the family of the lawyer who originally defended him. And it's just starting.* Adeline adjusted her pillows as the opening credits appeared on the screen.

The movie was creepy, but she could see why Nina liked it. One was always waiting for the sleazy guy to jump out at the lawyer or the bitchy kid. She munched on some popcorn and sipped a diet coke as she watched. During a commercial, she thought of Carol. *Carol should be watching this with me. God I miss her.* The commercial ended and she was again totally engrossed in the movie when something odd happened. The same scene started to play over and over again, looping at the point where one of the characters said, "I keep feeling that there's some animal out there, stalking us," while another added, "I think he wants to hurt us in the worst way." The scene repeated itself at least a half-dozen times. She picked up the remote and changed the channels, but everything appeared normal with the other programs. When she switched back to the movie, the scene continued to repeat itself, with the same actors uttering the same dialogue. Adeline turned the TV off, somewhat annoyed by this apparent technical problem. She sat and stared at the gray screen for a minute or two. She turned it back on and heard, "I keep feeling that there's some animal out there, stalking us," and, "I think he wants to hurt us in the worst way." She sat there, mesmerized, as the scene continued in its endless loop.

She was roused out of her stupor by Roger rubbing up against her. "There's got to be an explanation for this, right cat?" Adeline picked up the TV schedule and looked to see what local station was showing the movie. She went over to her desk, looked up the station's number in the phone book, and dialed. "Hi, I'm watching *Cape Fear* on your station and the movie seems to be stuck or something; it's just repeating two lines over and over. Are you aware of the problem?"

A deep voice on the other end said, "Just a minute please" before she was put on hold. After two or three minutes the voice came back on. "We've got no problems to report here. The movie's running just fine. It's at the part where they're on the houseboat in a storm. The problem's got to be with your TV, ma'am. Better check on that again. Anything else I can help you with?" the voice asked, somewhat sarcastically.

"Uh, no. Thanks anyway," Adeline answered, feeling a little perplexed. She put the phone down, walked back over to the couch, and slowly sat down. She looked at the screen: same actors, same scene. Once more she flipped through other channels. Still nothing unusual on the other stations. She was starting to feel upset. The words *I think he wants to hurt us in the worst way* were beginning to give Adeline the chills.

"Shit, I don't like this at all," she said to Roger. Adeline pushed the off button threw the remote down on the couch. *This is too weird to be a coincidence. It's almost as if someone is either trying to warn me or to scare me, and I don't like it either way.* Roger jumped off the couch and ran into the kitchen; he didn't like it when anyone got angry or upset, and Adeline was definitely both.

She paused for a second before she got up and went over to her desk. She quickly ran a finger down her phone list and dialed. "Mr. Stafford! How are you?"

It took less than a half-hour for Adeline to pack a bag and to ask her neighbor to feed the cat. She then got in the car and headed toward the Stafford home in St. Catharines, about an hour's drive at this time of night. She figured that a couple of days at the Stafford's was just what she needed.

Chapter 47

Palala

Yerf was stepping out the door on his way to work when he called out to Kebeck: "I smell company."

Kebeck dashed over to the door just in time to see Agara round a corner and come into sight on the path leading to the house. Yerf and Agara exchanged a showing of palms as they passed each other. When Agara reached the door where Kebeck was standing, he smiled, held his upper two hands up in the air and exclaimed, "High five!" Kebeck laughed and slapped the extended hands with his upper two hands.

"I am excited about our trip to Earth, are you not?" asked Agara.

"Yes, now that it is just days away, it is beginning to seem real. I am sure that I glow every time I think about it."

After his conversations with Yerf and Namucal, Kebeck had decided that he should not discuss his concern for Adeline with anyone else. He was very excited over the Earth visit but the anxiety caused by Erwin Bercic's statement had cast a shadow over his enthusiasm. One of his most precious desires was to see his Adeline in person. As she always went out in costume every

Halloween, it had seemed to Kebeck to be a real possibility to see her up close, in her natural environment. But now with this Bercic being's murderous intentions, he not only wanted to see her, he wanted to find a way to save her.

"I do not sense total happiness in you at this moment. Is there a problem?" asked Agara.

"There is no problem with our visit to Earth," said Kebeck. "It is but minor bits of my private reality that weigh on me. Again, do not be concerned; all will go well with our Earth visit."

"We had better enjoy it and make sure it goes well, because if Jarrell has his way, it could be the last Earth visit, ever. But let us not talk of him now. We have plans to make. I think we should …."

"I was thinking," interrupted Kebeck, "that I would like to bicycle to the launch site. I would have to start early tomorrow. It's a beautiful part of the country and I need the exercise."

"But I have reserved a landmobile to get us there and back. And, if you have an accident or get lost, they would cancel the flight." Agara looked somewhat upset. His neck was pink.

"Do not worry, Agara. I will carry a communicator. This Earth visit is very important to me; I will be there." Kebeck paused. "You are welcome to bicycle with me."

"No, thank you. I would not enjoy pedaling through the jungle for hours. I will take the easy way." Agara cocked his head and smiled. "Then there is nothing else to arrange. The costumes will be at the launch site, waiting for us. I have been told that we merely have to board the ship, fly for approximately forty-eight hours, and we are there. The excitement of it makes my heart flutter. I will leave you now. I suggest that you rest to prepare for your long bike ride. Remember, we meet at the launch site on day 235, at the fourteenth hour. Do not be late!" Agara flashed the palms of his hands and dashed out the door.

As Agara's scent faded from the air, Kebeck wandered over to his computer to see if there were any messages waiting. The only urgent message was from Samot; he wanted a face-to-face conference as soon as possible.

Kebeck's neck glowed with color. He had been expecting to hear from Samot. He knew his action could not be hidden. He felt heavy with dread as his hands pressed the keys to connect to the committee leader.

Samot appeared on the screen, an obvious frown on his face. "Greetings, friend. We need to talk."

"I wish you clear water," replied Kebeck.

"It seems you have muddied the water, my friend. I have received a report that indicates you manipulated a section of an Earth TV broadcast, and I see by the color of your neck that this report is correct." Samot looked puzzled. "Why did you do such a thing?"

"I was trying to prevent the killing of an Earth being that I watch."

"Out of curiosity, I must ask if you were successful; did you indeed stop it from being killed?" Samot inquired.

"Maybe, but I cannot be sure. I do know that I have frightened her so that she is now aware that something is amiss. I feel that I have helped her, but I have not necessarily saved her."

"As you are aware, this is a serious breach of rules that will call for a hearing. This could get you removed from the committee and thus change the committee vote on Earth-Watching. Jarrell, therefore, will get what he wants. Was helping this one being worth all of that?"

"Yes and no." Kebeck paused and thought for a moment. "I do not know. Emotion was involved."

"Jarrell will appear on your computer and on mine any time now. He will demand a hearing as soon as possible. Your Earth visit could be canceled."

"It occurs to me that we, you and I, are speaking of Jarrell as if he is evil. Of course no one is truly evil. Jarrell is just doing what he thinks is best for our planet. Some combination of logic and emotion has formed his opinion of Earth-Watching. His thinking has to come from somewhere; I want to find out what has made him close his mind to discussion." Kebeck leaned his head back on the slantboard. "I may have a strategy for handling this situation. I wish to discuss it further with you. Would it be possible for you to come to my house?"

Chapter 48

Earth

Erwin was doodling on a notepad, lost in thought, when Zoey entered the room. As always she looked fantastic; the red suit was just that right balance between professional and sexy. Many a time he had thought about seducing her, but he was sure that taking her as a lover would destroy a great working relationship.

"Mr. Bercic, I got your email telling me to find out which adult Halloween costumes were the most popular. You gave me your size, but I just needed to confirm your instructions about buying the top five costumes." She put down the files she had brought in with her and put her hands on her hips. "Do you really want me to buy all five costumes?"

"I sent that to you last week. Are you telling me you still haven't done it?" Erwin was angry. "Get going right now and go buy those costumes; they could be sold out by now. Look, we'll talk about this later. But from now on, when I give you instructions ... unless it's illegal or impossible, just do it. Immediately!"

Zoey grabbed the files and rushed toward the door. "Of course, sir. I'll go right now."

As she left, her high heels clicking down the hall, Erwin got up and stomped around the room, incensed at the woman for not following his instructions. Thoughts of punishing her ran through his mind. And he knew some very appropriate ways of punishing people.

Since his last facial-reconstruction surgery, he rarely had needed to draw from his considerable repertoire of punishment techniques. Ever since his move to Toronto, he had played the good guy; it was boring, but necessary. One of the topics Erwin had studied during his time in prison was psychology and from that he had devised some nasty ways of messing with people's minds. One day, while poring over a psychology textbook, it occurred to him that a few well-chosen words could have a devastating effect on most people. He had perfected his system during his years as a hired assassin. He found he needed something for amusement between jobs.

His first victim was a boy who looked to be eleven or twelve years old; the kid was irritating him by making lots of noise while Erwin was trying to relax by a motel swimming pool. As Erwin was leaving the pool area, he stopped beside the boy and stared at him for a second before saying, "I'm a physiologist and I can tell by the shape of your body that your penis will never be as big as a normal penis. I just thought you should know so that when it happens … well, just don't be too concerned."

The boy looked startled and said, "Wh-what do you mean?"

Erwin patted the boy on the shoulder, nodded his head, and said, "Small still works, so don't worry about it." Then he went inside and packed his bags to leave.

He once punished a waitress who took too long bringing him his water by mentioning her weight. He noticed that she kept pulling down the front of her top when it slipped up over her little round belly. As he got up to leave, he said to her, "You look good with those extra pounds on you. Some women would look fat at your weight, but you look good." Then he slipped out the door.

And Erwin didn't just use his talents for revenge. When he got bored while traveling on planes or trains, he would sit beside someone who looked a bit unhappy, let the person spill their guts to him, and then select a weakness to zero in on. He would convince these hapless travelers that he was on their side as he highlighted their doubts and fears. It gave him a malicious pleasure to know that his words would most likely have a lasting effect throughout his victims' lives.

The sound of the phone ringing brought Erwin back from his stroll down memory lane. "Yes, this is Erwin Bercic. Oh, hi Charles. What's up?"

"I'm just reporting in to let you know that the cars are all arranged. The rental company will deliver two economy size tan or white cars to the parking lot at the Gerrard Street store at noon on Halloween. They have agreed to leave the keys at the store's main desk, just as you instructed. Mr. Bercic, if I may say so, it's really nice of you to rent cars for your Halloween house guests. Mind if I ask why you chose those specific colors?"

Because they're less conspicuous, you dolt, Erwin thought. "Well, my cousin's a bit quirky. Says he only feels comfortable driving light-colored cars. He says that red cars get hit more often than any others and that black and blue cars blend in, so they get hit too. So let's just humor him, shall we?"

"Very considerate."

"Thank you, Charles."

"Is there anything else I can do for you Mr. Bercic, before I fly off tomorrow?"

"No Charles, you have a nice vacation. And thank you for getting the cars in your name; that saved me some time and trouble. But I'll be responsible if anything happens to either of the cars, so don't you worry. Have a great trip."

Erwin hung up the phone and paced around the oak paneled room as he reflected on his plan. He would park both cars on Adeline Morgan's street, one facing in each direction. Each car would have two costumes in the back seat. He would sit in one car while wearing the fifth costume and act like a patient father waiting for his kids out trick-or-treating. He knew Morgan was going out to meet friends, but he needed to find out what time. That was the only part of the plan that needed to be addressed. Both cars would have the keys in the ignition so that when she backed out he could jump in the car that was parked in the right direction and follow her. He scribbled on a notepad, "two nondescript bags." He would need something to carry the extra costumes in. A change of costume was vital to the plan. As he walked pass the mirror, Erwin looked over at his eye-catching reflection. *Yes, soon that handsome devil will be mayor.*

Chapter 49

Palala

Kebeck and Samot made themselves comfortable on the sleeping platform. Samot was munching on a green fruit and had a piece of smoked fish in another hand. Kebeck began. "I apologize for the inconvenience I have caused you. I asked you to come here in person because I did not want our conversation to be put through the computer network. I think it best that no record of our conversation be made."

Samot sat up. "Now, I am curious. What are you up to?"

"I want to go on the visit to Earth and deal with any hearing on my supposed infraction of the communication rule after I return."

"I have no problem with that, but I think Jarrell will object."

"The rule concerning relationships with other planets indicates only that we are not to communicate with the beings of other planets. Technically, I did not really communicate. I just caused a malfunction in a single Earth TV appliance."

Samot interjected: "Well, that is true, but ...."

Kebeck interrupted his friend: "But I do recognize that some people would construe that as communication, and I will have to deal with that when a hearing is convened." Kebeck tilted his head to one side. "Now, as I understand the law, there can be no hearing without me being present. Is that correct?"

"That is true," said Samot, nodding his head.

"Good, then my plan should work."

"What plan?" Samot was growing agitated. "You speak of a plan but do not explain it. And I see redness at your neck. Please, explain!"

"With apologies, I cannot. We have known each other for more than one hundred years and I have called you here to ask that you trust me." Kebeck paused, decided that he would take Samot's silence as an indication of trust, and then continued: "I ask that you go home now and check your messages two hours from now."

"That is all the clarification I get?"

"For now, yes. All will be clear water later," Kebeck told his friend.

Samot sat and stared at Kebeck for moment, then said, "I will do as you ask, but understand that I do not like this." He moved off the sleeping platform and started toward the door. He turned to face Kebeck when he reached the doorway and said, "I think ...."

Kebeck shook his head and motioned him out the door. Samot carried on, chewing on the smoked fish as he walked out of the house.

Kebeck moved into action the minute Samot was out the door. He typed the following note:

"I apologize for manipulating an Earth TV in such a way that it has caused some alarm and I understand that a hearing is necessary. I have informed Agara that I will not be able to accompany him on the upcoming Earth-visit. I will be available to meet with the committee on day 324, the day I was scheduled to go to Earth, at the fifteenth hour. I now need to walk down paths of reflection to think. I will return and check my computer on the fourteenth hour of day 324. I wish you all clear water."

He set his computer to send the message in two hours' time to all of the committee members except Agara. Kebeck's neck glowed a deep red from this deception, but there was no one there to see it. He printed out a map of all the roads and paths between his house and the launch site. Then he grabbed a rain poncho, his water cup, his hand communicator, and a bunch of fruits and vegetables and put everything in his backpack. He then went back to his computer and sent a note to his roommate, Yerf: "I will be gone a few days. Worry not. More later. Kebeck."

Kebeck stopped and looked around the one-room house to see if he had forgotten anything. He realized that he felt very odd. He had never deceived anyone before and it made him feel both insecure and free. *Maybe Earth-Watching is having a bad effect on me*, he wondered. *I never would have thought to lie to my friends and fellow workers before I started studying the beings of that odd little planet.* Kebeck went out the door, climbed on his bicycle, glanced at the map in his hand, and started pedaling.

Chapter 50

Earth

Adeline could feel her shoulders relax as she turned the corner onto the street where she had grown up. She slowed down as she passed the house where she had lived while in elementary school and high school. It looked much the same as it had when her family had stayed there, except that the trees were bigger and the garden was bit different. The front porch light was on; she remembered the sometimes awkward and sometimes passionate kisses that were exchanged on that little porch at the front door. It had been a wonderful place to grow up in and she had cried as she signed the papers to put it up for sale. She had thought that it would always be the family home, but the deaths of her mother and father had changed everything. She was sure her mother's two-year fight with breast cancer had contributed to her father's heart problem. Watching his wife die had literally broken his heart.

She pressed the gas and moved on down the road to the house where Carol had lived. With her parents gone, Adeline had no relatives in this part of the world except her Aunt Gloria in Calgary, and she was not someone Adeline could get close to. Mr. and Mrs. Stafford, on the other hand, were almost like family. As her car entered the driveway she heard Mrs. Stafford call out, "Frank, she's here." The house was all lit up. They were waiting up for her. Before she could get out of the car they were both standing out on the porch, waiting to greet her. It was hugs and kisses all around, and as they entered the house they were all wiping tears from their faces.

Except for the funeral, this was the only time that Adeline had been in the Stafford's house without Carol being there. In the back of her mind she felt that Carol could come around a corner any time, yelling, "Hey, Babe, what's up?" She tried to ignore her friend's ghost by chatting with the Staffords about everything and anything. Soon it was one a.m. Pie had been eaten. The teacups were empty. A sad silence fell over the threesome and Mr. Stafford did something he had never done before. He offered Adeline a drink, an alcoholic drink. Starting in junior high, Mr. Stafford had lectured both girls on the evils of alcohol. As far as she knew, there was never a drop kept in the house. Adeline agreed to a rum and coke, and almost fell off of her chair when Mr. Stafford opened a secret panel in the kitchen wall and exposed a well-stocked bar.

Adeline got up and ran her hand over the opening. "How long has this been here?" she asked.

"About forty years. I put it in when we bought the house," he replied.

"We never suspected …."

"Of course not. You girls weren't supposed to find it. Now take your drink, luv, and toddle off to bed. It's late. We'll talk over tea in the morning."

The next morning when Adeline came down, Mrs. Stafford was already gone. "She works as a volunteer at the hospital most weekday mornings," Mr. Stafford explained. Tea and crumpets were on the kitchen table. "Well, luv, we need to talk about the little break-in last week. I didn't bring this up last night because I feel that it is better that my lovely wife not know everything I do. She's always been steady as a rock about my work, but, I'm supposed to be retired, you know. First, I want to apologize for scaring you. But I broke into your house precisely because I didn't want to scare you."

"What? What do you mean?" Adeline was puzzled.

"You see, luv, I wanted to see if you had any information in your papers or computer files that might lead me to Carol's murderer."

"But you could have asked …."

"Yes, luv," he interrupted. "But, I didn't want to frighten you. I didn't want to say to you, 'Adeline, there's some bastard out there who killed Carol and who might now want to kill you because of some bit of data, so mind if I go through your files?' That wouldn't have gone over so well."

"So it was you who broke in?"

"Yes, and I found nothing that would be reason enough to harm you. You would have never have known I was there if one of your neighbors hadn't been a bit nosey. I had to leave the window open and dropped the screen behind the bush. Sorry, luv."

Adeline got up and hugged him, then went back to her tea.

"And about the rat chewing the insulation off your stove connection, I went on the Internet and according to the pest control companies it is quite common for rats to chew on electric wires. Isn't that amazing? I had no idea that rats had a taste for electrical insulation. Funny, the stuff you can find on the Internet."

Adeline poured herself a bit more tea. "So what about last night? Can you explain why my TV got stuck on one section of a movie that kept repeating itself? 'I keep feeling that there's some animal out there, stalking us,' and, 'I think he wants to hurt us in the worst way.' That was spooky."

Mr. Stafford looked down at his cup. "No, I have no explanation for that. If you were somebody else, I'd think you had just imagined it, or fell asleep and dreamed about it." He looked up and smiled at her. "But I know you, luv, and if you say it happened, it happened. I'm doing a little research to see how one could do that to a TV. Meanwhile, the guest room is wired for the Net so you can work from there as easily as you could from your own home. And call anywhere you like; we're on a one-fee system. Annie and I are just glad you're here; having you around makes us a little less lonesome for Carol." Mr. Stafford stood up, ruffled her hair, just like he had always done, and left her to her tea.

Chapter 51

Palala

It had been years since Kebeck had ridden alone in the jungle. Usually he biked with a friend or with his son. With no one to distract him, he was able to get into the moment and see the details he usually missed. He had forgotten how beautiful it was. He saw every hue of green that the mind could conceive. There was an occasional dash of red or white or purple as little wildflowers poked through the maze of greens. Ancient trees towered over him, blocking out the sun. Just when his eyes had adjusted to the darkness, a blaze of light would blind him. The shafts of light cut through the canopy and spotlighted little sections of the lush forest.

It made him think of some of the Earth art he had viewed. He did not understand why Earth beings had to paint or make photographic reproductions of scenes like these. *Why did they not just enjoy nature where it lies?* He had examined Earth art and many of their paintings seemed to be a display of skills used in an attempt to accurately reproduce scenes like these. *Since much of Earth was polluted and covered over with buildings and roads, I should not blame the Earth beings for wanting to use their art to bring beauty inside their buildings. But, why paint? The Earth photography seemed to be an easier way to share the beauty of a location with others.*

He slowed his bicycle to a stop and examined the lively jungle scene before him. *It is good that I live amongst a people who have chosen to preserve and maintain our vegetation. I could not bear to live in a land of cement, metal, and plastic.*

Still, he had to admit to himself that he did find some of their paintings appealing, especially the ones that used exaggerated color and form. Painting was rare on Palala. Kebeck did appreciate the creative painting he saw on the inside walls of some public buildings, but its purpose was to amuse the eye and decorate the building, not to imitate nature. And photography was mostly used for practical purposes. Builders displayed examples of types of buildings they could build and doctors documented medical conditions. There had been some discussion about having Agara take a camera on the Earth visit to take photographs for the Earth museum, but it was decided that sections of Earth-Watching data taken from Earth TV monitors could be displayed much easier.

Kebeck had been so deep in thought that he almost missed a turn. He quickly jerked his bike around and soon found that he was approaching the city wall. The wall was only two hands tall. It was not intended to keep anyone out or anyone in. It was only there to mark the border between the jungle and the city, and in some places the jungle was still crawling over the wall and into the city. Dopala was the fourth or fifth largest city on the planet, and had a population of about 130,000 people. In recent years, Kebeck rarely visited the city. He knew it well because he had spent three years in university here. And later, he had lived in Dopala for twenty years with his first wife. His son Prigo had been born and raised in the city. Kebeck had never liked the smells of so many people living so close together. As he peddled between the tall three-story buildings, the scents of thousands of people overpowered his nose and almost made his head spin. Trucks passed him. Multi-passenger vehicles zoomed by. The sound of the music coming from each of the vehicles combined to make a painful cacophony when one was not used to it. Because compressed air engines were so quiet, every vehicle that drove in the city was required to play recorded music so bikers and pedestrians would be aware of them. It reminded Kebeck of why he liked living in the country. He treasured the sound of the wind in the trees.

A four-sided tower marked the center of the city; each side was painted a different color so that people could tell where they were in relation to the tower. Kebeck's first wife lived four blocks from the tower, on the red side; her name was Syron. Actually, her name was Syron Epa Lebar Vilspa Napar Badu Nilar Karbo. When a child is hatched on Palala, the child is referred to by the prefix "Ta" followed by the mother's name (Ta-Syron in this case) until he or she is twelve years old, at which point the child is allowed to choose a first name. Before a name is chosen, the child must complete a one-week course on the significance of names. The official name is made up of the child's chosen name, followed by his or her mother's first name, then the father's first name, followed by the first names of the maternal grandmother, the maternal great-grandmother, the maternal great-great-grandmother, and so on, until the child has eight names. But, unless a Palalan is signing a legal document, most go by their first three names. Kebeck had noticed that lately some children had chosen Earth names. He personally had met a David, a Sarah, and an Abraham.

As Kebeck pedaled past the town tower he spied a welcome sight: a small, one-story building with two colored triangles on top. One of the triangles was brown, signifying that this was a place in which one could dispose of body wastes and the other triangle was blue, the color of water, the basis of life, signifying that this building held food and water. Kebeck leaned his bike against the building and entered the door with the brown triangle. After relieving himself he went back outside and went to the other side of the building and through the doorway that had a blue triangle above it. Inside were four other people standing around, eating from the bowls on the shelves. The room had four water hoses coming out of the ceiling, two refrigeration units, shelves on the walls, and several slantboards. A tall grayish fellow caught his attention; he had on clothes. He wore a yellow sleeveless top and a piece of red fabric was draped around his lower body, much like the garment known on Earth as a skirt.

Kebeck rinsed his hands and drank some water before he turned to greet the fellow who was wearing clothes. "Greetings, we do not know each other but I wish to talk with you. Do you mind?"

The fellow showed his palms to Kebeck and said, "It would please me to meet you. I am in no hurry. Let us sit on the slantboards and eat as we talk."

They sat.

"If I may ask, who are you and where do you come from," inquired the clothed fellow.

"I am Kebeck Rofel Warnon from Sango. And you?"

"Sango is a research village, is it not?"

"Yes, it is." Kebeck bit into an orange fruit.

"Well, I live here in the city. I am Rolee Kerson Seebo and I work at a factory that makes the transport vehicles that move large goods. What kind of research do you do?"

"I study Earth ecology."

"Really? I am much enthralled with Earth." Rolee's neck started to change color and a big smile lit up his face. "I am so glad to meet you. You are an Earth expert. I have so many questions. For instance …."

Kebeck interrupted. "First, let me ask you a question. Why are you wearing that clothing?"

Rolee looked down at his skirt. "Oh, this. Well, I belong to a group and for fun we get together and wear Earth-like clothes and pursue Earth activities. And you, being an Earth expert, must wonder why I, a male, am wearing female Earth clothes."

"Not really, as many males in less developed areas of Earth wear skirts."

"They do?" Rolee looked down and touched the edge of his skirt. "I tried wearing pants and found them very uncomfortable. I find I like the feel of a skirt."

"You said you are involved in Earth activities. What types of activities do you do?"

"Last week we tried to play baseball. It did not go well. We could throw the ball, but hitting it with the bat was very difficult. Are you familiar with baseball?"

"Yes, I have watched it on Earth TV. My friend Yerf likes it, but it does not amuse me. It takes so long to do so little. I find soccer a little more entertaining, and basketball can be diverting. But with the Earth sports I do not care who wins because I do not know the individual beings. I know people on many sports teams here. Speaking of sports, I hope to see the waterball game scheduled for today. I know three people on the Topala team and I hear that the team is very good this year."

"Yes, they are fantastic. The city hired a new coach and it has really made a difference. I understand that on Earth, in some sports, players are paid to play. We should do that; I would contribute to a fund if we were to do that."

Kebeck took another bite and cocked his head to one side. "I have been thinking about this. I was discussing it with my friend and now that I have given it further thought, I do not feel it would be right to cheer someone for merely doing his job. Maybe it is adequate that we pay coaches."

"Enough about sports! I have other Earth questions I would like to ask you. Why did the Earth beings evolve to have fur on random parts of their bodies? What purpose does it serve? It is not sufficient to keep them warm. Furthermore, they decorate and color the fur on their heads and hide the rest under clothing. Why is this so?"

Kebeck stopped in mid bite and stared at the fruit in his hand. He put the fruit on the shelf, leaned back, clasped both sets of hands across his scaled belly, and gazed at the ceiling. Finally, he turned to Rolee and replied: "I have no idea. But then I have no idea why they only have two arms. On Earth there are creatures such as the octopus and the crab and insects that have multiple arms. Why then did the Earth beings evolve with just two? And their eyes, they are located in front, not allowing them to see anything at their sides. Their bodies are not of a practical design. But evolution results in many curious creatures, as we can see on their planet and on ours."

"Do you know why they choose to live in the cold parts of Earth and leave some of the warm areas underpopulated?"

"I know that because their bodies produce heat they are able to live in cold places, but I do not understand why they choose to live in areas where the water freezes. When I was in school, as an adventure, some of us used our spare credits to purchase insulated heated clothing and took a vehicle so far north that white flakes of moisture fell from the sky. It was quite beautiful, but most unpleasant. Also, fruits cannot grow in such cold areas, so we almost ran out of food. I do not understand why any being with a brain would choose to live in such a place." Kebeck sighed. "Sorry that I do not have better answers for you, but even after years of study, there is much about Earth beings that we do not understand."

"One more question. Do you know why they use so many artificial lights? In general, we go to bed when it gets dark and get up when the sky begins to glow with light. They seem to ignore the light and dark cycles of their planet."

Kebeck perked up. "This one I know, somewhat. Because the Earth tilts on its axis, the length of the light and dark periods varies during the year. They do not have the consistent twelve hours of darkness and twelve of light that we enjoy. So, there are long periods of darkness in some areas at some times, especially in the colder areas near the poles. Thus, they make use of artificial lights. Also, biologically speaking, they seem to need less sleep than we do."

"Interesting. Thank you." Rolee reached into a pocket of his skirt and brought out a communicator. "I see that it is almost time to meet my friends. Today, we are going to attempt Earth-style dancing. And, we are going to try to smoke. One of our group has gathered several harmless plants, dried the leaves, and rolled them as they roll cigars on Earth. We are going to light the ends of these and suck air through them. Of course we will have a physician and a plant biologist there to record the experiment. I must go now. I thank you for a most engrossing conversation and I hope to see you at the waterball game this afternoon." Kebeck watched as Rolee left; his skirt swished from side to side as he walked out the doorway.

After a brief rest on the slantboard, Kebeck was back on his way. He knew he was going the right way when he passed a building in which computers were both made and sold. He had once purchased a computer there. He then passed the school where his first wife worked as a counselor.

A block later he was at Syron's door. As usual, her door was half open. Syron had said she had adopted the custom of leaving her door half open so that her students would always feel welcome, yet still respect her privacy. Kebeck raised a hand to ring the bell beside the door but stopped before he touched the bell. He heard voices in the front room.

It was Syron talking to someone. "I have not seen Kebeck in weeks. Why would you think to find him here? We are friends and we share a grown child, but rarely do I see him. But now that you mention his name, I should communicate with him soon. Have you heard? Our son Prigo has opted to have a child. I am excited to see the child of my child. It is unfortunate that my mother did not live to see this; as you remember, a disease took her before she reached age 175. I wish it to be a female, but of course that is a decision for Prigo and his mate. I have not asked Kebeck what sex he desires it to be."

A voice interrupted. "I was just wondering if you had seen Kebeck." It was Jarrell's voice. Kebeck backed away from the door. It was fortunate that all the smells of so many people in the city made it almost impossible for Jarrell and Syron to detect Kebeck standing there. He grabbed his bike and peddled down the street. Listening to Syron chatter on reminded Kebeck of why he moved out as soon as their marriage contract had expired. Syron always said three times more than necessary; it had driven him crazy during their marriage.

Kebeck turned onto a small street, then turned again onto a bike lane that went between two industrial buildings. There he saw the park he was looking for. He had spent many happy hours in this park when his son Prigo was small. He propped his bike against a tree and lay on the grass by a small pond. He suspected that Syron's prattle would probably have sent Jarrell out the door by now.

Three very young children walked by. Kebeck thought them to be too young to be out without an adult. Then he noticed that each had a communicator securely strapped to their front. He had heard of this new custom of letting children roam wearing activated communicators; the parent, at home, was able to see and hear everything happening in front of the child. He thought that both of his children would have loved to be able to do so when they were five or six.

Seeing the communicators also reminded Kebeck that he had not heard from Namucal Dulmal. He took his communicator out of his pack and accessed the memory. Namucal had left a message.

"I recorded and sent you this because knowing the past of the Earth being Erwin Bercic seems to be very important to you." Namucal paused. "As I indicated I would, I continued my research on the Erwin being. Earth police use ridges on the skin of digits, fingerprints, to identify specific individuals. It seems that each digit has unique patterns. Realizing that I needed fingerprints from the Erwin being, I fine-tuned the definition on my computer and searched his offices and home for his fingerprints. I was able to take a print off of a glass he placed in front of a small TV in his kitchen. I am searching records of criminals, Earth beings who committed crimes and were caught. I will get back to you if I find a match." Kebeck could feel the muscles tighten in his neck as he thought about his Adeline and this Erwin being. He stretched all four arms in an attempt to defuse the tension.

A loud noise made him look over at the pond. An adult male had just dumped a basket of underwater balls in the pond. He then noticed the two teams of ten- to twelve- year-olds waiting for the signal to start the game. He had loved the game when he was a child. The balls were weighted so that they would float about five hands underwater. All sixteen balls were numbered. Each team of four players was supposed to retrieve eight balls. The numbers on the balls were added up and the team with the largest number won. The fun was trying to wrestle the bigger numbered balls away from the other team while underwater, because whoever held the ball when it got to the surface got it for his team. Most people liked to swim with their lower arms as they tried to capture the balls with their upper arms. Also, Kebeck had enjoyed the strategy involved. He and his friends had spent hours discussing whether it was better to work in pairs or to work as individuals. Some preferred to have individuals going for the balls, with a second person hovering underwater ready to help any team-mate who needed help. Another strategy was to have guards follow the better players on the other team. As the adult clapped his hands to start the game, Kebeck got up to leave. *Jarrell should be gone by now.*

Again, Kebeck approached Syron's half-open door. He stood by the bell and listened. He heard the voice of a student, then another student, then Syron's voice. They were creating a group fantasy story. When he had lived with Syron, one of his pleasures was to listen as she guided groups of students in the creation of fantasy stories. More than once, their stories were so good that they were animated and shown on computer TV for children. Kebeck was deciding whether to ring the bell when he heard a voice behind him.

"Father, what are you doing here? Should you not be at the launch site preparing for your trip to Earth?"

Kebeck turned to see his son Prigo coming toward him. "Prigo, how are you? How is the digit you injured?"

"It is healed. I had to spend two days in a medical hot room. Such a waste of time. Are you not going to Earth?"

"Yes, I still plan to fly to Earth, but that is not until tomorrow afternoon. It is nice to see you."

"Father, I got messages from Jarrell saying you were not going to Earth and that he is trying to find you. He is quite anxious to find you; he left four messages on my communicator. Is there a problem?"

"Yes and no," Kebeck answered. "Jarrell has a problem and I have a problem, but it is not the same problem."

The door to Syron's house was thrown open and Syron stepped into the doorway. "I thought I smelled you two, then I heard your voices." As she touched palms with Kebeck and then Prigo she said, "This is quite a surprise. Come in."

Kebeck shook his head. *It still amazes me that she can pick out our smells in this sea of people.*

Syron led the two into the front room. "Jarrell was just here looking for you, Kebeck."

"Yes, I know."

Syron gave him a strange look and then proceeded to introduce both Kebeck and Prigo to the four students who were sprawled on cushions in the front room.

"It would please me if you two will wait in the family room while we work another fifteen blips on our fantasy story. I have things to say to both of you."

Kebeck and Prigo stepped into the next room and closed the thick wood door. Prigo plucked a piece of fruit from a bowl on the shelf and flopped down on the sleeping platform in the middle of the room. "May I be of any help with the problem you mentioned?"

Kebeck sat beside him. "Not really. The only thing you can do for me is to not mention to Jarrell or to anyone that you have seen me."

Prigo jerked up to a sitting position. "You are hiding from Jarrell?"

"No, it is more like I am avoiding Jarrell. And I shall continue to dodge him until it is time for my flight to Earth. After I return, I will meet with him."

"Why do you avoid him now?"

Kebeck took a piece of fruit from the bowl. "It is a long story. A story that has no ending as of yet. When I return, I should know how it ends and it will be my pleasure to tell you the whole story."

"You leave me in suspense. Does mother know about this?"

"No. You are not to mention anything about Jarrell to your mother. She is a wonderful person, but she talks a lot and she talks to everyone. I want to see the waterball game this afternoon, spend the night here, and travel on toward the launch site tomorrow. Would you like to watch the waterball game with me?"

"I would enjoy that." Prigo jumped off the sleeping platform and opened the refrigeration unit.

The door to the front room opened and Syron breezed into the room. "My son with his head in the refrigeration unit, as usual. Welcome home, Prigo. I cut the session short. The sudden presence of both of you distracted me. I am happy to see you both, but I am curious to know what brings you two here on this particular day?"

Kebeck stood up and turned toward Syron. "The final waterball game is this afternoon. Would you like to see it with us?"

Syron screwed up her face and tilted her hear to one side. "You know I do not enjoy watching sports."

"But I do, especially waterball."

"You came into the city just to see a waterball game?"

Kebeck's neck was turning red. "I do want to see the game."

Prigo, fruits in three of his hands, stepped between Kebeck and his mother. "I came to discuss my marriage contract party with you. Remember, you asked that I come by some time so we can plan it?"

"I would have liked some notice, before you just show up at my door. I am anxious to plan the first marriage contract party of my only son, and it will be a pleasure to do it today. But as for you, Kebeck." She stepped around Prigo and faced Kebeck. "Why are you red? You did not come here just to see a game."

"I decided to stop by on my way to the launch site. Our son has chosen to have a child. Is it not an occasion for a visit?"

"Kebeck, your neck glows like a ripe pele fruit. You do not enjoy my company; I understand and accept that. We were different people fifty years ago. I have good memories of raising Prigo with you. And here you are at my door today, the same day that Jarrell comes here looking for you. What is the real reason for your presence?"

Kebeck looks at Prigo. "Prigo, you get all of your brains from your mother, but you would never learn diplomacy from her."

Syron stepped a bit closer to Kebeck. "Well?"

Kebeck hopped up on the sleeping platform. "I came here to avoid Jarrell. I did not think he would seek me at the house of a wife that I left almost thirty years ago. I also thought it would be nice to see you since we are to have a grandchild, and I do want to see the waterball game."

"Why are you hiding from Jarrell? He is an old friend and a work mate, is he not?"

"First, I am not hiding; I am just avoiding him for a couple of days. We differ on an issue and I prefer to handle the issue after I return from Earth. So, may I stay the night here?"

"Of course you are always welcome on my sleeping platform, but I suggest you forgo the waterball game if you do not want Jarrell to know you are in the city."

"Brown water! You are right. See, my son, what a smart one your mother is, and much more experienced than I at dodging people she does not wish to encounter. Jarrell or someone he has questioned about me might be there. But I really did want to see that game."

"If you do not want to be found by Jarrell you should probably not go anywhere in the city," Prigo advised.

Kebeck stood up and waved his upper hands in frustration. "I am not going to hide in the house all afternoon. This is not what I planned. I thought I could have a nice afternoon in the city; I am not skilled at deception and evasion. You are both right. So I will change my plan. If you do not mind, Syron, I will visit with you and Prigo for a few blips more, then I will be on my way to a more secluded place for the night."

"I would enjoy a chance to plan the marriage contract party with the two of you," Syron smiled at her son. Then she glared at her ex-husband: "But first I want to know more about this situation with Jarrell."

Kebeck sighed, pulled a slantboard up to face her and said, "Well, I know both of you will respect my wish that you speak to no one of this." He paused. "Syron, please tell me that you will keep silent about this until I give you leave to speak of it."

She shook her head and huffed. "I will say nothing."

"Thank you. It is very complicated, but let me begin ...."

Chapter 52

Earth

After working for two hours, Adeline decided she needed a break. She really wasn't getting much done. Her mind kept wandering back to the TV movie that had sent her flying out her door. *What an appropriate name: Cape Fear. It sure scared me, alright. But something caused the TV to keep replaying that scene. That wasn't just some mechanical glitch. Somebody did something to my TV. Why is someone trying to frighten me?* She looked around the guest room that the Staffords had put her in. The old-fashioned striped wallpaper was topped off by framed prints of the English countryside. *This room is not my world. I want my life back.* Her computer chimed to let her know she had a new message; it was from Nina.

Without thinking, she picked up the phone and dialed Nina's number at her law office. "Hi, what are you doing?"

"I'm digging through some old cases; I need a precedent. But you don't care about that. What's up?" Nina asked.

"I just needed to talk to a friendly voice. I had a scare yesterday and, well … have you got a couple minutes?"

"Sure."

Adeline told her about the incident with her TV.

"Tell me again. What were the exact words being repeated?"

"I keep feeling that there's some animal out there, stalking us," and, "I think he wants to hurt us in the worst way."

"Okay, that's pretty weird and creepy. This has got to be a Halloween trick. Somebody has a nasty sense of humor. I'd be spooked by that too," Nina declared. "So why didn't you come stay at my place. Why are you staying with the Staffords?"

Can't tell her the truth flashed through Adeline's mind. "Well, I had just been talking to Mr. Stafford, and they are so lonesome, and I wanted to check on some details on a story here in St. Catharines. So, here I am!"

"Well, you're welcome to stay at my place anytime. And, you can bring the cat. I don't know how we can find out who played such a nasty trick on you. I'll talk to our tech guy. Oh, I'm sorry. My secretary is waving at me. I've got to go. We'll talk later, ok? Take care."

Adeline put the phone on the desk and looked up at a picture of a young Mr. and Mrs. Stafford standing in front of St. Patrick's Cathedral in London. They were holding hands like a young couple in love. *I just want my Jim. I want to tell him about this, but I don't want to worry him. Anyway, it sounds so silly. Maybe it was just a trick. If Carol were alive, I'd blame it on her. It was her style, but she would have rang the phone five minutes after the trick to brag about it. I won't tell Jim just yet. That cop, Detective Hawes, said to call him if anything unusual happened. Part of me says to call him but it sounds goofy when I say it out loud. "Yeah, ha ha, my TV went crazy and repeated threatening lines from a movie for half an hour." I have no proof that it even happened. Hawes would just put me down as a nut case. I can't call him; it might just be a Halloween trick. I feel so fucking alone. And I'm scared. Mr. Stafford is the only person taking this seriously. I hope he can find an explanation for it; he's the expert.* Her computer chimed again; another message. This one was from Jim.

227

Chapter 53

Palala

Kebeck was getting tired. He was doing more pedaling than he had planned, but he wanted to be at the village of Mendo by dark. He had chosen this out-of-the-way route so that he would avoid Jarrell and he was anxious to stop in Mendo for the night and talk with Jarrell's son, Tabat. He had heard from Syron that Jarrell had disowned his son, a rare occurrence in Palala. *What could possibly make a man cut off communication with his child?* He had not seen Tabat in many years. When they were young, Tabat and Prigo had been good friends, and Tabat had spent much time in Kebeck's house.

A subtle clicking sound caught Kebeck's attention. It took him a moment to realize that it was the personal communicator in his backpack making the sound. He rarely activated the audio-alarm function of the device so he had forgotten what it sounded like. He stopped and took it out of his pack. He was surprised and delighted to see a recorded message with Namucal's face on the little screen.

"It is I, the Earth-like detective, still on the case. I found something very interesting. The digit print from the Erwin being's drinking vessel matches that of an Earth being who tortured and killed two older beings in an area known as British Columbia, almost forty years ago. At that time, he was jailed for ten years. When he was released from prison, he disappeared from all records. The criminal's name was Newt Clark. There are no other files on him. I searched tax records, driving licenses, credit cards, and many other places for his name, and I searched various photo-identification records for his face. Nothing. But because Earth beings have unique digit impressions, I have concluded that the Erwin being is indeed Newt Clark. He must have changed both his face and his name. I have included in this message a copy of the Erwin being's fingerprint and the criminal record and fingerprints of Newt Clark."

On the little video screen, Namucal took a breath and scowled. "Your mystery is solved. I advise that you take satisfaction from the knowledge you have gained and find another Earth being to study. From my studies of Earth crime, the Adeline being will probably soon be dead anyway. I thank you for the thrill of solving this Earth TV-like murder mystery. If you do chose to continue watching this Adeline, I would appreciate a copy of the killing if you happen to view it. I close, wishing you clear water."

Kebeck was ecstatic. He put the communicator back in his pack and pedaled quickly down the road, curving his bike back and forth like a twenty-year-old. After a while he slowed down and started driving more carefully. Thoughts rushed through his mind about how he might use the new information to save Adeline. *If I communicate this information to the police, I will really be breaking the communication rule and put the continuation of Earth-Watching in jeopardy. But I do not want Adeline to die.* From what Erwin said, he planned to kill Adeline on Halloween night. Kebeck decided that he would have to think more on this as he journeyed toward the launch site.

It was growing late and the sun now cut through the bushes at an angle. A bopper hopped across the road in front of him and he abruptly stopped to avoid hitting it. The spiny little animals were common in the jungle; their erratic hopping pattern, green and gray coloring, and tough hide allowed them to survive in a forest stocked with bigger carnivorous animals. He now noticed the loveliness of the rampant foliage that was highlighted by the afternoon angle of the light. Lacy leaves almost as big as a bike wheel cast unique shadows on the road. He stood and took in their beauty, then continued on toward his rest stop for the night.

He reached the little village just at twilight. He only had to ask one person in order to find directions to Tabat's house. As he approached the dwelling, a familiar voice called out, "I smell someone I have not smelled in years. Could that be Kebeck, Prigo's father?" Tabat's happy face appeared in the doorway just as Kebeck got to the door. Both of them extended all four hands and touched palms, standing silent for a few moments. Then Tabat backed up, gestured for Kebeck to enter and said, "God has blessed me with a surprise visit from an old friend. God is good."

Kebeck was shocked. He had never heard a person say anything like this. He had heard these types of things on Earth TV but never had the words been uttered by a Palalan. Even though he was trying to hide his astonishment, he was sure his neck had reddened. "You look well," was all he could manage to say.

"Come in and recline. I see by your bike out there that you traveled by foot power; you must be tired," Tabat grinned. "I see also by your color that you are taken aback by my gratitude towards God. Relax. I am not the type of Christian that kills people. Those are fanatics, or rednecks, and the only red neck here is you," Tabat chuckled. "Obviously, my father did not tell you that I had converted to Christianity."

As Kebeck stepped into the house a smile crossed his face. Now he knew why Jarrell was so opposed to Earth-Watching. "No, he did not."

"He is quite ashamed of me, but I love him and God loves him. Truly, it is wonderful to see you. I will, of course, share my food and sleeping platform with you. There is a lake one thousand steps behind this house if you would like to rinse the dirt off." Tabat was charged with excitement. "We have much to talk about, not only as friends, but I am thrilled to talk to one of our foremost Earth experts. I have many questions. Also, I have several friends here who I am sure would also like to ask you questions about Earth. If you are not too tired, may I invite them over later?"

"I would be pleased to meet them after I jump in that lake and have a bite."

An hour later, as a cleaner, fatter Kebeck lay down on the sleeping platform, four of Tabat's friends appeared at the door. Both the two males and the two females were close to Tabat's age; they were mature, but still young. Kebeck could feel excitement in the air; he had not realized that his visit would cause such a commotion. The group gathered around Kebeck and Tabat introduced each of them: Luca, Kimva, Wesra, and Hoden.

"We all Earth-Watch, some more than others," Tabat glanced at the female Luca standing beside him. "And there are many behaviors we do not understand. I have noticed that in North America, many of the older Earth beings spend much time growing and trimming plants surrounding their houses. It seems a futile task to water and then cut the same plants over and over. Why do they do this?"

Before Kebeck could say anything, Kimva interjected, "Yes, why? They see on their TVs that many beings on their planet starve to death. Why do they not plant food instead of wasting hours on this vegetation they refer to as lawns?" They all stared at Kebeck.

"The grass known as lawns is a decoration they treasure …."

The tall male, Wesra, interrupted: "Why do they spend so much time and effort on decoration? They decorate their bodies and their buildings. What is the purpose?"

"Well, I do know that the body decorations are a part of their sex practices. And the sex customs are very complicated and vary in different regions. The decorating and the absurd size of some of their houses seem to be related to status."

"What is status?" asked Wesra.

"Status is a rating of one's power," Kebeck replied. "In North America they display their status with objects such as cars and houses. Bigger, more elaborate houses and automobiles indicate more status. But in some less developed parts of Africa, status is determined by how many cattle one owns. The symbols of status vary on different parts of the planet, but it is usually related to work credits. They call it money."

"Fascinating," said Wesra.

"I would like you to explain their wars," asked Hoden. "I watch and see beings working many hours to buy homes and possessions. Then I see a war happen and the homes and possessions are blown up by bombs. Many of the beings are killed; there is much sorrow. How can their disagreements become so big that this happens? Why do they not work out their differences with words and logic?"

Kebeck shook his head. "I also find their wars disturbing. I do not understand why they seem to prefer fighting more than negotiating. I am not an expert in the field of Earth politics, my specialty is ecology. But from my observations, these wars often happen in areas where there is much religion and little science education."

"But are wars not also fought when one group wants what another group has?" asked Hoden.

"Yes, they do not have our sense of planet. They see themselves as parts of groups that compete for food and objects. They do not view all the beings of Earth as being equally deserving of food, water, and respect."

"I wonder if there is something in their genetic code that makes them so destructive," Hoden speculated.

"Kebeck, we need you to settle a much debated question for us. Is it physically possible for Earth beings to insert their heads into their own posteriors?" asked Kimva. "I have often heard them claim that some Earth being or another 'had his head up his ass' but I have yet to witness any such insertion. "I would think it is not something that their anatomy would allow."

"But," added Wesra, "if it is not possible, then why would so many of them say such things? Just because we have not seen it does not mean that they do not do it. After all, their young come out of the bottom of their bodies. So those areas do stretch."

Both Wesra and Kimva waited for Kebeck's answer.

"I must agree with Kimva. I think that their body waste opening is insufficient in size to allow them to place a head there. And, I do not think they have enough flexibility to bend in that way. I also have heard that same phrase, but I think it is said to denigrate others. It seems to indicate that the being is not considering the welfare of others and is only concerned with his or her own self. But it is vague and can be interpreted in different ways. I have found that in the Earth's English language, there are quite a few things said that we should not take literally."

Kimva beamed at Wesra. "I win."

Luca spoke up: "I have watched two families who live in the same town in the United States area. One family is what they call working poor. The female works serving food in a restaurant. The male works for a company that puts tops on houses, so-called roofs. They make just enough money to feed their children and pay their bills. They have no possibility of doing anything except working long hours all of their lives. "The other family is what the Earth beings call well-off. The male is a doctor of animals and the female works as an administrator for a big company. These beings live like little gods. They fly away on vacations whenever they wish. They use earned credits to purchase objects whenever they please. They hire other beings to clean and maintain their possessions. They have accumulated so many work credits that they will soon be able to stop working and pay others to do everything for them." She paused. "The Earth beings are violent. We see this in their news. And they only live a short time. So my question is this: Why does the poor couple that I watch not rebel and take the food and possessions from the little gods? How do they live with such unfairness?"

"Some poor do rebel by taking the possessions of others," answered Kebeck. "Those beings are considered to be criminals because that is counter to the laws of all the nations on Earth. These persons are put in jails. I think that North America has many beings in jails because they have many poor and many little gods. I read on their Internet that in the United States, one in every 136 beings resides in jail."

"That number cannot be correct," Tabat said.

"It was written on an official government Internet site," Kebeck replied.

"That is both amazing and terrible." Wesra shook his head in disbelief. "I watched an Earth TV documentary on prisons. I thought only a few incorrigible beings were put in those brutal places."

"Let us not just dwell on the negative aspects of the planet," Tabat interjected. "They have introduced us to some wonderful things. I am excited by winged flight. I plan to go to the hang-gliding center at Lake Lecit next week and experience flying. Kebeck, did Prigo not tell you that he plans to go with me?"

"No, he probably wished to shelter me from worry. He knows I would not feel comfortable with the idea of having my son leaping off a mountain wearing a fabric and plastic contraption copied from a design found on the Earth Internet," Kebeck replied.

"Speaking of things that fly, you might see a live bird on your Earth visit. How exciting! Now that I have seen them while Earth-Watching, I wish that our planet's evolution had included animals that can fly," Hoden said.

"No you do not," Luca chimed in. "All animals release dung. I would not want to live in a place where a thing flying over my head might discharge dung any time. Yuck!"

"I probably will not see a bird, but I might see some flying insects. Our brief visit to Earth will be at night and for some reason birds fly very little at night; they hide in trees when it gets dark. I will have to take precautions not to be bitten by the flying insects; we know some of them bite and we are not sure what it could do to my body."

"I am most impressed! I did not realize that the insects could be dangerous. You are going to be doing something dangerous and amazing," Kimva exclaimed.

"Yes," Tabat added, "and he should get some sleep so he can be alert for the experience. So, I ask you all to leave now." Tabat shooed them toward the door.

Luca extended all four palms toward Kebeck. "We thank you for talking with us and invite you to stop by after your Earth visit."

"I will," Kebeck stated. "You are all a pleasure to talk to."

After all good-byes were said, Kebeck and Tabat were alone in the house. As they prepared to go to sleep Kebeck turned to Tabat and asked, "Tell me, do you really give credence to this deity theory, with a god and a heaven?"

Tabat nodded. "Yes, I am sure it makes no sense to you. I experienced what they call a leap of faith and now truly believe there is a god and I will join him in heaven when I die. It is easier to live when I know that death is not terminal. I understand that it is a leap of faith and could possibly be an illusion, but living with a belief that could be either delusion or truth is more pleasant than facing a finite end of life."

"This leap of faith ... what are you leaping over?" Kebeck asked.

Tabat chuckled. "It refers to the fact that we Christians must leap over a big chasm of science and reality in order to trust that our god is there for us."

"That would be difficult. In fact, it would be impossible for me to do so; I could not accept a concept that is counter to my reality. But, as long as no one is harmed, I see no problem with you having the right to believe in a deity. And when your three hundred years on Palala are over, only you will know if you go to heaven or into oblivion."

"I thank you for your understanding," Tabat paused and smiled. "I have a request." He paused again. "When you return from the Earth visit, would you talk to my father and try to get him to understand? He is quite upset."

"Yes, he is. You have turned his world upside down and now he is trying to turn my world upside down. I will speak with him, but I do not think it will do much good."

When Kebeck laid his head down to sleep that night, thoughts of Adeline and Erwin, Tabat's views about religion, and the flight to Earth zipped around in his head. Just when he had decided that sleep would be impossible, his tired body overruled his mind and knocked him out.

When Kebeck awoke the next morning, Tabat was rushing in from a morning swim. "You look like a person in a hurry," Kebeck observed.

"Did I not mention it last night? There is to be a last-day ceremony today. I have much to do this morning; I am responsible for coordinating everything for Ello's last-day party."

"I could help," Kebeck suggested. "I do not have to leave yet."

"That would be much appreciated. I was going to ask if you would go over the eulogy I have prepared and suggest improvements. Tabat took some paper off the shelf and handed it to Kebeck.

Kebeck leaned back against the pillows and read through it as Tabat stood staring at him.

We are sad that Ello is going to die and will no longer be here with us. But he is one of the fortunate ones … he was born. He was born to be a unique individual, unlike any that came before him or that will come after him. He is fortunate that generations of genes combined in such a way to make this man; he was the result of thousands of years of mating and chance. There are countless combinations of genes that will never be. We will never meet those people ... they did not happen. But Ello did. He was intelligent, creative, and interesting. And we are glad to have had to the opportunity to share time on this planet with him. Soon he will no longer be. But he and everyone who knew him delight in the fact that ... he was.

Kebeck finished reading the eulogy and smiled up at him. "Most excellent. I could not improve it."

"Thank you. I am pleased. Now I must get this ceremony organized."

Kebeck followed Tabat to the village recreation hall and helped him set up tables outside and put food out on the tables. "Tell me about your friend. Why does he choose this day to die?"

"Ello is two hundred and eighty-six years old. His aging body has caused him pain for the last twenty or thirty years. Not long ago he decided that his pain was greater than his pleasure and he selected this day as the time to take the little red pill and suffer no more. He was planning to have a quiet last-day, with friends just dropping by, but I talked him into a traditional last-day party. It was much work to arrange the games, music, food, and the decorations, but I know he will enjoy it. He is, like me, an Earth-Watcher. Ello especially enjoys their music. We will have the usual drums and horns for dancing today, but he has requested as his pre-pill music the sounds of an Earth being named Ella Fitzgerald. And his after-pill music will be a very dramatic instrumental called 'Bolero.' Ello was a famous speed swimmer when he was younger. Have you ever heard of Ello Abat?"

"No, I do not remember that name."

"Well, that is the man we honor and say good-by to today." Tabat looked up at the sky and said, "Thank you God for not letting it rain."

Kebeck was surprised at what he had just heard; he stopped what he was doing and said, "Tabat, do you really think that there is a powerful being that controls the weather and will adjust it just for one person?"

"I hope so. I like the idea of having an intimate connection to the universe. It feels so much better than merely being a leaf in a stream."

"So what happens if another deity believer on the other side of the village is praying for rain to water their plants?" Kebeck asked.

Tabat smiled. "I guess God will have to make a judgment call."

Kebeck chuckled. It was good to see that Tabat had not lost his sense of humor. He looked at the sky and realized that the morning was passing. "I have enjoyed your company very much, but now I must go. Please continue with your preparations; it is a good thing you do for Ello. I am proud of you, Tabat." Kebeck extended his palms and Tabat touched them with his own.

As Kebeck turned to go, thoughts of his Adeline nagged at him. "Tabat, is there a path of meditation near here? An important decision hangs over my head. I need to sit and think for a few blips."

Chapter 54

Earth

Lunch had been another unhealthy British meal. Adeline loved cheddar cheese and mango chutney on white bread, but she felt guilty eating it. She found an apple in their fridge and took it with her just to have something nutritious to munch on. As she walked down the hall toward the guest bedroom she passed the door to Carol's old room. She paused, looked down the hall to see if the coast was clear and quickly opened the door and entered the room. She stood facing the door she had closed behind her. *What am I doing?* She turned and looked around the familiar room. Carol's parents had left it just as it was the day Carol went off to university. Carol said that every time she came home and slept in that room she felt like she might wake up to find that she was still a teenager. Adeline went over to the bulletin board on the wall by Carol's desk. There were photos of Carol with her basketball team mates, faded newspaper photos of Carol posing by trophies and another showing Carol making a shot. Up in the corner of the bulletin board there was a picture of Adeline in her cheerleader uniform; she was all mouth and curly hair. She touched the photos and smiled. Her eyes moved to the movie poster beside the bulletin board. She and Carol both were quite definite in believing that Sean Connery was the only actor who could or should play James Bond. She sat down on the bed and ran her hand over the purple print bedspread that Carol had bought when they were in the eighth grade. Mrs. Stafford had thought the bedspread was hideous and was never shy about mentioning that fact. But, here it was, still on the bed because Carol had loved it. On the dresser there was a collection of cut glass perfume bottles that Carol had bought, one by one, as they went through junior high and high school. Carol had had mixed feelings about the fact that her parents had kept her room like a time capsule. Many times she had told her Mom to just clear it all out and give away or throw away everything in the room. Her mother would say, "No, but you can take the stuff with you if you want. When I go in that room, it feels like my little girl is still living with us." Adeline shook her head. *I should get back to the real world. Time has stopped in this room. Now that Carol is gone, I wonder if her mother will ever do anything with this room?* Adeline quietly snuck out of the room and went to the guest room. As she sat down at the desk, her cell phone rang.

"Adeline Morgan. Can I ... Oh, it's you Nina. What's up?"

"Well, first, do you know where your wedding dress is?"

Adeline searched her mind. "At my house?"

"Wrong, you left it in my car; I went to put groceries in the trunk, and there it was."

"I'm sorry; I'm such a bubble-head lately. I've had a few weird things happening around me and I guess I'm spooked."

"Not to worry, your guardian angel is watching over you."

"I wish I had a guardian angel." Adeline's eyes wandered over to the screen saver on her computer; it showed an idyllic beach scene with a ray of sunlight beaming through the clouds.

"Hey, bubble-head, what I'm trying to tell you is that I've finally decided on a costume. I'm going to be a guardian angel."

"Ok, I'm game; so what does a guardian angel wear?"

"This guardian angel will be wearing a fabulous fluffy pink dress with big white feathered wings, with cartridge belts crossed on her chest, and carrying a machine gun."

The image made Adeline laugh.

"Are you really going to be a witch for Halloween? That's just so common. I expect something fabulous from you, like that backward-man thing you did last year. You getting old and lazy?" Nina teased.

"You'll love the witch I've cooked up. So shut up about it and tell me why you're calling."

"I just wanted to check on the time. I hate standing around in a bar, in a costume, all alone."

"I'll leave the house exactly at nine-forty; so, with traffic, I'll get there just before ten. Will you phone everyone else? I've got a deadline staring at me. Ok?"

Nina agreed to call them and let Adeline get on with her work. Before Adeline could get a sentence written, Mr. Stafford tapped at the door.

"Sorry to disturb you, luv, but I thought you'd like to hear what I've found out."

Adeline turned in her chair to face him. "Of course, come in."

Mr. Stafford came in and sat on the corner of the bed. "Well, I called some people I know, old work colleagues, and your fiancé is all right; he's a bit of a straight arrow. I had done a preliminary search on him when you became engaged, just to see if he was good enough for you, luv. It's too bad about his father, but that's no reflection on Jim. But now that I've done a total work-up on Jim, I see he's a good lad and I'll be proud to be dancin' at your wedding. Now about …."

Adeline moved forward in her chair, a look of disbelief on her face. "I can't believe you checked up on Jim when we became engaged!"

"Well, I only want the best for you, luv."

"Did you check up on any of my other boyfriends?"

"Just that Andy fellow you dated for over a year. Did you know he had sold a little marijuana in high school? And … as your relationship neared the end he had another girl on the side."

"What! That bastard! And I felt guilty breaking up."

"That's history, luv. Forget it. Now about your television incident. My sources told me that it's possible for someone to send a command to a television to behave as yours did. They said they don't know exactly how to do this but they're sure that someone with a sophisticated knowledge of electronics could do it." He shifted his position on the corner of the bed and scrutinized her. "Have you pissed off a computer or electronics genius?"

"No, I don't think so." She glanced at the ceiling and reflected for a moment. "I don't think I even know any computer or electronics geeks. I tend to associate more with artsy types."

"Who fixes your computer?"

"Some guy the company hires. I just leave it at the front desk with a note and he picks it up, fixes it, and leaves it with the receptionist. I've never really met him. Just talked to him on the phone," Adeline replied.

"Then I've got nothing, luv. But not to worry, I'm on the case and you're safe here."

"Mr. Stafford, I'm grateful for what you're doing, but I'm going home tomorrow. I've got to get back to a normal life. I can't let a weird TV run my life." She grinned. "And tomorrow is Halloween!"

"Of course," he grimaced. "You're going out, aren't you? You girls always made such a fuss over Halloween; I never understood it. Just do me this favor, luv, put your cell phone in your pocket. Then, if I learn anything, I can contact you. And be careful."

Adeline got up, went over, and planted a kiss on top of his head. "I'll be careful."

Chapter 55

Palala

Shortly after Kebeck left the village he saw a path marked with stones that indicated that it was a path of meditation. He hid his bike under some bushes beside the path. Thievery was extremely rare, but he thought it best not to tempt any mischievous youth who might come by and borrow the bike. As he strolled down the path, Kebeck could not help but notice the beauty of the forest as blowing trees made bits of light bounce around on the big shiny leaves of the undergrowth. The path ended by a small stream that fought its way through a maze of boulders. Kebeck reclined on the grass and cleared his mind of all but the problem of Adeline. Then he attempted to work through the problem logically, as he had been taught in school.

I must get the information about the Erwin being's history to someone on Earth who can stop him from killing my Adeline. If I phone or email the police it will be detected, I will be removed from the committee, and probably all Earth-Watching will cease. Is my desire to Earth-Watch more important than Adeline's life? Is Earth-Watching good for my people? And what about me? If I am detected communicating with an Earth being, I will be disgraced for the irresponsible act of breaking a contract. I will have to live like Karna. My children and friends will still love me but they will be saddened by my disrepute. I will live in ignominy. I will be cut off from the community and my work. But I love my Adeline.

Logical problem solving was not working for him this time. His mind was dashing around instead of approaching the problem analytically. Kebeck was startled by a sound. The bushes moved on the other side of the stream. He listened and heard the thumping of a creature hopping through the undergrowth. The sound reminded him of the bass rhythm of certain Earth music. He liked much of the Earth music. The Earth beings had developed some unique instruments and the sounds they call singing interested him. It had never occurred to anyone on Palala to use their voice for music; music was always made on instruments.

Yes, it is good for us! Earth-Watching has introduced us to many new ways of thinking, different ways of doing things. We need to be exposed to these new and different things so that life does not become stale and routine. We can choose whether to try some of these new things or just be amused or disgusted by them. But it is important that we are free to view what we please.

And I do not want my Adeline to die, at least not yet. Her life span is only twenty-five to thirty thousand days. I do so want to watch her live through it all. I want to see the wedding and the children. I want to see her as a mother. Will she write the books she hopes to write? How will she adjust to becoming old? I want to see it all.

Kebeck stood up. He had reached a decision. He looked at the shiny rocks, the clear water, and the variegated tangle of lush bushes and said to it, "I will go to Earth and if I can think of a way to save her that cannot be detected from here, I will do so. But this Earth-Watching is a very good thing for my people and ultimately more important than any one Earth being." With a determined stride he started down the path toward his bike.

When he was almost back to the head of the path a thought occurred to him. He had gone many hours without viewing Adeline. He took his portable communicator out of his pack and set it to connect with his home computer. He then quickly reviewed the scenes of Adeline at the Stafford house.

As he listened to the conversations between Adeline and Mr. Stafford he began to see Carol's father in a new light. *Maybe he can help my Adeline.*

Kebeck clicked a few keys on his communicator and the face of Namucal appeared on the tiny screen. Namucal greeted him hurriedly and asked, "Have you a time and place for the killing yet? Some of my friends and I would be most pleased to see it as it happens."

Kebeck was disgusted with Namucal's fascination with violence but decided that this was not a good time to voice his feelings. "No, I do not know that yet, but it would be helpful if you would check out another Earth being for me." He gave Namucal all the information he had on Mr. Stafford.

"This Stafford being sounds very interesting. I will get on it immediately. He could be an international spy or a contract assassin, like in the Earth movies. This excites me. I will contact you as soon as I find anything on him." Namucal's face disappeared from the screen.

Kebeck gathered up his bicycle and pedaled down the road toward the launch site. After two hours he started to pass people on the road and saw houses tucked into the jungle along the lane. He could feel warmth in his neck as he thought about what was to happen on this day. This trip to Earth had been planned over a year ago, but now that the day was here he could not help but be excited. As he rode into the small town that surrounded the launch site, a wide smile stretched across his face. He was so distracted by his thoughts that he was almost hit by a supply vehicle. The compressed-air engine of the transport was so quiet that it was only two arm lengths away when he noticed it and quickly dodged to one side. He got off the bike and stood for a moment trying to calm down. The driver must have forgotten to turn on his music when he drove into town. Just as he was getting back on his bike, his communicator made a sound. He pulled the bike off the road and activated the communicator.

"Greetings, I see that this is the day of an Earth flight and remembered that you are one of the two researchers embarking on this trip. You are a fortunate person; I would like to be with you," said Namucal. "But that is not why I am interfacing with you at this moment. I have already found information on the Frank Stafford being. Most interesting. I thought you would like to hear this before you go. Frank Stafford went to the University of Toronto and received a political science degree. He then spent four years in the Canadian army. After he left the army, he was on the Canadian government payroll for thirty-seven Earth years; his title was military consultant. During that same time, this Frank Stafford was listed in the tax records as working for the Royal Canadian Insurance Company. His Canadian government salary was paid to the Insurance Company, who then paid him. Also, during those years, he went on many business trips to countries all over Earth." Namucal paused and took a breath. "I think, from my study of Earth movies, that the insurance job was what they call a 'cover' for his secret job as a government spy or assassin." Namucal beamed.

"I thank you. Your research confirms my thoughts. I must go now. I need to be on time for my flight to Earth. Again, please accept my appreciation." Kebeck cut off the communicator. He did not want to give Namucal the opportunity to ask, once more, about the imminent death of his Adeline.

Kebeck looked both ways down the road; then he got on his bike and pedaled in the direction of the launch site.

Chapter 56

Earth

Sam was prancing and dancing as Erwin entered the room; the dog was ready for his walk. Erwin squatted down to Sam's level and let him nuzzle and lick his face. "What big wet kisses. You're my happy puppy. Wanna go for a ride with daddy?" Erwin gave Sam's ears a good rub, stood up, and went into his office. Sam followed. Erwin went over to the built-in bookcase that covered one wall, took out five books, and laid them on his desk. He then reached into the space where the books had been and pulled out a black metal box. It was about the size of a fist and looked like a little audio-tape player. Erwin went to the kitchen, with Sam following of course, and took three plastic grocery bags out of a container on the counter. He put the black box in one of the bags and stuffed the other two in his jacket pocket. He pocketed a handful of dog treats and then grabbed a leash from the hanger on the wall and leaned down to hook it onto Sam's collar. Sam stood up on his hind legs, looking like he was auditioning for Riverdance. "Sam, cool it! Settle down." It took a few tries before Erwin was able to get the leash attached. With the bag holding the black box in one hand and Sam's lead in the other hand, Erwin headed out the door.

Erwin pulled the car over to the curb in a middle-class neighborhood of thirty-year-old bungalows and split-levels. Sam started leaping around the back seat as soon as the car engine was turned off. As he whined and yelped to get out, Erwin took the black metal box out of the bag and clicked a switch on it. He put the box back in the plastic bag. Within seconds he was walking down the sidewalk with the bag in one hand and Sam's lead in the other. He walked two blocks then paused on a corner to lean down to pet Sam. From the corner he could see Adeline's house, about six homes down on the other side of the street. He pretended to pick up some dog poop as he listened to the slight humming sound coming from the box inside the bag. The sound stopped and Erwin turned and started back to his car. He now had what he needed from Adeline's computer. He was pretty sure that reading her email would tell him what he wanted to know.

Chapter 57

Palala

This was Kebeck's third trip in a space transport but it was the first for Agara. When Kebeck arrived at the launch site he found Agara pacing back and forth in front of the small interstellar vessel that was to take them to Earth; he looked worried and scared. Laniff was sitting on the ground beside him; he just looked irritated.

Agara looked up as Kebeck approached him and a big smile spread across his face. "You are here! I was so worried that I would have to go without you. Laniff got up and greeted Kebeck with his palms up. Agara ran up to Kebeck, "Samot said you would stay here and attend a hearing this afternoon. He sent Laniff to take your place. What happened? You are coming with me, are you not?"

"I am going to Earth, if Laniff does not mind. We can have the hearing another day, after we return. It will be very interesting." Kebeck smiled at Laniff.

"You go," Laniff motioned toward the transport. "As you all know, I went last year and I did not enjoy the experience. Samot thought it best to land in the United States region of Florida because it would be warm. That was a big mistake. We landed out in the bush by a river and while we were dressing to exit the vessel a very large alligator came out of the river and decided to lie in front of our door. The creature had many large teeth. Much time passed and those costumes were most uncomfortable. Then two dogs came and barked at the creature. It went back to the river. One of the dogs urinated on the vessel. Such a smell I will never forget. After the dogs went away we got out and we only had time to visit four houses. But we were so frightened by the alligator and the dogs that we could not enjoy the experience. You have all heard this story but sitting here by this vessel brings it back to me. No, I do not want to go. Enjoy the trip, Kebeck." Laniff turned and started toward town.

Kebeck smiled at Agara. "It is time to go. Have the engineers programmed the transport for the trip?"

"Yes, everything is done. You just missed Sheme and the other engineer. They are in that building doing something technical." He pointed to a building fifty steps away. "They said I am to push the red button to start the trip. After we land, we push the green button to activate the holographic illusion camouflage. Then we are to put on the costumes and exit the vessel. After we return, we are to turn off the camouflage by pushing the green button. Then we push the red button and it will fly us home. It all sounds so simple."

"From what Sheme tells me, it is." Kebeck looked toward the building beside the vessel. "Do you mind if I take a blip to have a private word with Sheme?"

A sly smile crept across Agara's face. "I will wait here."

Sheme stepped out the door just as Kebeck reached the building. "Greetings," she said as she extended the two hands that did not hold tools. "I am happy to see you."

Kebeck touched the extended palms. "It is nice to see your smiling face."

"Is the redness of your neck from your joy of seeing me or the excitement of the trip?"

"Neither. It is from embarrassment that I want to ask a favor of you."

"Of course I will do what I can, for you." Sheme put down the tools and crossed her arms as she waited for his request.

Kebeck took off his backpack and pulled out a map from one of the pockets. "Uh, well … I would like you to make a small change in our landing location on Earth." Kebeck held up the map. "Here is the park in Toronto where we had planned to land and here is a park in a small town near Toronto. I would like to land there, in this wooded section, instead."

Sheme took the map out of his hand and studied it. Then she looked up at him and smiled. "No problem. It is a simple adjustment. For you I will do it."

"And …."

Sheme smiled even more broadly. "And I see no reason to mention this change to anyone unless I am asked about it. Are you going to tell me what reasoning is behind this change of landing site?"

Now Kebeck was smiling just as broadly as she. "Later, after I return. I thank you for your understanding and assistance. I should probably help Agara now. He is acting as if he had a bopper in his belly; he has never flown in one of these vessels." Kebeck dashed over to the vessel, where Agara was waiting.

He heard Sheme call out, "Have a nice trip! I look forward to seeing you when you get back."

Agara was still wearing the sly smile when Kebeck got back to the vessel. "Agara, come; let us get in. I will show you how to buckle into your seat." Kebeck climbed through the vessel door and looked out at Agara, who looked most unhappy. "What is it?" Kebeck asked.

"We are landing in the southern area of Canada, right?"

"Yes"

"Are there alligators in this region?"

"No."

"Good." Agara climbed into the transport.

After both were securely buckled in, Kebeck reached out and touched the red button. "This first part is powered by compressed air, but soon it will switch to a fuel-burning engine that will speed us out of the atmosphere. So get ready to be pushed back into the seat." Just as Kebeck had predicted, the vessel slowly rose from the planet for a few minutes and then roared into action. Agara squealed when his head was thrown back by the change in speed. Kebeck tried to comfort him but found it almost impossible to talk. After a while, the engine cut off and they were in free-fall.

Except for the initial takeoff, the trip was easy. There was really nothing to do. Because of the lack of gravity, Agara spent the first hour of free-fall playing with floating objects through the air. "Look how long this bottle continues to spin."

Kebeck chuckled. He had done the same thing the first time he was in a gravity-free atmosphere. While Agara experimented with free-fall, Kebeck passed the time reading the messages on his communicator; he found notes wishing him a good voyage from his son, his daughter, his good friend Yerf, and other friends. He dozed off with his communicator in his hands and woke up to see that Agara had also fallen asleep. As Kebeck lay there half awake, half asleep, he thought about a trip he took about fifty days earlier to visit his uncle in Nedow.

It had been a wonderful visit. Kebeck had not been to Nedow Village in many years. Everyone knew about Nedow but only people who were invited by the residents ever visited the village. It would be considered impolite and improper to try visit the area just as a tourist. Kebeck was one of the lucky few who could visit it anytime because he had an uncle who chose to live there. Kebeck was always welcome at his Uncle Pason's house. Nedow was a unique place where people still lived in the primitive style of thousands of years ago. About nine hundred years ago, the people of Nedow decided that they wanted to live without electronics or sophisticated tools. They decided to go back to doing all their work by hand. The only modern things that were retained were twenty computers in the library, so they could vote on eight-day. The village became a living museum, but a museum with few visitors.

Nedow was also unique in the way it was built. Solid rock hills surrounded a lush valley that had a small river running through it. Thousands of years ago people carved into the stone hills to make their homes. They carved winding steps that connected five or six levels of homes. They carved planters all over the hillside, filled them with soil, and planted flowering vines. The fields beside the river were cultivated with fruits and vegetables. The result was a beautiful thing to see. Every Palalan school child had seen pictures of it and heard about it.

The population of the village was never allowed to go much over one thousand. Most of the children raised there moved on to other places to continue their education and usually settled elsewhere, coming back only to visit. But the city hall was always stacked high with applications from people desiring to move to Nedow. A city committee sat once a year and picked their new citizens. It was not a place to retire to; they selected people with the skills and strength to keep the village alive, interesting, and self- reliant. Almost nothing was imported into Nedow and nothing was exported out of Nedow. So, people moving there had to be prepared to work hard.

Since Kebeck could not call his uncle to ask permission to visit, the process of sending a message to the village library, having someone post a message on the village bulletin board, and waiting for his uncle to notice it and reply took almost a week. This procedure reminded Kebeck that he had better be prepared to live a different way of life during his week visit with his uncle.

When Kebeck arrived, the first thing that struck him was the different sounds. It was a loud place in the daytime and very quiet at night. When someone in a hillside house wanted to talk to someone in the valley, they just yelled: "Meet me at the river for a swim," or "I have Kala fruit, want some?" On the rest of

Palala this would be improper and is rarely done, but the people of Nedow have no communicators, so they yell. But only in the daytime.

Also, the independent lifestyle took some getting used to. If one wanted fruit, one had to go pick it and all visitors were expected to work either in the fields or at some other task for one hour per day. Everyone drew their own drinking water from the village well and those wanting a clean towel had to wash it themselves.

The reason for Kebeck's visit to Nedow had been twofold. He had always enjoyed spending time with his Uncle Pason, but moreover, he felt he really needed a week away from everything complicated. In Nedow, life was simple and the freedom from work problems and responsibility allowed him the time to think about his life and discuss his feelings and possible life plans with people who cared. Nedow was unique in the way that everyone in the village cared about everyone they met. People asked others how they were feeling and they really wanted to know the answer. The whole village seemed to flow into a continual conversation about the feelings of the residents and visitors. The people of the village wanted everyone to be happy, not happy in the grinning, laughing sense but content and positive about their lives and their world. Kebeck would never want to live there permanently; the intimacy would drive him mad. But he had appreciated spending the week folded in the arms of the villagers who had genuine affection for everyone.

One thing he had wanted to clarify in his mind while in Nedow was his feelings toward Adeline. Since none of the village residents Earth-Watched they would have an unbiased view of Kebeck's affection for Adeline. Most nights a fire was lit and people gathered around it to talk. Kebeck took a small slantboard from his uncle's house and joined a group.

"What is it that you enjoy about watching these Earth beings? I hear their lives are quite unpleasant," asked a female on the other side of the fire.

"Most Earth beings do have difficult lives. Many do nothing but work from childhood until they die. But there are many others who have the time to live interesting lives. Their lives are somewhat like the fiction stories we used to read as children, but they are real," Kebeck replied.

"But as adults we do not read fiction because our mature minds will not accept the lies necessary in fiction. On the subject of fiction, as I understand it, these beings are able to lie without it showing."

Kebeck looked up from the fire. "That is true. And viewing Earth is different because we can view real deception. It is a part of their daily lives. Most of the duplicity is delusion and half-truths such as their television advertising. But there are big frauds, like when a country's ruler takes the people's credit units and lets the beings in that country starve; that occurred on the island nation of Haiti. Many Earth beings lie to get what they want and it can be sometimes amusing or sometimes distressing to watch."

A male beside him named Tallha turned and looked at him. "I know studying Earth is your job, and from what I have read in our library, it is very different from our world … violent and unorganized. You say you have watched an Adeline being for many years. Why did you choose to watch one being and allow yourself to form an attachment to a being that exists in such a chaotic place?"

"Because, as you would see if you watched an Earth being for a while, they are intelligent creatures with feelings and desires as real as mine and as yours. Seeing her reality is better than any fiction or re-staged biography we have on Palala. Just the possibility of falsehood and violence adds excitement to their lives."

"Do you want that kind of excitement in your life?"

"No, the anxiety would exhaust me. As it is, I find watching Adeline's life too much for me sometimes."

"They are not as developed as us but you say they are intelligent and perceptive. Is it not an invasion of their privacy to watch them?"

Kebeck thought for a second. "No, I think that because they will never know of us, it does not harm them. And, I am beginning to think that viewing them is good for Palalans. It opens us up to some new ideas."

"Do we want new ideas?" asked Tallha.

"Probably not in this village," Kebeck smiled. "But, the rest of the planet is seeing some changes brought about because of Earth-Watching."

Kebeck had left the fire and Nedow feeling more centered and secure in his feelings about Earth and Adeline than he had been before the visit. The magic of Nedow worked because the residents questioned but nevertheless understood and cared.

Kebeck looked over just as Agara was opening his eyes and asked, "Have you ever been to Nedow?"

"Where?"

"Never mind, go back to sleep."

Kebeck and Agara slept, talked, and nibbled the hours away until a chiming sound caught their attention.

Agara looked around. "What's that?"

Kebeck examined the panel of gauges mounted on the wall of the cabin. "I forgot to tell you. I asked Sheme to have an alarm notify us when we are getting close to Earth so we can watch our landing."

"Oh, this is going to be something to see." Agara raised the cover of the little window beside him and looked outside. Kebeck did the same. "This is scary!" Agara exclaimed. He closed the window covering and looked over at Kebeck. "We are rushing at such a speed toward the planet. I know this ship is programmed to land us safely, but I cannot help but be alarmed by the speed at which we plunge." Agara slowly opened the window covering again and peered out. "I am terrified!" He slammed the cover closed and turned his back on the window.

Kebeck kept his face pressed to his window and reached out with one hand to touch Agara on the shoulder. "All is well, my friend. I have flown in one of these three times before and we are in no danger. Oh, just look. It is wonderful to see so much blue water and the varying shades of the planet's different areas. The land is mostly green. Now I can see the deserts of Africa. You should look."

Agara sat with his back to the window, hands at his sides and as stiff as a tree. "I cannot look. Will this part last much longer?"

"No, we should be on the ground very soon. I see the large cities! There are so many buildings … and so many roads. It is amazing. We just passed over the country of England. Did you know that there are more Earth beings on that little island alone than we have on Palala?"

"We have Earth beings on Palala?"

"Of course we have no Earth beings on Palala. You know what I meant. The population of that island is more than the population of Palala. Oh, you should see this. The fields look like little squares, countless little squares and rectangles. This is most enjoyable." Kebeck patted Agara's shoulder. "We will be down in just two blips."

Agara cocked his head. "We see them, the beings down there. Why do they not see us flying by?"

"Their detection systems are quite primitive and easy to fool. Ah! Do you feel that? We are slowing down to land."

The vibrations of the vessel made Agara's neck go from pink to red. The tiny ship turned and gracefully touched down on Earth. Kebeck reached out and pushed the green button to activate the holographic illusion camouflage. Agara came out of his fear-induced stupor and yelled, "We are here! Push the green button!"

Kebeck grabbed Agara's upper hands as they flailed in the air and said, "The green button has been pushed. Calm down and look out the window."

Agara flashed a smile and brushed away Kebeck's hands. In no time he was glued to the little window on his side of the vessel. "Some of the plants are green like ours but the shapes are very different. But many of them also have red or yellow or brown leaves. That is because their tilted planet has seasons; I remember that. So this is what their fall season looks like, very colorful. But I see no animals or people. Why is that?"

"We landed in the back section of a big park. This area is only used for organized picnics on certain designated days they call weekends. If there had been people here, the vessel was programmed to stay in orbit until the area was clear. Note that it is getting dark. This is the best time to land unnoticed. As soon as it gets a little darker we can put on our costumes and go to the habited area and examine the people."

"This is most frustrating," Agara grumbled. "I am on Earth but seeing less of it than I could on my home computer."

Kebeck was not really listening to his friend. He was studying a map of the area that he had printed off from the Earth Internet. It would be difficult to read the map after he was in the ghost costume. Frank Stafford lived at 132 Highland; if the map was correct, that was just six blocks from the park entrance.

He still had not decided whether or not he was going to try to get a message to Mr. Stafford. Any form of communication with an Earth being might be detected by his committee on Palala. He was pretty sure that he would get away with his manipulation of the TV broadcast that had repeated the same scene, but he knew that they would not tolerate any direct communication. Maintaining the current Earth-Watching program was the greater good. He had no doubt about that. And, he had been taught that emotion should never overrule the greater good. He had looked forward to this Earth visit for a long time and now that it was here, he could not enjoy it because he was torn with emotion about his Adeline. His original plan had been to land in her neighborhood and try to see her. That would have been wonderful. Now, here he was sitting in this little space vessel, trying to decide whether he should try to communicate with the only Earth being who might be able to save his Adeline's life on this very night.

Chapter 58

Palala

Samot was on a slantboard nibbling at a handful of purple kaka fruit when Jarrell crossed the ceramic floor of Committee Room 4 in the science building. Samot turned as he heard Jarrell's bare feet slapping against the hard floor. "Greetings, pardon my full hands; you are early."

"My anger would not let me sit still. You do know that Kebeck will not be here today because he is now flying toward Earth?" Jarrell's neck was a livid red.

"That is fact?" asked Samot. "But I received a message from him saying he would be here for his hearing today." Samot was puzzled. He could not remember when or if anyone had ever lied to him. "Are you sure?"

"Yes. It was in the news, so I checked with the launch site to see if it was a mistake. It was no mistake. He is on the vessel. My head spins with rage. I had also received a message saying he would be here today for the hearing."

Samot gobbled down another piece of fruit. "He must have changed his mind and decided to go at the last blip. He would not deceive us on purpose."

"Yes, he did!" Jarrell roared. "Before we started Earth-Watching he never would have thought to send a note that was not truth. This again proves my point about the evils of Earth-Watching. We must remove him from the committee as a punishment for this lie. And, we must stop all Earth-Watching activities!"

Samot stood up. "First, there can be no hearing without the accused being present. Second, we have no punishment for lying. Almost always, what is thought to be a lie turns out to be a misunderstanding. And with discussion, misunderstandings can be fixed. And finally, we will have a committee meeting to discuss the possible termination of Earth-Watching only when all of the committee members are present."

"But he did lie!" Jarrell bellowed as he extended his upper two arms up in the air in frustration.

"Maybe he did and maybe he did not. But nothing can be done until he returns. For now, I suggest that you calm down. This agitation is only bad for your health. If there was a deliberate falsehood then we will have to research how it might be handled and call a vote on how to deal with the untruth." Two distinct scents made Samot turn toward the doorway just as Leto and Laniff entered the room.

Both paused and extended their hands with the palms facing toward Samot and Jarrell.

"You two look like you have just got news of a last-day ceremony," said Leto.

"We are here for the hearing."

Samot quickly turned his palms toward the two and said, "The hearing will be rescheduled." Samot glanced at Jarrell, who was still waving his arms and sputtering with rage. "Jarrell is just leaving to go on a long swim. He has allowed his emotions to overpower his reasoning."

Leto and Laniff moved to one side and Jarrell stomped past them out the door.

"What was that all about?" asked Laniff.

"He is upset that Kebeck is not here for the hearing," Samot replied.

"I thought everyone knew he is on the Earth flight."

Leto asked, "He is?"

"He is," replied Samot. "So there will be no meeting."

"Good. Now I can use this time to play waterball. There was a game being organized just as I came out of the river." Laniff flashed his palms and hurried out the door.

Leto stared at Samot. "Why is Kebeck there and not here?"

Samot climbed back on the slantboard and snatched a handful of the kaka fruit from the bowl beside him. "That we will only know when he returns and tells us. Meanwhile, life is long; let us enjoy it." Samot held out his hand, offering some fruit to Leto.

Chapter 59

Earth

Kebeck and Agara were having a difficult time squeezing into the bodysuits that they had been given to keep them warm. The vessel was too small for both of them to dress at the same time. A quick game of finger matching decided that Agara would get dressed first. As Agara pulled the top half of his bodysuit over his head, Kebeck took some papers out of his satchel and put them in the bottom of the treat bag he was to carry. Having rarely worn shoes, Agara found the Earth-type shoes to be confining; he said that they did not allow enough space for the webbing between their toes. The long white gloves that fitted on their upper arms had a fake extra finger that would move along with their fourth fingers. Agara had to stop and laugh at that. After putting on the shoes and gloves, he put an Earth-being mask on his face and then covered his whole body with the long ghost costume. Then, finally dressed, Agara backed up against a wall and helped Kebeck into his outfit.

When they were both totally satisfied with the adjustments on their costumes, Kebeck pushed the button to open the door. As soon as they were outside Agara looked back at the vessel and exclaimed, "It is a tree! The illusion device makes our vessel look like a big green tree, like the ones the Earth beings decorate at Christmas. Now our only problem is to remember which tree is the vessel."

Kebeck shuffled his feet and kicked up a few red and gold leaves. "We are really here! My insides are bubbling with excitement, but I must control it in order to do what we came here to accomplish. We must remember to gather samples of some plants and soil when we get back to this park and prepare to leave."

"Yes, we will collect leaves before we leave. Ha! I made a rhyme. This language can be fun. But now, let us go and see the beings. I want to see real live Earth beings."

Kebeck led the way as the two four-foot-tall ghosts shuffled down the road that led to the suburban neighborhood, their custom-designed trick-or-treat bags in their white-gloved hands. "Remember, you should let me do all the talking. Since you learned your English mostly from British movies, you do have a bit of an accent. That will sound unusual in this neighborhood."

Agara protested" "I can speak North American. But since you wish it, I will not say much. Just 'trick or treat' and 'thank you,' if that is all right with you."

"Very well, but nothing more. Because …." Kebeck stopped in mid-sentence as he now saw an Earth house with a witch and a superhero of some sort standing by the front door of the house.

Agara looked at Kebeck then turned to see what had caught his eye. "What should we do? Shall we communicate with those young ones?"

"No," Kebeck replied. "I think we should keep our communication with the juveniles to a minimum. They are erratic and could, as they say in movies, 'blow our cover.' If we walk slowly they will probably complete their candy-receiving activity and move on down the street before we get to that house. Then we may ring the bell at that house and see our first Earth beings. I am quite excited, but it is important that we do this right."

"Do not be concerned. In preparation for our visit, I reviewed many Earth movies which included this 'trick or treat' custom. I know what to do and what is expected of the candy-givers. Also, there is no problem with expressing stimulation in our tone of voice because many juveniles are enthusiastic about this holiday."

"True. Excellent point." Kebeck saw that the young ones were now moving away from the house. "I suggest that we now walk faster and approach the house."

Kebeck could not believe the excitement that coursed through his body as his gloved digit touched the doorbell. It was on the same level as watching his children crack out of their eggs. He wanted to leap with joy that he finally was going to see an Earth being. But in the back of his mind remained a sadness, knowing that the being he was about to see would not be his Adeline. He also mourned the fact that tonight she was probably going to die. He hoped that his plan to save her could be implemented. Unfortunately his plan depended on luck and he, as a person raised in a science-oriented society, did not put much trust in luck.

A tall, adult female Earth being with short gray hair opened the door. "How cute! Two little ghosts. Now what do you say?"

Kebeck nudged Agara.

Agara sputtered out, "Trick or treat!"

"Well, since I don't want to be tricked I'd better give you some candy. Now hold out your bags," said the Earth being.

Both Kebeck and Agara presented their bags and the female dropped several pieces of candy in each. Kebeck said, "Thank you" and turned to go. He was halfway to the street when he realized that Agara was not beside him. He turned around to find that Agara was still on the porch in front of the closed door. Kebeck ran back to him. "What are you doing?"

"I spoke to a real live Earth being. I am overwhelmed. Of course you smelled the interesting odors that came from the being and her house. This is very exciting."

"Good. I also appreciate the moment and recognize the unique odors, but we must move on and act the part of an Earth juvenile. Come. We must move faster. The normal time for Earth children to do this is from dusk until about nine o'clock, so they tend to move quickly in order to get as much candy as possible."

At the next house, Agara said "trick or treat" as soon as the door opened and turned to go as soon as Kebeck uttered his "thank you."

After the fourteenth house, Agara said to Kebeck, "This holiday is a way for the powerless juveniles to extort a type of desired goods from the beings with power, the adults. Very interesting. And I am enjoying the experience. We have accumulated much of this candy food. I wonder what it tastes like." They crossed the street and headed toward a house decorated with cardboard skeletons and witches.

"Agara, we were warned not to eat the candy. We will take some of it back with us and after the appropriate scientists have tested it, we can probably taste it." Kebeck looked for a doorbell and when he found none, he knocked on the door.

As the door opened, a voice rang out: "Harold, you should see these sweet little ghosts; they're adorable." A plump, short female, not much taller than they were, wearing a garment covered with images of bright flowers stood in the door; she was so wide that her body almost filled the doorway. "You kids come in and have some hot chocolate." She backed out of the doorway to let them in. Agara already had a foot across the threshold when Kebeck grabbed his arm and pulled him back.

"No thank you," Kebeck blurted out. "Mother said we were not to go in any houses."

The female stepped up to the door and looked them over. "Well, I suppose you'd better obey your mom. You two are brothers? Do I know your family? I'll bet you two are the Thompson twins."

Kebeck and Agara had backed up so far that their heels were hanging over the top step. Agara spoke up, "We be from England, having just moved here."

"Well, I'll be. Two little Brits. This is your first Halloween, isn't it? Open up those bags. I'm going to load you up." The large female dumped two big handfuls of candy in each bag. With his British accent, Agara said "Thank you, Mum" before they turned and ran out to the street.

As they strolled down the sidewalk, passing Earth children in costumes, an agitated Kebeck whispered to Agara. "Did the flight rattle your brain? You know that we should not enter an Earth house."

"I apologize," said Agara. "There were wonderful smells in that house. I very much wanted to see what made those aromas. I ask that you do not report this mistake to the committee when we return."

Kebeck stopped walking and took Agara's arm to stop him. "I will agree to not report it and I ask you to not report what I am about to do. Agreed?"

"What will you be doing that I will not be reporting?"

"I will talk to a juvenile. That is all."

"But why?"

Kebeck thought for a moment. *Agara cannot see my neck grow red under this costume.* Then he said, "Because I want to."

Agara paused before saying, "I can agree to that. Tell me when you intend to do this and I will turn my back. I cannot report seeing what I did not see."

They collected candy at three more houses before Kebeck said to Agara, "I think it is time to turn your back. Stand here and face that big house with three pumpkins on the porch until I come back."

Agara did as he was told and Kebeck ambled over to two young male Earth beings that were coming down the sidewalk. He said to them, "Hey, you guys want this candy?" He shook the bag of candy in his hand.

"Sure, don't you want it?" asked the taller one.

"No, I have much at home. I will give you this if you will deliver a note to that house." He pointed to a house across the street.

"That's the Stafford's house," said the shorter of the two males. "Why don't you do it yourself? They're not bad people."

Kebeck was getting agitated, but was trying to not let it come through in his tone of voice; this was so important to him. "If you will just hand whoever opens the door this note and then return here, you can have this candy. Here, I will give you half of it now." Kebeck grasped the side of the shorter Earth child's treat bag and dumped half of his candy into the bag, then he held a folded piece of paper out to him.

The child looked down at his bag and said, "Charlie, he's got full-sized chocolate bars!" The child reached out and snatched the paper from Kebeck's hand. "Sure, I'll do it. Come on Charlie, the Stafford house was next anyway; they always give good stuff."

As the Earth children crossed the street, Kebeck walked back over to Agara and stood next to him, facing the Stafford house. "May I move now?" Agara asked.

"No, just stand there a couple of blips longer, but then be prepared to rush back to the vessel."

"It is already time to go?"

"Almost. We should be in the vessel by eight. Studies show that there is an increased presence of larger, more aggressive Earth children after eight." Kebeck watched as the two male children rang the bell at the Stafford house. He saw the shorter child hand his note to a gray-haired adult female. Just then, a loud group of six costumed Earth children walked by, blocking Kebeck's view. Kebeck fiddled with the candy in his bag as they went by. As soon as they moved out of his way, he saw that the two males were leaving the Stafford house and heading toward him. Kebeck dropped his treat bag on the sidewalk, tapped Agara on the shoulder and said, "We must go, now, but do not run." Kebeck and Agara moved quickly down the sidewalk toward the park and their transport.

They walked in silence until they were two blocks from the park entrance. Then Agara slowed to a stop and said, "Please let us do just one more?"

They were on a corner. Kebeck looked around. He could see a small group of trick-or-treaters at the end of the block on his right and two Earth children on the sidewalk six houses down on the street in front of him. He looked to his left and saw no one. The second house on his left was a small dwelling with many lights on; an Earth-being effigy was hanging from a rope in the tree by the door. He pointed to the house. "We could do that one, but then we must go."

Agara pranced up to the door and rang the doorbell. Kebeck followed. A voice rang out, "John, will you get the door?"

"Sure! I got it!"

A middle-aged Earth male with a smile and a mustache opened the door, stuck out his hand, and said, "Hi, nice to meet you two ghosts!" The male held his hand in the customary position that indicated that he expected Agara to grasp and shake the hand. Agara had seen this hand-shaking in many movies and on Earth TV. Agara reached up and gripped the male being's offered hand and gave it a little shake. The hand came off of the Earth male's arm. When Agara realized he was holding the detached hand in his gloved hand, he screamed and dropped it as he jumped back! He stood there in shock until he realized that the Earth male was laughing and waving two hands at him, saying, "It's all right, it's all right! It's just a plastic arm!"

Kebeck quickly grabbed Agara's arm and pulled him down the steps and toward the road.

The Earth male called out, "Hey, look, I'm sorry! Come back! You didn't get your candy! Come on, it was just a joke!"

The two little ghosts ran all the way to the park entrance. Once they got in the park and away from the houses they slowed down to a walk.

"Should we not start gathering plants now?" Agara asked.

"Yes, I almost forgot," Kebeck sighed. "My mind was elsewhere." Kebeck was thinking of Adeline and hoping that his note to Mr. Stafford would be enough to save her. Kebeck began to tear leaves off trees and bushes as they walked toward their vessel. As he leaned down to uproot a small plant next to the path, he heard Agara laughing behind him. He stood up with his now dirty white-gloved hands full of leaves and plants and asked, "What is so funny?"

"I am," Agara answered. "The trick of the artificial hand amuses me. The Earth male was clever to fool me so. I now find humor in it. But at the time, when I saw it on the floor, I was quite terrified that I had torn the hand off an Earth being."

"I will laugh about it when we are safely off this planet," Kebeck replied. He felt heavy with worry about the note he had sent to Mr. Stafford. "Please walk faster. We need to get in the transport before anyone sees us."

Finding the big fir tree was easy, much easier than getting out of their costumes inside the small vessel. But after pushing the green and then the red button, they were on their way home.

Chapter 60

Earth

Frank Stafford was sitting in a worn leather chair in his little office at the back of the house, flipping around websites on his computer when he heard his wife call out. "Frank dear, please come out here. There's a note for you."

Mr. Stafford had been avoiding the whole Halloween nuisance by spending the evening in his office. He was still mourning the death of his daughter Carol and he knew that watching the costumed kids come and go would be too much for him to bear. His wife had a different and maybe better attitude about the whole thing. Ever since they first discovered the strange holiday the first year they lived in Canada, Anne had reveled in the costumes and the children's visits. Since Carol's death, she often had long crying sessions while thinking about her daughter, but the tragedy had not affected her love of Halloween. She had carved three pumpkins, decorated the front of the house, and was wearing a good-fairy costume complete with a musical wand that chimed when she waved it.

Mr. Stafford came into the kitchen. Anne stuffed a piece of paper into his hand and rushed back to the living room to look out for more trick-or-treaters. On the face of the folded paper was written in big letters:

MR. STAFFORD, CONCERNING ADELINE, VERY IMPORTANT.

Just below this heading was the following text: *Respecting your past as a military consultant requesting that you not open this note until exactly 8 p.m. this night. Also, ignore child who gave you this note. Only innocent messenger. Note has been through many rubber-gloved hands.*

The letter was signed, *Friend of Carol and Adeline.*

He called out to his wife, "Annie, who gave you this?" Then he realized that there was no way she could hear him over the CD of Halloween sounds that she had playing in the living room. He reread the front of the note, then his eyes darted up to the big clock on the kitchen wall. It was five minutes until eight. Should he wait the five minutes? Should he rush outside and try to find the kid who gave his wife this note? Just seeing Carol's name on the note left him torn between wanting to rip the note open and wanting to rush out to find the kid who delivered it. But the words, "your past as a military consultant," told him that chasing the kid would be a futile waste of time and that the note was sent by someone who knew a lot about him. He sat down at the kitchen table and watched the clock as the seconds ticked by. His wife dashed in just long enough scoop up another bag of candy and ask, "What's up, luv?"

"Nothing, dear. An old friend just sent me a note." At exactly eight he unfolded the paper and read the note:

Please contact Adeline Morgan immediately and instruct her to not leave her house tonight. The male who killed your daughter Carol will be outside her house intending to follow her and kill her. The name of the male is Erwin Bercic. He was called Newt Clark when he went to jail for killing an older male and female in Vancouver. Erwin Bercic has had facial surgery to disguise his identity but his fingerprints still match those of Newt Clark. Attached here are two fingerprints from Erwin Bercic. Please discreetly get this information to police.

Mr. Stafford read the note twice before he stuffed it in his pocket, grabbed the nearest phone, and ran to his desk for his little phone directory. Adeline answered the phone on the second ring. "Adeline," he asked, "are you all right?"

"Yeah, I'm fine. I was just sitting here having a talk with Roger about sleeping on my sweaters. I've got to find a way to keep that cat out of my closet. You sound a bit out of breath; is there a problem?"

"You're still planning on going out tonight, aren't you?"

"Of course. I'm not going to let a crazy old TV set scare me. My costume is laid out on the bed. I'm meeting three girlfriends and we're going to barhop and see who shows up this year. Last year there were some fantastic space creatures. Why do you ask?" she said.

Mr. Stafford took a breath. "Adeline, you must not leave the house tonight. I have reason to …."

"But it's Halloween!" she interrupted.

"Just listen to me! I have reason to believe that the person who killed Carol is planning to … well, he's targeting you tonight. He's going to follow you from the house and …."

"And what? Some guy is planning to kill me? Why? What did I do?"

"Do you know Erwin Bercic?"

"Well of course. He's running for Mayor. I interviewed him; so did Carol." Adeline paused. "Him?" Mr. Stafford could hear her breathing hard and fast. "That slick weasel murdered Carol? Why?"

"It seems he has a past that needs hiding. I've got to check it out. Meanwhile, call your friends and cancel this evening. No, wait! Don't do that. He might have the phones bugged. I hope he's not listening to us right now. On second thought, don't phone or email anybody until … what time were you supposed to meet your friends?"

"At about ten, at the Lazy Lizzard."

"Here's what to do, luv. You lock the doors and stay in the house. Don't talk to anyone except me. You don't answer the phone unless you see this number on the phone display. If he had this call bugged, then he's heading out of town as we talk. If he doesn't know we're on to him, then I'll be taking care of him. Now I know he'll probably be in costume, but tell me what he looks like."

"Oh, I can do much better than that. Just have a look at the Toronto Globe from two days ago and you can see the bastard's picture."

"I'll do that. But I need two more bits of information. How tall is he and what size shoe does he wear?"

"What? What does that matter?"

"Just tell me; approximately … compare him to Jim."

"Well, I did notice that he has big feet. Maybe a size eleven or twelve. And he's shorter than Jim. Jim is exactly six feet. So Bercic must be about five-ten or five-eleven. Does that help?"

"Helps a lot. Now you just stay put and let me handle this. I've got to check some sources to make sure it's him. Now, don't unlock the door for anyone and don't answer the phone unless you see this number on the call display. I'll be talking to you in a bit. Bye, luv."

Mr. Stafford pushed the disconnect button on the phone and sat down at his desk. He reached down into his shirt and fished out a small key that was attached to a long thin gold chain that he wore around his neck. He then unlocked a drawer in his desk. He pulled out a notebook and flipped through it until he found the code and password that would allow him to access police and government records through his computer. He typed in the code and password. He pulled the note out of his pocket, looked at it, and typed the name 'Newt Clark' into the search field. He easily found a Newt Clark who, with an accomplice, brutally tortured and killed a couple in Vancouver years ago. There was a photo of Clark; he looked like a tough kid. He was described as being five-eleven, 175 pounds, with green eyes. According to the files, Clark disappeared off of all records shortly after being released from prison; it showed that there was a warrant out on him for not reporting to his parole officer. Mr. Stafford pulled up Clark's fingerprints and compared them to the two prints on the note. Sure enough, the prints on the note matched the thumb and forefinger of Newt Clark. *I don't know who gave me these prints and if they really belong to Erwin Bercic. Maybe someone is trying to use me to do their dirty-work. I need more information.* Mr. Stafford then searched the name Erwin Bercic; he found the man's driver's license; it described him as five-eleven and 180 pounds, with green eyes. Mr. Stafford went back and forth between the photos of the two. Both had green eyes, but that was irrelevant because who knows when people are wearing contacts. He knew what could and couldn't be changed with plastic surgery and he had to allow for the difference in age. Chins, cheeks, noses, eyelids, eyebrows, and lips could all be changed. But the distance from the eyes to the top of the head, the distance between the eyes, and the distance between the eyes and the mouth never change. Mr. Stafford printed both photos and with a ruler compared the two. Both Bercic and Clark had the same upper-head shape and the eye placement was the same. He growled, "That's definitely him." He grabbed the phone and hit the redial button. It rang three times.

"Is it him?" she asked.

"Yes, it's him."

"I sat and had coffee with that bastard. How could he...? What did...? "

Mr. Stafford interrupted her. "I know you're a bit shaken up, luv, but now it's important that you do exactly what I say. You should be safe for now if you stay in the house. Do not answer the door. Do not go on the Internet. Do not answer the phone unless you know it's me. Tell me again. What time were you planning to leave the house?"

"About nine-thirty."

"That gives me some time. Just stay put, luv. And do not deviate from my instruction, no matter what happens. Stay put with the doors locked. I'll take care of this." He put the phone down and sat back in his chair. *I could phone the police, but it would take too long to get to the right person. And this guy is smart; he'd get away. If I called the nearby fire department and reported a fire at her house, she would be safe, but the commotion would allow him to disappear. I can't bear to let him get away with this.*

He leaped up and started toward the living room yelling, "Anne, where did you put that box of costumes?" Within minutes Mr. Stafford had a tattered Emmett Kelly clown costume in his hands. His wife had made it for him years ago and seeing it made him remember the times he had worn it to take Carol and Adeline out trick or treating. He shook his head. This wasn't the time for memories and tears. He went to his bedroom closet and dug back behind the hanging clothes until he found a large black umbrella. He then went to the basement and opened the door of the freezer. In the far right corner, under packages of meats and ice cream was a plastic container labeled 'rat poison.' He took out the container and read over the manifest that listed what was in the six vials in the container. He selected one and as he started to close up the plastic box he hesitated. *I don't need to burden my soul with another death.* He put the vial back and selected another one. He checked his watch. *Good thing she lives on the west side of Toronto and just off Islington. I can easily make it to Adeline's by nine-thirty. I'm sure I can.* He only needed one more thing. Best to have a fake I.D. in case he was stopped on the highway. Something told him he would be going a wee bit over the speed limit. He went to his bedroom and in the bottom drawer, under his socks, were two black leather wallets. He flipped one open. Tonight he would be Leonard Horne; at least that was what the license and registration said. The wallet also contained a couple of hundred dollars and a Visa card in the name of Leonard Horne. The real Leonard Horne was somewhere in Toronto; he had stopped driving two years ago when he was blinded by a construction accident. As Mr. Stafford started to close the drawer, he hesitated. *It's always good to have a plan B.* He pulled the drawer all the way out and laid it on the floor. Then he removed the small loaded pistol that was taped to the back of the drawer. He had made this chest of drawers just after he left the army; it was full of such surprises.

Five seconds later Mr. Stafford was high-tailing it down the hall, trying to get out of the house as fast as possible, when he noticed that the door to his daughter's room was ajar. He stopped dead, and opened the door. His wife was sitting on the bed, crying. She looked lovely in her baby-blue fairy costume. The rhinestone tiara was tilted to one side, and there were stains where tears had ran down her satin bodice. He squatted down in front of her and took her hands. "Darling, I know who killed our Carol."

She stared at him, a glazed look in her eyes. "Oh my god! Who? Why?"

"We'll discuss that later. I've got to go. He's going to kill Adeline."

"No!" She squeezed his hands so hard it hurt.

"No, I won't let him. I couldn't save Carol, but now that I know who he is, he's not going to get Adeline too." He gently pulled loose from her iron grip. "Now go wipe your face. I think I heard the doorbell. You've got to give out candy." He got up and rushed out to his car.

Chapter 61

In transit from Earth to Palala

As soon as they were released from Earth's gravity, Agara commented, "This candy stuff smells like it would have a good taste. It tempts me, but logic restrains me. I hope the tests discover that it is edible so that I can then try it."

Kebeck said nothing.

"You are quiet for a person who has just had the biggest adventure of his life."

"I have concerns. For one, I have apprehensions about how our committee will vote on Earth-Watching," Kebeck said.

"So do I," added Agara. "I doubt Jarrell will change his mind. But I plan to speak with Leto and Laniff, and explain to them what it was like on Earth. I hope to influence them. Our experience was much nicer than Laniff's. It is good that there were no alligators in Canada."

Kebeck lifted a hand in a sign of exasperation. "Remember, tonight we were seeing a middle-class North American area where the beings live like little gods. Laniff not only fears alligators, he sees a very different world as he studies Earth crime, war, and violence. If we had visited one of the economically deficient, lawless countries of Africa, we could have been killed. And Leto, he fears that some of our people will choose to replace logic and science with religion. There is a lot of good and bad to be said for Earth."

"That is truth. But from the posture of your body and your facial expression, I think there is also something else causing you distress."

"I worry about the Adeline being that I have watched for many years. Tonight I tried to stop her from having an early death."

"So that was why you spoke to the young Earth beings. Did it work?"

"I do not know if I succeeded. Their lives are very short as it is. I want her to have as long a life as is possible for her kind." Kebeck stopped and shook his head. "I will tell you no more because I do not wish to burden you with more secrets."

"Then I will speak more about our Earth-Watching committee. I have been thinking. It is my opinion that even if we have a vote as soon as next eight-day, the people will vote to keep Earth-Watching. Palalans will be unwilling to ban the dramas we see in Earth TV shows, movies, and in the lives of the Earth beings themselves. We only had historical stories to amuse us before we started Earth-Watching. Also, there are many people, like you, who have adopted Earth pets that they watch regularly. Let Jarrell put it to a vote; he will lose."

Kebeck was overjoyed to hear Agara speak this way. "What you say may be truth. When I visited Tabat on my way to the launch site, he and his friends were greatly involved in Earth-Watching. I am sure his village will vote to keep it." Kebeck smiled. "You give me reason for optimism and hope."

Agara twisted his neck and stretched his arms. "I find that I am tired. We should sleep a bit."

Kebeck agreed and as he laid his head down, he noticed a map on the floor. It was the map he had shown Sheme. *She will be waiting at the launch site when we arrive; she will want an answer soon. Do I want to spend the next twenty years being a parent? Do I want to spend the next twenty years with Sheme? She is fun and intelligent and caring. If I were to parent again, she would be the right person to partner with. It is an honor that she chooses me to share her second child. This will be the last child she is allowed to have. They say the first one is just practice for the second one. Do I want to share a house and a life with Sheme and a child? It will mean less time watching Adeline. That could be a good thing. Maybe I have been spending too much time watching this being on another world. But I so enjoy watching my Adeline. I only hope she survives and is not killed by Erwin Bercic.* Kebeck continued to think both of his future and Adeline as he drifted off to sleep.

Chapter 62

Earth

After Adeline got off of the phone with Mr. Stafford, she sat down on the chair by her desk and just stared into space for a few minutes. Then thoughts came drifting into her mind. *Erwin Bercic killed Carol. He wants to kill me.* She leaped out of the chair and prowled through the house, checking every door and window. *If he plans to follow me, then he must be waiting outside for me.* She looked out the front window, carefully holding the curtain so that no one outside could see her. *I should have something to defend myself with.* She remembered that there was an old baseball bat in the basement, but she didn't dare go down there. She had seen too many movies with villains lurking in such dark spaces. The heavy old basement door was securely locked, and it was going to stay that way. She went into the kitchen and rummaged through the utensil drawer. She selected a sharp little knife that she used to cut vegetables and put it in the front pocket of her baggy cargo pants. The knife bounced against her leg as she walked back into the living room; it reminded her that she wasn't totally helpless. She so wanted to call Jim and be comforted by the sounds of his voice. She took her cell phone out of her purse and sat down on the couch holding it in both hands.

The doorbell rang and she jumped up off the couch, fumbling for the knife in her pocket. She then heard young voices yelling, "trick-or-treat, trick-or-treat." She sat back down, listening as the door bell chimed again and again, but she didn't move. After a minute or two they went away. She looked at her watch; it was a bit past eight. *That's probably the last of the trick-or-treaters; they usually stop between eight and nine.* The doorbell rang again. This time she went to the window and looked out. There were three older boys standing in front of the door. One had on a hockey jersey and a goalie mask, another had on a fedora and a torn overcoat, and the third one was wearing a baseball uniform that looked a bit too small for him, with the words 'Roger's Dodgers' written across the front. They looked harmless enough, but instead of going to the door Adeline moved away from the window and just stood in the middle of the room, with her arms at her sides, as they rang the bell again and again. After a couple of minutes, they went away.

She looked at her watch again. *It's not even eight-thirty.* She squared her shoulders and took a deep breath. She approached the door and hit the switch to turn the porch light off. She then retreated to the couch. She reached for the remote with her left hand, the cell phone still clasped in the other. As her hand touched the remote, she pulled it back. *I'm afraid to turn on the TV.* Roger moseyed into the room and jumped up onto the couch beside her. He rubbed against her, wanting to be petted. She put the phone down long enough to scratch him behind his ears. "Roger, I'm freaking out here because supposedly some guy wants to kill me because he thinks I know something that I don't know." She released a huge sigh. *Crazy friggin world!* She rubbed her hand across the smooth old leather couch and remembered the hours she and Jim had spent cuddled up on it. *I would give anything to have him here now.* Adeline jumped up. "I can't stand just sitting and waiting," she told Roger. Adeline made another quick turn inside the house and then discretely looked out the window towards the street. The kids were all gone and many of her neighbors had turned off their Halloween decorations and porch lights. She noticed that there was an unfamiliar tan sedan parked on her side of the street, about three houses down. *Probably just someone visiting a neighbor.* It had a car rental sticker on the back bumper. Roger sat on the couch and watched as she paced the living room floor. She sat back down beside him and picked up the remote. "Roger, I'm not going to be afraid of a TV set. Let's see what's on, shall we?" Boris Karloff smiled at her from the TV screen. She quickly moved on to watch Abbott and Costello playing hide and seek with Frankenstein. *Too silly!* On the next station Jack Nicholson was running through the halls of an old hotel, waving an axe. *Too scary!* She moved on. As she then watched Anthony Perkins checking a young couple into a seedy motel, she quickly turned the TV off. *I've already got a psycho in my own life right now, thank you very much.* Now there was only silence. She realized that she wanted the house silent so she could hear if anyone was creeping around or breaking in.

The silence and waiting were driving her crazy; she went to the window again. Adeline saw another unfamiliar car, another tan sedan from a rental company; this one was parked on her side the street, in front of her next-door neighbor's place and there was a person in a pirate costume standing beside it. *Probably just a parent, waiting for his kids.* She looked at her watch; it was after nine. She looked down the street in both directions. There were no kids in sight. *Could that be Erwin Bercic in that costume? His height and size are about the same....*

Suddenly she saw a man in a clown costume with a big black umbrella perched on his shoulder walk up to the pirate; they exchanged a few words. The pirate put his hands out with his palms up as he shrugged and shook his head; she thought she heard the pirate tell the clown to get lost. The clown then proceeded to take the umbrella off of his shoulder and, using both hands, he stabbed its pointed end directly into the top of the pirate's foot. The clown sauntered away as the pirate fell to the sidewalk, grabbing his foot as he yelled out in pain.

Adeline stood there with her hands grasping the window frame, watching the man writhe on the sidewalk. She didn't know what to do. Now the pirate was yelling for help and porch lights were coming on. *Good, someone will call an ambulance.* The clown was nowhere in sight. Two neighbors came out and tried to comfort the pirate. They took his mask off. Because he was lying flat on the sidewalk she couldn't see his face. *Is that him? Is that Erwin Bercic?* She was just about to go out the door when the phone rang. Adeline ran over to her desk and looked at the display screen on. It was Mr. Stafford. She picked up the phone.

"He won't be bothering you again, luv. Not tonight, not ever. Go to bed. All is well. Now, don't speak to anybody about this. We'll talk later." He hung up, leaving her listening to a dial tone.

Adeline went back to the window. The man in the pirate costume was still on the sidewalk. He was sitting up now, holding his foot. Someone had put a blanket over his shoulders. There were six or seven neighbors standing around him. She could hear an ambulance siren in the distance. She watched until the ambulance took him away, but she never got a good look at his face. The phone rang. She went over and looked at the call display; it was Nina. *I'm not up to talking to anyone right now.* She picked up her cell phone and sent Nina a text message: "Can't make it tonight. Sorry. Will explain tomorrow."

Adeline didn't sleep much that night. Next morning she stumbled into the kitchen half-asleep and, as usual, she turned on the radio. She was pouring a cup of coffee when she thought she heard the DJ say the name Erwin Bercic. She walked over to the radio and turned up the volume: "Well folks, if you were thinking of voting for Erwin Bercic for Mayor, then you'd better make some other plans. Looks like old Erwin's in the hospital right now being treated for some rare flesh-eating disease that might cost him a leg. And if that's not bad enough, city police have just confirmed that he isn't even who he claims to be. Turns out that his real name is Newt Clark, and get this: he's an ex-con who served ten years for murder. And we were going to elect him Mayor? Yikes!" Adeline turned off the radio; she couldn't believe her ears. *That was why he killed Carol. He thought she knew. And if Carol had known that he was an ex-con, she would have told me, and he figured that I would have known all about him.* She sat down at the kitchen table and stared out the window as tears of relief and sorrow flowed down her cheeks.

Chapter 63

In transit from Earth to Palala

Kebeck and Agara were so tired that they slept through the first ten hours of their flight. Kebeck woke up to see Agara watching him.

"What is it?" asked Kebeck.

"I did not wish to wake you, but I am most anxious to discuss our wonderful visit." Agara was pink with enthusiasm.

As consciousness returned to Kebeck his first thought was of Adeline. *Is she alive?* "Agara, I know you want to talk about our adventures now, but I ask that you wait a couple of blips while I check something on my communicator."

Agara nodded and grumbled a bit.

Kebeck set his communicator to access his home computer so that he could see into Adeline's house. He first looked in her bedroom; the bed was empty but the fact that it had been slept in was a good sign. There was no one in the living room. But he smiled and relaxed when he saw Adeline sitting at the kitchen table with her usual cup of coffee. He flipped off the communicator.

"Now, Agara, tell me your thoughts of our visit.